ALSO BY CHRISTOPHER TILGHMAN

Roads of the Heart
The Way People Run
Mason's Retreat
In a Father's Place
The Right-Hand Shore
Thomas and Beal in the Midi

On the
Tobacco Coast

FARRAR, STRAUS AND GIROUX

NEW YORK

On the Tobacco Coast

CHRISTOPHER TILGHMAN

Farrar, Straus and Giroux
120 Broadway, New York 10271

Title-page art by makar/Shutterstock.com.

Library of Congress Cataloging-in-Publication Data
Names: Tilghman, Christopher, author.
Title: On the tobacco coast / Christopher Tilghman.
Description: First edition. | New York : Farrar, Straus and Giroux, 2024.
Identifiers: LCCN 2023045453 | ISBN 9780374226060 (hardcover)
Subjects: LCSH: Family farms—Fiction. | Families—Eastern Shore
 (Md. and Va.)—Fiction. | Chesapeake Bay (Md. and Va.)—Fiction. |
 LCGFT: Novels.
Classification: LCC PS3570.I348 O5 2024 | DDC 813/.54—
 dc23/eng/20231004
LC record available at https://lccn.loc.gov/2023045453

Designed by Gretchen Achilles

Our books may be purchased in bulk for promotional, educational, or
business use. Please contact your local bookseller or the Macmillan Corporate
and Premium Sales Department at 1-800-221-7945, extension 5442, or by
email at MacmillanSpecialMarkets@macmillan.com.

www.fsgbooks.com
Follow us on social media at @fsgbooks

1 3 5 7 9 10 8 6 4 2

For my father, Benjamin Tilghman, 1917–1997

"Oh, I'm not afraid of history!"

—MAGGIE VERVER, in *The Golden Bowl*

The Masons of Mason's Retreat

Richard Mason and Mary Foxley Mason immigrate to the New World in 1659 and settle on Maryland's Eastern Shore. Mary Foxley outlives her husband by twenty-five years and is recognized as the real founder of the large estate called Mason's Retreat.

Their son, Richard, marries Anna Maria Lloyd. Their eight children establish the Mason name and influence for several generations to come.

Ophelia Mason inherits the Retreat after her two brothers are killed in the Civil War and marries Wyatt Bayly of Baltimore, who turns the Retreat into a vast peach orchard. They have two children, Thomas and Mary.

Thomas Bayly falls in love with Beal Terrell, daughter of the farm's orchardist, and because she is Black, they must escape to France to marry. They start new lives as owners of a neglected winery called St. Adelelmus. Before Thomas and Beal leave America, Beal's brother, Randall, Thomas's best friend and a brilliant student, is murdered on the farm, a crime that is never solved.

Mary Bayly remains single. After the failure of the peach orchards, she leads the Retreat into the twentieth century as a modern sanitary dairy. Upon her death she bequeaths the farm to a direct descendant of Richard and Mary Foxley Mason, Edward Mason of Boston, who is about to move to England.

Edward Mason, failing as a manufacturer, and his wife, Edith, withdraw to the Retreat from 1936 to 1939, until the coming war revives Edward's business prospects in England. They have two children, Sebastien and Simon.

Sebastien Mason hates his father, and in August 1939, he drowns in an attempt to avoid having to return to England with him. His mother, Edith, never recovers from her grief.

Simon Mason grows up in Chicago and pursues a mostly unsuccessful career in advertising in California. Along the way, he sells Mason's Retreat. He has one son, Harry.

After making his fortune investing in the dot-com bubble, Harry Mason buys Mason's Retreat back from its indifferent owners. His wife, Kate Lorenz, with some complaint, agrees to relocate to the house she calls Harry's Folly. They have three children, Rosalie, Eleanor, and Ethan.

Julien Bayly, great-grandson of Thomas and Beal, and his daughter, Céleste, expand the family's wineries in France and abroad. On July 4, 2019, he and Céleste accept Harry Mason's long-standing invitation to visit the family seat of their American ancestors.

On the
Tobacco Coast

In the beginning, for your husband, it was the promise of land, an unimaginable prospect for the son of a grocer, for a man whose first career had been as a surgeon in the Royal Navy. It could not have been for what had once been supposed might be in the land—gold, silver, iron; there was none of that in this part of the New World, and he knew that now. It wasn't for what was already growing on it: there was no profit in trading in its chestnuts and cypresses and oaks, as much as England could use the timber. It wasn't for what he would almost certainly be doing with the land: planting tobacco. He had no interest in tobacco, loathsome to the eye, hateful to the nose, dangerous to the lungs. And it wasn't, finally, flight to a land more hospitable to Catholics; your husband was more than willing to barter away his allegiances to Rome, if that's all that might have stood between him and what he desired.

For him, it was just the land, a good in itself, an object and an end, the soil and the dirt, the sound and feel of it under his boots, the pleasing rise and fall of its contours, the fingers and fists of it thrust into the

3

Bay, the paper-thin but immutable shroud of ownership, the blessings and documents, the greetings and the seals that would make it his forever, the permanence of it (so he thought). Why would that matter so much, be worth leaving all that was known, the gentle landscapes of Kent, the advantages of his family's well-established enterprise? Well, it just did matter that much to him.

But no one ever asked you what it was for, did they? No one saved a scrap of your words, though you must have had some education; no one preserved your account books, though you must have become one of the shrewdest planters in the colony. The date and place of your birth, the date of your marriage, the dates of your children's births, the date and place of your death are all that is known of you. We must string your life between these points of light. Of you in the world after your death, besides the two of your six children who survived you, there is just a portrait: a young woman with hooded eyes, a sharp nose, but oh the beauty of those set lips, the skin, that long neck, and those tight ringlets of auburn hair. It hangs in the stairwell above the similar oval of your husband's likeness; it is you, three hundred and twenty years after your death, who oversees all who enter and depart, who permits and denies. After all, it was you who built this place.

See it now, the slight smile of an eighteen-year-old woman who knew that in the end she would prevail.

1

"Have you heard about our French cousins?"

Ethan was standing at the top of the stairs on the land-side porch of Mason's Retreat when they arrived, in the time-honored stance of welcome to this historic property. He'd come out when he heard the car pull through the gateposts at the bottom of the lane, but he made no motion to help them unload. He wore the bemused, self-satisfied look of one who has thus far not had the pleasure of packing or unpacking a car for an overnight with a two-year-old. He was twenty, with only one more year of college before he had to, as Rosalie thought it, get real. He was wearing a ragged, de-sleeved T-shirt that revealed his long, skinny arms and his tattoo. There had been family fretting about this tattoo; first of all, what was it, a bird in flight or a flaming car wreck? Eleanor had said she thought it was "cute." Bullshit, thought Rosalie. A bullshit word from Eleanor, who knew nothing, and cared nothing, about cuteness. Rosalie believed that Ethan, the delayed last-born and only son of this generation of

Masons, had been spoiled irretrievably, and she accepted some of the blame: they had all four raised him like a puppy.

"You mean one of the Frenches?" Rosalie asked. "Those people from the house?" Oral and Alice French had managed the Retreat more than a century ago, and the house they lived in was still referred to as the French House. Their descendants practically ran the county, but none of them was named French; they'd had only daughters, but Rosalie did not know that.

"No. French. As in France. Cousins."

"Do we need the BabyBjörn?" asked her husband, Paul.

Of *course* we need the BabyBjörn, thought Rosalie, not that Daniel would sleep a wink in it. Paul's wasn't a question that required an answer; it was a complaint. And it wasn't really a complaint about the crib or any of the other gear required to keep Daniel safe and happy; wasn't really a complaint about the challenges of parenthood, although parenthood is never as insipid as it seems when arriving for a weekend; but it was most definitely a complaint about the event, Fourth of July at the Retreat, all this family tradition. "*Almost three hundred and fifty years! Are we going to get there in time for the brunch?* Did you remember the *salmon poacher?*" Paul had mimicked on the way over the Bay Bridge. "Do you think that's enough *peas?*" All this Masonizing, as he called it, and it wasn't as if any of them, except possibly Ethan, had been born to this manor, or raised in its histories; if anything, it was a windfall to them, or a curse, a family relic Rosalie's father had salvaged out of some desperate desire for meaning after cashing in on a start-up IPO; the shares had tanked and never recovered, but the farm remained.

"No," said Rosalie. "I don't know anything about cousins from France. Will you help us, please?"

Ethan idled down the steps and poked a diaper bag as if it were a dead cat.

"Hold it by both handles," Rosalie snapped.

Paul had released Daniel from his car seat, and he headed off in a chubby run toward the graveyard, which was a few feet from the house. All those Masons, and Goldsboroughs and Hollydays and Lloyds, intermarried as if they were the marooned survivors of a seventeenth-century shipwreck, which was not so far from the historical truth: with settlement spread out over miles and miles of riverbanks, the Chesapeake families had married, and remarried, their neighbors, who were usually their cousins as well. "Not many branches on that tree," her father had said, an old joke apparently.

"I'll get him," said Paul.

"Don't let him climb on the graves."

"Someone has been bitten by the bitch bug," said Ethan.

Rosalie did not favor Ethan with a laugh, but he was right. A beautiful day, unusually dry and cool for July on the Chesapeake; even the city had been lovely, the air clear, with that intimate, emptied-out ease of the northwest neighborhoods on a long holiday weekend. As soon as she woke up and felt the breeze through the window, she knew Paul was going to be disagreeable about leaving; he was a city boy—Cleveland—and summer weekends like this could never be savored and treasured more than staying at home, on your own block, in your own corner of the park. On days like this, breakfast was never better than in your own cramped city kitchen. Taking the toddler for a walk, letting him stumble-walk behind the stroller, pudgy hands gripping the handles, was never better than on days like this. And in the afternoon, when that same child, tired out from all the fun, obligingly settled down for a deep nap, married sex, as the sun-brightened curtains flapped luxuriously in the breeze, was never as voluptuous. In fact, she and Paul could really, really use such a day right about now; how long had it been since they had had that kind of fun? And sure enough, Paul woke just after she did, rolled over to look out the window, and then let out a groan and a "*shit*." "I know," she said. She could see the appeal of staying home, of course she could. This might not be the easiest of the Fourths at the Retreat, and as much as to remind herself as to forestall the slightest debate with her husband, she said, "This could be the last."

"How is Mom?" she asked Ethan now.

"Oh," he said, casting his eyes away from hers. "Okay. I guess. Everyone keeps telling her how much better she looks."

"What do you think?"

"She looks okay, I guess."

"And?"

"And yes," he answered curtly; and *What the fuck*, he meant. At that, he took hold of the crib and one of the suitcases and trudged up the stoop and into the house. The louvered screen door crashed heavily after him; from the inside came a muffled bark about letting the door slam: their father, Harry. Ethan was in college in New York, but on his vacations, his summers, he had borne the weight of their mother's illness almost without complaint. And now, only a few moments after thinking of him as feckless and immature, Rosalie reflected that she, at eighteen, nineteen, had coped with not a fraction of Ethan's lot, none of the terrors of a child losing a parent, none of the burden of carrying on—because that's what he was ordered to do, to carry on as if all were fine, to demonstrate on a daily basis that he wasn't being scarred by his unwelcome assignments: cheer up and distract Dad when they ate alone at home, drive Mom across the bridge to Annapolis to get her wig and her prostheses fitted, come to the phone and for the eight-*millionth* time tell his sisters, or his grandmother and aunt, or Myrtle, their well-meaning but incorrigibly nosy cleaning lady, how the latest round of chemo had gone, to tell everyone *how good she looked*. God, why had she asked him that? Rosalie was now pissed off at everyone—herself, Paul, Daniel, Ethan, the trunkful of luggage, her blameless ill mother—but what she was really angry at was having to make this visit to a house where, to read the grave markers, many of the women of the family had died young.

During the time when Rosalie was castigating herself, Eleanor had come out onto the porch. She watched Rosalie's lips move and decided not to interrupt, but that would not have been Eleanor's m.o. in any case. Eleanor was a lurker, a watcher with a voyeur's lust in every glance, an aspiring writer trenchantly storing away whatever unguarded moments she could steal, a dream catcher, someone ancient peoples would have feared, with good reason. She watched Rosalie run one hand along her temple, patting a strand of her blond hair behind her ear. Rosalie had been heavy as a child, good German American stock like their mother, but she came into her own as a three-season jock in school and college, and even now, in her bright Patagonia tank top and violet trail shorts, she looked ready to kayak across the Bay, which, of course, she had already done several times. Eleanor had always been skinnier, and in her black leggings and racerback she might have looked equally athletic, but it was all show. She was dark, and proud of it, and she played up to it; she didn't mind that the two of them used to be called Sunshine and Shadow. If those were the available choices, she was content with the one that had been made for her; she believed that the men who were attracted to the shadows were more interesting than those looking for the sun, though Eleanor did quite like her brother-in-law, Paul Gottlieb—and never more than when he was mocking or complaining about Rosalie. Aside from that sisterly pleasure, his take on almost any subject often surprised Eleanor; he was, after all, an academic, a climate scientist, a prophet. Paul, Eleanor had once concluded, was a person of sun *and* shadow. Her current boyfriend was all shadow, almost ghostly; in the sunlight he looked exposed, desperate, hunting for a place to hide.

"Am I supposed to not realize you're standing there?" said Rosalie.

"I was letting you finish your conversation with yourself."

Rosalie looked as if she might snap back, but then she let her shoulders slump. "I was mad at myself for asking Ethan how Mom looked. You know. As if I wouldn't be seeing her in about two minutes and could answer that for myself. As if I couldn't face it. God!"

"I *do* know," said Eleanor. The truth was, sisterly rivalries apart and despite every possible appearance, she and Rosalie could still finish each other's sentences, duplicate each other's thoughts, mirror each other's instincts and impulses with cellular precision. Eleanor sometimes felt bad that Ethan, coming when she was nine and Rosalie was twelve, would never share in this spooky affinity. But no one was tighter with their mother than he was; no one could give her the comfort he was giving now that she needed it so badly. In a certain cul-de-sac of her mind, Rosalie believed that Ethan deserved this unique burden as a kind of payback for being their mother's favorite.

"Actually, she looks fine," said Eleanor. "She's very excited about today, but she does get a little spacey. She's in a panic because she can't find the salmon poacher. I told her you would know where it is."

There was a shout from the graveyard; Paul and Daniel were playing a form of hopscotch on top of the slabs. "Shit," said Rosalie.

"I'll get them," said Eleanor, and headed over. There had until recently been a massive beech tree in one corner of the burial plot, and under its dense, low-hanging boughs nothing grew and the ground was covered with spiky nut husks. This was what Eleanor remembered from the first time she'd come here. She was six; the family lived in California, and Eleanor had no idea what this place was, and no idea that her parents were making this trip east because they were debating moving to New York and had taken this detour to the Retreat on their last day because her father was considering buying it. Buying it *back*, really. It hadn't seemed remarkable to Eleanor that this was the seat of their family in the New World, or that it was her grandfather Pop who had given it up—the Mason who lost it. What Eleanor remembered most vividly from that first visit was piling out of the car in front of this empty, hulking house, following her parents in her bare feet to the graveyard, and then being punctured by those nut husks and trapped by them and crying until her father picked her up and deposited her on a grave slab. The ancient stone was cool and soothing on her scratched soles, and she looked down to see a skull and crossbones at the top of the epitaph, which seemed pretty neat. No one had told her that her family had been pirates. She believed this well into her early teens.

"Rosalie says not to step on the stones," Eleanor said.

"Uh-oh," said Paul. "Are we riling up the ghosts?" He looked down at the inscription at his feet: "A blessing she was / God made her so."

"Oh, nothing disturbs *their* slumber. It's them you have to worry about." She pointed to the back of the graveyard, into a scraggle of trees, where slaves and servants had been buried over the years, mostly in unmarked graves. "Joe," proclaimed one low stone.

"Indeed," said Paul. Somehow every reflection about his wife's family ended up in a grave somewhere; the Retreat was Halloween the year round. Paul supposed that life everywhere ended up in a grave, but here that ordinary fact seemed noteworthy, as if the Retreat had found a way to contain the multitudes. In Paul's mind, nothing ever left this farm, certainly not by way of anything as trivial as death.

"Hello, Daniel," said Eleanor in a cutesy auntie voice. The child ignored her. Perhaps this was typical behavior for an almost three-year-old with grown-ups he saw rarely, but the truth was, Eleanor found him unappealing, wide-set eyes in a broad, bruiserish face: not the sort of child people gazed at. Possibly he sensed her reserve; the worry was that Rosalie might have sensed it also.

"So, who's here?" asked Paul.

Eleanor was taken aback by the question—this was hardly Paul's first visit—but in response she dutifully began to describe the two oldest graves—Richard Mason "the Emigrant" and his wife—and then their son with his wife, a daughter of Philomen Lloyd. "The big family next door, much more interesting history than ours," she explained, and it was only then that she realized Paul's expression had gone from an equal amount of surprise to high amusement. "Oh," said Eleanor. "Shit. You mean, who's here for the weekend?"

"Yes. I wondered how far you'd get in the genealogy."

"I've been at this too long," she said. She was working on a novel set in the first decades of the Chesapeake settlement, based on the life of Mary Foxley, the Emigrant's wife, and she had been at it for long enough within her own cone of silence—and despair—that "working on the novel" had become a sort of family code for Eleanor going nowhere. What, after all, was a master of fine arts degree from Columbia for if it didn't get you published within a year or two of graduation?

"You don't have to apologize to me," said Paul. "All I think about is carbon dioxide absorption."

"At least what you do matters. 'Poetry makes nothing happen,'" she quoted. "Not that anyone is listening to you these days."

"So we're in the same boat."

"Anyway . . ." she said. Daniel was now bored with the gravestones, and it was time to get going. "Mom and Dad are here, of course. And Ethan and his girlfriend from Vassar, and Dad will be bringing Pop down from Osprey Neck. And later, I think my friend Vittorio is going to come for dinner. But maybe he isn't. I don't know," she said. "I don't care if he comes or not."

"I see," said Paul.

"And Alice Howe. I think you met her once? She's ninety-six, and lived across the creek when my grandfather and his brother lived here in the thirties. It was her boat that Pop's brother, Sebastien, was sailing when he drowned. Her cousin Margaret is bringing her over from Weatherly and everyone is hoping Margaret won't stay, but she'd never pass up free food. And then there are these cousins from France, and who knows how much English they have."

"Ethan mentioned something about them," said Paul.

"Some kind of Mason," she said carelessly, but actually, she knew very well who they were, the descendants of the family's famous Thomas Bayly and Beal Terrell, the scion and the servant, an interracial couple who had escaped to France in the 1890s. She understood, as her sister and brother simply refused to grasp—*I never can figure out how the Baylys get into this*, said Ethan quite recently—that Thomas's mother, Ophelia Mason, had inherited the Retreat after her two brothers were killed in the Civil War, and that she had married a man named Wyatt Bayly. And after their son, Thomas, had renounced any claim to the Retreat and never returned, his sister Mary Bayly took over, and before she died, without issue, she gave the place *back* to a Mason, Eleanor's great-grandfather Edward. *I mean, Ethan, is that really so complicated?* The American Masons and the French Baylys: two families bound by blood, by history, but mostly by what remained of the ancestral property called Mason's Retreat. She could tell

Paul all this—not that he hadn't heard it before—but there was a distinction here that was important to her: yes, she was writing a novel based on the life of one of their forebears, she was using some of the material, but no, she was not a damn family historian, a tedious elitist genealogist, a little twit clucking about Aunt So-and-So. "Cousins from a different branch," she allowed.

"Hmm," said Paul. Once again, one of those old family stories edged into view; it was so often like this when living in a repository of tales, each one writ on a single card in a trim stack of moments and episodes ready to be pulled out of the deck, held up a sleeve, or hastily shuffled back in.

They had wandered back to the car and the stoop, and Daniel had clambered up to the landing. To either side of the door there were green benches piled with baby paraphernalia waiting to be brought in, as well as a pair of lacrosse sticks—just exactly *who*, wondered Eleanor, did Rosalie expect to play catch with—a drinks cooler, and a bag of trash. Daniel was whining to be picked up so he could give the door knocker a good thundering smack—a sound, Eleanor assumed, they'd be hearing plenty of during the weekend, along with the dinner chimes in the butler's pantry and the fire bell in the "servants' wing." These were the noisemakers children always loved. They were only a few of the sounds this house made; most of the others, the more interesting ones, never rose above a murmur, a whisper, scrutable but nonverbal.

"I'll let you go in and make your hellos," said Eleanor. "I was going out to the rivershore anyway."

Paul watched her march off. She'd grabbed the trash bag, apparently headed to the river by way of the dumpster at the farm, and he was dismayed that even this heedless and homely act seemed vaguely erotic to him. It was the sense of weight on those narrow shoulders, the straining of that lovely flesh at the hairline on the back of her neck, the curve of her waist emphasized in the extreme by her skintight shirt. Many of Paul's undergraduate students dressed exactly like Eleanor, but for all their beauty they were students, kids, untested and finally not all that interesting to look at. Eleanor had seemed thus far unlucky in love, or had made choices—like this scumbag Vittorio—that seemed designed to have the same result, all of which did nothing for Paul but increase his interest in her, as if in some unimaginable and unwanted far-off future he found himself alone, she would still be available to him.

He had now pulled the heavy louvered door open, and from the darkness inside he heard Ethan saying to Rosalie, "Mom can't find the salmon poacher."

"Yes," Paul called in, "but has she found the salmon? Is it the same one from last year?"

He got no response. Paul knew he had gone too far. Even Daniel, who was suddenly still, standing at his side, knew it. "I'm sorry," he called into the bruised silence, though he didn't know if anyone heard it. He'd have to apologize to Ethan more convincingly, but the truth was, he had never bought into the cult of "Ethie." Ethan reminded him of the underachieving boys in his classes who were his very least favorite cohort; their capacity to bullshit others and to patronize their betters—"Hey, *Paul*, what's up, man?"—was boundless, especially for the good-looking kids like Ethan. *Rich WASPs*, he might have said.

He held out his hand for Daniel. "Hey, Bear. Dad said a mean thing. Let's go inside and face the music."

"Here it is," said Rosalie. She had brought over a stool and was reaching blindly into the recesses of the cabinet above the refrigerator. She handed down the long oblong pan to her mother.

"I'm sorry. This isn't chemo brain," her mother said. "This is just me getting old and stupid."

"And your habit of asking questions and then not listening to the answers."

Oh, Kate thought, I probably deserved that. It felt good, after all, to be discussing her normal failings after the past five years, when so much had been extraordinary, terrifying, painful. "Ordinary heartbreak," Nadezhda Mandelstam had called what she yearned for in those years of exile, her husband's imprisonment— what Kate reminded herself she had enjoyed enough of in her life: miscarriages, a thwarted academic career, bad years in California before Harry quit drinking. All of which, now, was hers and hers alone; recalling these heartbreaks made her feel glad to be alive.

"It's a miracle all three of you survived into adolescence," she said.

"It's a miracle at least one of us isn't still waiting for you to pick us up at soccer practice."

"That was *once*," she protested. But yes, the incident had involved the police.

Starting out, Kate had never imagined any of this, and by *this*, she meant the life she had lived. She had grown up in Connecticut, followed her mother dutifully to Mount Holyoke College, but when the time came, she bolted, moving as far away from all that as she could, to Berkeley, to graduate school in what used to be called comp lit—German, Russian, French. She introduced herself to her new classmates and professors not as the bland "Kate," but as Käthe, much more suitable with the last name of Lorenz; she'd been planning that switch since high school. She had a little third-floor apartment just down the hill from Shattuck Avenue, and when the wind was right she could hear the coffee impresario, Peet—was that his first name or last, it took her months to find out because she never had the courage to go into the shop—trashing out some customer for asking a naïve question. She could smell the espresso even now, the dangerous aroma leaking from the café just up the street; her parents drank Nescafé. The Connecticut suburbs, whiter-than-white New England: done with all that. In every part of her life in California an *old* was being shoved aside by a *new*: nothing about food was being left unchallenged. The New Critics, even the French structuralists, were in full flight; she was swimming joyfully in the newest of directions. One more kick of her little feet and she would be free, but a last thrash of an octopus tentacle caught her by the heel, and before she knew it, her degree was an ABD, she had a child, Käthe was no more, Kate was back. The octopus, of course, was a Stanford Business School student—of *all* things— named Harry Mason. It didn't help that she had declared as her dissertation topic the poetry of Paul Celan—might as well write a paper on life on Mars as attempt to explicate Celan—but the tentacle was the thing.

She tried to refocus, tried to get some lines from Philip Larkin about being "linked to losses." She was searching for this one, from "Reference Back": "Truly, though our element is time, / We are not suited to the long perspectives / Open at each instant of our lives. / They link us to our losses." Ever since the last round of chemo ended several weeks ago, Kate had been rereading Larkin; she forgave him nothing, but he had a way of ripping her heart from her chest and leaving it thumping on the table in front of her, which served her mood very well. She wanted to see her heart thumping. Larkin had been with her ever since she'd gone to a poetry recital at Mount Holyoke given by some English actor. Over the years, as a parent, "They fuck you up, your mum and dad" had been her argument of defense, the faux confession she had used when the girls were teenagers. "'Well, useful to get that learnt,'" she would say when they told her what an awful, careless mother she was. "'Home is so sad,'" she said when they were grounded, not taken to the mall. Years later, Eleanor realized that her mother had been quoting Larkin all along. "Figures," Eleanor said. "He was a misogynist bigot."

"Mom," Rosalie said.

"I'm sorry," she said. "For some reason I was thinking about Berkeley. The smell of the coffee, I think."

Rosalie gave her a calculated look, an appraising one-to-ten on some scale of dementia, but then—how Kate needed this—the look, urgent with concern, softened into pure love. What is pure love? Well, forgiveness, of course, but also admiration for what you are, what you have done; it is sympathy, because everyone has a corner of the soul that needs to be pitied; it is boredom, because a fully lived life is after all a tedious slog. More than any of all this, one feels that love is pure when no one else on earth gets this particular mishmash from this lover, this parent, this child.

"Thank you, sweetheart," said Kate, and what she was thanking her for needed no explanation. "I am really only about a third in the room these days. It's actually not so bad. It's kind of druggy, and I know it is irritating to be around, but the memories are very strong."

"You're doing great. This Mason pageant. I think it's no one's favorite thing, but it always seems right at the end of the day. To honor the place, if not the people."

"That's very nice, dear, but I don't know about what we owe to this house. This day is for Pop," she said.

"Not that he's willing to spend a night here. Not that he really grew up here."

"Oh, don't get him started on *that*."

Rosalie handed her the poacher and left the room. Kate stared down at the pan, wondering, for a moment, what it was, but then the day ahead snapped into view and she worked that logic back to the pan. That was the way her thinking went these days. Was the salmon she had ordered big enough? Did they have enough peas? She counted through the guest list for the millionth time: the seven of them, counting Daniel; Eleanor's awful Victor, maybe; and Ethan's girlfriend, what's-her-name? Kate went to the window facing the water, and there she was, down on the lowest terrace with her sketchbook in her lap, so hunched over her work that she looked, way down there, like a porcelain figurine called, maybe, *The Artist*. A pretty girl. Her face was slender and flawless, and she wore big, heavy glasses, which Kate found endearing, even a little sexy—a naughty librarian. Kate didn't know where the girl had slept last night, one of the advantages of living in this monstrous ark, with airless maids' rooms under the eaves of the third floor and a whole wing of summer kitchens and laundries and cooks' quarters. The house was a cocoon wrapped in privilege; it had sucked the blood out of the people who worked in it and left their souls in limbo. That's what Kate thought about its history, when she thought about it, which she tried not to do very much, especially these days.

But back to the girl. Kate didn't care where she slept. Heidi, yes, that was it. So with Heidi and Victor, or *Vittorio*, as she reminded herself, maybe, there were nine of them—did I count Daniel? she wondered, and then started all over, not counting Daniel. Pop made eight, not counting Daniel. Then Alice Howe, who had been living on the farm across the creek, Weatherly, since forever. For a time she had owned a small local publishing company that concentrated on the Chesapeake Bay; they made lovely books on obscure bits of local history—the Oyster Wars, the steamship lines, Hooper Island workboats—but they never made any money. Her cousin Margaret would be bringing her over, pretending she couldn't stay because she had a roast something in the oven but of course, staying. How many was that?

Where were the dogs? she wondered. Rowdy was probably out rolling in a dead fish carcass or feasting on rotten deer haunch. Disgusting animals, dogs.

And then the cousins from France. Julien Bayly's great-grandparents had grown up here, an old family story. This was in the 1890s. Julien had long been interested in seeing the place his father's family sprang from and had been in contact with Harry for some years about a visit to the Retreat, and this, finally, was the first time it had worked out. He was bringing a son or a daughter and maybe a grandchild—here is where the head count really fell apart, as many as fifteen, but no matter what it was, they would still need to set a place for Daniel, or Rosalie would complain. Kate had ordered a monster-size fish; the young man at the fishmonger offered to help her load it into her car. Fortunately, this late in the mid-Atlantic season—salmon and peas for the Fourth of July was a New England thing after all, her one contribution to the event—fresh peas could no longer be found, which took the guesswork out of peas in the pod. She had one whole freezer shelf given over to bags of frozen *petits pois*. French had been the third language she learned, after English and German and before the smattering of Russian she had acquired before Harry took her for that weekend in Monterey. *That* weekend. If these cousins had little or no English, she figured she could saw through the day. She had resolved to practice her French in advance but had not. Of course they might be able to connect in German; hers was still pretty good. It was a Lorenz family affectation, conversing in German; whether or not the French Baylys spoke English, if they did speak German, her cousin Lotte would simply eat them alive. Poor Lotte. Did I count her? And her husband, Hector? Is the fish big enough?

Looking out the window, she saw Ethan approach his girlfriend on the lawn. The girl kept her eyes glued to her drawing as he came upon her, even as he stood over her. Hmmm. She'd been out there since Kate came downstairs: trouble, or was it simply that she was very serious about her art? Last night at dinner she'd said, "Drawing landscape is about capturing a moment of change." Very nice. Kate wasn't sure whether this was a girl for Ethan—maybe a little too intense for her floppy-headed boy?—but time would tell, and let it. Let it be for now. Her people were gathering—Paul's booming voice and Daniel's exuberant squeals, the screen door slamming, and Harry, from somewhere in the house, bellowing his complaints—and here she was, still in her pajamas, fixating on a fish. A beautiful, clear day, a day that made up for a month of Chesapeake haze, as if a single day like this could add a month to one's life span. A beautiful day for doing this thing again, this homage to or apology for history—take your pick—in this strange house, Harry's Folly, as she thought of it. It was all either unbearably pointless or the last stop between them and the abyss, but either way it was a beautiful day to do it.

Eleanor heaved her burden into the dumpster and listened for the boom as it hit the bottom, an oddly satisfying sound, except, in this case, for the smashing of glass, not the tinkle of a respectable jelly jar, but the detonation of wine bottles. Infuriating. Number one, her mother shouldn't be drinking so much, there was no need for it; and number two, why was recycling so hard for her to do? Even in Brooklyn, most people could get that together. There had been, against all odds, an improvement in human civilization in regards to its trash: in fact, there were noticeably fewer plastic bottles, Styrofoam containers, and worn-out tires washed up on the rivershore these days, and about half the boats going by on a weekend were flying blue Trump flags. Even those turds knew how to take care of their trash.

Eleanor was never far from criticizing people, she knew that. She had vivid, cringe-inducing memories of herself as a sullen, judgmental child, hardly anyone's favorite. And more recently, in her MFA workshop at Columbia she was not widely loved, and she professed not to care. Her group—Vittorio, Letitia Mower, Deirdre McGonagle, Monroe Monroe (not a typo), ann smith (yes, always lowercase, but with a name like Ann Smith, with not so much as a middle initial, what's a writer to do?)—could hack harsh criticism, *wanted* harsh criticism. As a sign of respect they saved their most scabrous comments for each other—"Eleanor, this story is *a fecal embarrassment*" (whatever that meant)—but the general population felt it introduced bad karma into the discussions. One of their detractors had posted a manifesto of sorts on the department bulletin board, "Constructive Criticism in a Nutshell," which Vittorio had defaced to read "in a Nutsack." Especially galling that this person, "Miss Decorum" they called her, had just published her second novel, and the first had been a Notable Book.

But enough of these disappointments. Eleanor was working on a bigger thing, her world was a broader canvas than four college friends intersecting in Manhattan or a mother and daughter making a pilgrimage to Lake George with the grandmother's ashes. No little domestic dramas for Eleanor. Broader canvas, in time and place. "Sweep," if she must reveal how she saw it. That is what history can give us. There was history everywhere in this place, brick foundations peeking through the topsoil in the yards and pastures, the few remaining pilings where the peach dock had once jutted far out into the river, Wicomiss Indian middens of oyster shells and bones, dinosaur fossils. People claimed that dinosaur fossils had been found on the Eastern Shore, but Eleanor did not believe it: this land didn't even exist back then.

She turned, looked back at the sheds, the weathered silvery gray of the barns and corncribs, the silos, the gutted milking parlor: there was a history of maybe a hundred and fifty years of farm technology in these structures, almost all now unused. Technologies came and went; men wielded them, women did everything else by hand, a cast, over the years, of hundreds. Only three of the dwellings that once housed the families who worked here remained; the main farmhouse was rented to an accountant, the French House had become home base for a hunting club, and in the third lived Bo Handy, a longtime farmhand, and his son, Francis. The arable acres were leased to an organic farmer next door who harvested the corn and beans with lumbering combines as big as houses.

She left the farmyard behind and headed toward the waterscape, bands of land and expanses of river and bay, a water world. The corn was still low enough for her to see the distant Fourth of July parade of boats on the river, and beyond them, the far bank, another low swath of land, Eastern Neck Island, shrinking and sinking. There used to be family farms on Eastern Neck, but they had been abandoned long ago, the spit of land turned into a wildlife refuge, but the geese, swans, mergansers, loons, and grebes that could be seen there today would be wise to scout out other places to land in the years to come. Yes, history is the history of change, a washing away. What was it that Heidi had said at dinner last night about drawing landscapes? Capturing time? Something like that. Maybe the first time the girl opened her mouth, and out comes a bombshell like that! So where does that leave literature, especially fiction, especially historical fiction?

She had turned off the lane and was walking straight toward the water, a quarter mile or so away. In the distance, upriver, there were stands of loblolly and white pine, and the air was so clear on this remarkable day that Eleanor could almost see the needles and the pine cones, could smell the pitch. Ahead of her, at the edge of a small drainage gulley, a fat woodchuck scurried back to its burrow. The road was dusty, and these flat lands offered no refuge from the sun. Eleanor wished she had worn a hat. Long ago these fields had been scrub oaks and hickories, then tobacco and grain, then peach orchards, then hayfields and cow pastures, and now corn, wheat, and soybeans—oh, Eleanor knew everything about this farm, who had lived here, who had died here, who had gotten away. She didn't care about the begats, but she did care about the lives. All this agriculture, she thought, was kind of indecent, a sort of male dominance, forcing the land to produce this or produce that, an imposition of will, forcing fertilizer down its gullet like force-feeding a goose to make pâté. Yes, the Indians of the Eastern Shore had grown corn and beans and squash in these better-drained flatlands, but that was a kind of subsistence, living with the land; it was the English, the English *men*, who raped it.

She reached the end of the lane and glanced over the low bank onto the modest band of sand and stones and, in the old days, oyster shells that, in this place, passed for a beach. The wakes of the boats out in the channel were lapping the shoreline. It was up this channel that the English came, scouting for that perfect combination of inlet, creek, and deep water; they looked for nut trees because the hickories and pecans grew best on well-drained soil; they looked for fields that the Indians had kept open for planting; they looked for any kind of elevation or rise upon which to build and defend their houses. That was what the English *men* did, and when they found what they were looking for, they "discovered" it. Which is to say, took it. Eleanor imagined herself standing on this very spot three hundred and fifty years ago, not as a wary indigenous inhabitant—even for a novelist, some circumstances are impossible to conjure out of nothing—but as a recorder, a timeless person who hears and sees, seeing in this case a two-masted ship—a pinnace?—the *Elizabeth and Mary*, coming up the river, anchoring, lowering its boats, which were then rowed ashore. She could see figures in the lead boat, six men rowing, a gentleman on the tiller at the stern under a broad-brimmed hat—feather?—and in the bow, her shawl and bonnet flapping, feeling God knows what as she surveyed the scene, was Mary Foxley, holding a child. Did she see it as wilderness or Eden? What would *I* feel, wondered Eleanor, gazing out into the broad river, two miles wide at this point, if I were she? Mary Foxley, Eleanor's God of all things, and this, as Eleanor had long planned, was where her story must start, at the very beginning.

THE EXILE'S WIFE
A novel by
ELEANOR LORENZ MASON

(From the time when she learned the alphabet and began to read, she had loved the fact that all the letters in her first name could be found in her middle name and last name, with just an *m*, an *s*, and of course a *z* (!) left over. And now, for professional purposes, she valued her middle name even more, as it gave her, she hoped, a bit of global cred.)

Finding the Haven
This is how it happened for me, Mary Mariana Foxley.
I was born at Foxley Hall in London in my parents' bed, and
I was the death of my mother, as she had been for her mother,

as I came to expect my first child to be for me. Soon after my birth my father relocated the family to Rochester on the River Medway, where the ships of our day were built, or rigged, or provisioned for voyages to all the new worlds that were just then becoming visible to us. Besides this commerce, which was my father's business and trade, there was little remarkable in Rochester except for a castle in ruins and a Catholic sanctuary that was to be sacked by the Parliamentarians at the outbreak of the war. The grand highway of my youth was our river, and I could watch the trade on it from the nursery window, tell the time of day and the month of the year by the cargoes piled on those decks. I marveled at the diversity of goods and wondered who had grown those vegetables, raised that livestock, milled that flour, gathered those hops and apples; in years to come, no lesson from my childhood was to prove more valuable to me than these reflections on the nature of trade.

I was raised by my father's sister, who blamed me daily for my mother's death. She was a widow, and none of her children had survived, but of all these passings she had chosen my mother's to express her rage against fate. "Where is Elizabeth?" she would ask, using my mother's Christian name so that I could not forget that it was not just my mother I had killed, but a woman who would be alive today if it weren't for me. "She is dead, Aunt," I would say. "Why did she die?" asked my aunt, and there was no reply I could give, because the answer was that she died because she was female, and that I, a female child, had killed her and could only expect and deserve the same.

And so my early childhood years passed. Of food and clothing I was given only what I needed to survive. I had no brothers or sisters to play with, and I was kept apart from my cousins in London. I was given little education in the schoolroom; my only pastimes were the labors of the house. In this way my aunt offered me entry into a communion of suffering that is the female lot.

I might have succumbed had it not been for my father, who loved me and treasured me as a last gift from his departed wife. He was powerless to enact a better life for me in his own house, so he let me escape into his world. He loved to talk, loved the sounds and shapes and meanings of words and what they could unlock, and thus, he imparted to me—I do not remember exactly how this happened—the ability to write and read. My father was a large, burly man, and it pleased him to be seen with his little daughter at his side; wherever we walked, we went hand in hand. We went to the shipyards, where I made dolls out of the pristine mounds of wood shavings and built a house for them with wood trimmings. We went to the roperies and sail lofts, where in the trades of harnessing the wind there seemed to be magic at work. I learned much about the world of men in these places, and I saw kindness and also violence, yet I saw none of the cruelty that I endured at home. I became acquainted with everything to be known about ships and the commerce of the seas. After I had outgrown my pastimes on my father's rounds, I entered his sheds and his countinghouse, and though the clerks were less friendly to me than the tradespeople, I soon proved that I could do all the figures necessary to run an enterprise.

I met my husband's cousin first, a ship captain of whom my father was very fond. I was ten years old, I believe, and it amused him to be questioned about his voyages, not without perspicacity, by a girl. On this first occasion he was outfitting his ship Golden Fortune *to conduct trade on the great Bay of the New World, the Chesapeake, on behalf of the Mary-Land colony's proprietor, Cecilius Calvert. I do not know how a mariner of Kent had come under the employment of a family in the County of York, but by the time he was done, he had earned the title Admiral of Mary-Land. It was thus that, when it began to seem wise for my husband to emigrate, he knew of a place in the New World where he would be favorably received.*

Of the Interregnum, the wars of the three kingdoms and of the Commonwealth and the Protectorate, of the complaints between the Anglicans and the Catholics and the Quakers and Puritans, and of my husband's part in any of it, I will say little, because I knew little and understood less of the political rivalries in our country. When my father gave me in marriage, my husband was a surgeon in the Royal Navy, and my father believed this institution could be trusted, as mariners have always been trusted, to steer a middle course, to bend this way or that to gain favorable winds, to put in at the safest harbor, and thus, my father believed the same would be true for my husband. None of this went quite as he hoped. For some years the navy did indeed attempt to remain loyal both to the king and to Parliament, but that became impossible, and it was with the Parliamentarian fleet that my husband remained. I was never sure why, but it was not for me to question it. He was an impulsive man, a man of actions inspired not by logic or loyalty, but by dreams, and I learned upon his death that the year before we were married, he had signed a petition to have justice done to the king for his many lapses of honor and faith. I had always felt that my life was bent by a force or power that was unknown to me, and when I learned of that petition, I knew this was it. He signed it on a whim; his friends had done it, and my husband thought, Why not? Why should not justice be done, whatever justice was.

But in that way my fate and my future were sealed, even as we were living in comfort with his family in Maidstone. As I approached the delivery of my first child, I accepted that I might not survive, but in the end it was the child, a boy we named Samuel after my husband's cousin, who did not live out the day. He lies now beside my mother, who lies beside her mother; we can only consider our ends, and our time well spend. My second child, my daughter Maria, was born sickly, but she survived, and then William, a quick birth attended by wild cries and vigorous kicking, thrust himself into the world. This was in the year 1658, and by then my husband had left the navy and was deep in planning our removal to Mary-Land. With certain promises in hand and letters of introduction to Lord Baltimore, he left on his cousin's ship Golden Fortune *with five servants, to select and survey his lands, to obtain a patent to them, to build an estate. I departed with my son William, still not but two years old, a year later from Gravesend on the* Elizabeth and Mary. *Our daughter Maria, age five, was not healthy enough to survive the voyage, and I left her in the care of my husband's family; I never saw her again, but that did not mean we ceased to be mother and daughter. I saw my father for the last time, standing on the shore, waving his sad farewell, and though I knew that my life as I had known it was at an end, that death by a hundred causes might await me, I was content. I had outlived my aunt. I had survived my confinements. I had proved my abilities. I was ready for the adventure to come.*

The time of our passage had been chosen wisely, and our ship was never in danger. I endured none of the terrors of the seas nor likewise the monotonies and privations of the mariners' diet, as my father had arranged for me to dine at the captain's table, where we had fresh meat and pies at almost every meal, and where the captain and his gentlemen passengers drank gallons of rum and cider late into the evening. In addition to our cargoes of Spanish wine and cheese, clothing, shoes, candles, and nails, there were aboard perhaps thirty indentured persons who came out on the deck in fair weather. I had seen much poverty in my last years in Rochester and could only hope that these people would fare better in the New World. I tried to talk to them and learn about their lives, but they were mute to me.

On the fifty-ninth day we put in at Kecoughtan at the head of the Bay to discharge most of the cargo and the indentures, except for a few, including six who had been purchased by my husband. After taking on some ten hogsheads of tobacco, we continued up the Bay, putting in at several plantations to unload stores and persons and to take on tobacco. In this way I began to grasp trade in the Chesapeake, the extreme reliance on a single crop, the complete dependence on trade for the manufactured goods necessary to survive, and I understood as well the society of it, where each planter conducted business as his own merchant state. On land there was no village or parish, no road or public way, no government save the distant power of the Crown. On the Bay there were ports and landings, landmarks that stood like beacons for pilots who knew where to look, and for long stretches the low, verdant shores ran alongside our ship, guiding the way north; I was entering a drowned world, a water world upon which the land simply floated in an evolving array.

At each stop, even before our anchor was set, we could hear the sounds of rejoicing rising from the shore; our captain might have preferred to get the business done and then move on, but there was no way to accelerate these visits. "What news of home?" they asked. "Have the Stuarts been restored? Have you no letters for us?" I would never have foreseen such behavior from myself, even with the image of my father on the dock so recently engraved on my heart; I was puzzled by this unseemly *clinging to home when home could no longer provide comfort. I favored the mood of our indentured servants, who for the most part had left behind nothing but misery and looked forward to their years of service and their ultimate freedom with the certainty that a better life lay ahead.*

All this time we drew ever closer to the River Chester, where, if disease or Indian attacks had not put a swift end to this whole venture, my husband would be waiting for me on the patent he had earned the right to name, now and forever, the Haven. So it was that sixty-seven days after I said farewell to my father at Gravesend, we rounded Love Point on Kent Island—where Mr. Claiborne had established and fought for his claim—and anchored in the river. I do not know how our captain determined that this was the right place to put ashore my son and me, the other persons traveling with us, the goods my husband had ordered. Some of the shores we had passed were high yellow clay banks topped with pines, and some were wetlands where grasses waved like grain in the wind, but this was something in between, perhaps a mile of low coastline with what seemed to be a few open meadows and various hues of green, which even I, a girl of town life, knew promised good pasture and good fodder. In the center of this gentle expanse was what appeared to be an agreeable and sheltered rivulet, above which the land gradually rose to a level of perhaps twenty-five feet above the sea. At the top of this rise, an easy few hundred feet from the water, I caught a glimpse of something man-made, a dwelling or barns. As the boat rowed me into the creek, my son in my arms, I could see the logic of this place, each element of land and water supplying a piece to the puzzle, each crop and good fulfilling a purpose within this system. I had the feeling that my husband had printed his thumb on Lord Baltimore's map shrewdly. I did not miss the fact that he had chosen to posit us at the head of this fine river, with its many creeks and coves and shelters, and that any commerce flowing out of this watershed would pass not a half mile from our anchorage. I had grown up on rivers, and the sense of what this Haven could someday be was plain to me.

2

"Hi," said Ethan, as much to warn Heidi of his approach as to say hello. Still, she looked up, startled, her pencil point unmoved from its spot on the paper.

"Oh," she said.

Ethan tried not to be disheartened, though from the beginning of his relationship with Heidi he had felt he was playing above his game. The first night he made any real overture to her they were in a bar in Poughkeepsie with some of her friends, and he placed his hand strategically on her thigh, not so low as to be pointless, but not high enough to come on (too) strong. In the midst of the rumble of the bar and the conversation, she stared down at his hand as if it were a lizard or rodent, a small beast that had gotten there by mistake, and that withering glance had left Ethan wondering how and when to remove it. Not an encouraging start, but at the end of the evening she invited him into her room.

"'Oh,' what?" he said now.

She softened. "I mean, am I supposed to be doing anything?" She beckoned at her page, on which she was drawing not a sweep of landscape, as Ethan had assumed, but a single plant, a tall grass that, in her drawing, exploded into relief out of the backdrop of the marsh. "I should help," she said, but her pencil was still on the page.

"No. Keep out of it, is my advice."

There was a loud splash from the water, and they both looked between the cattails and sedge toward Mason's Creek, a not totally welcoming green in these flat conditions; the water was blue when there was a nice breeze from the south and turned copper when a squall was coming in from the west. But in stillness, a sickly green. The mouth of the creek had once been much narrower, with a natural channel sufficiently deep for ships to come in to take on tobacco; there was still a rubble of stones where the pier had been. But every year the mouth of the creek widened and the channel silted in, and now, unless one knew where to steer for the remains of the old entrance, you'd run aground in a kayak. Beyond the creek and across the vast basin of the river they could see Kent Island and, beyond it, in this extraordinary light, the spindly outlines of the towers of the Bay Bridge.

"Rays, probably," said Ethan. "We're seeing a lot of them this year. Wildlife comes and goes. This year, a lot of rays and foxes."

"Is your sister here? I thought I heard a baby. Is that what they're called, at two? Babies?"

"I think you call them toddlers," he said. And laughed. Talking about babies seemed, at that moment, wonderfully, enticingly erotic. It took *nothing* for the idea of sex with Heidi to spring to mind, which seemed the same for her too. "Come up when you're done. I just came to say that Rosalie and I are going to town to get some stuff for Mom. You're good here."

She watched him trudge off. This place, this whole deal, was not at all what she had expected. She was a Vermont girl, and she regarded anything south of Pennsylvania—before college, Heidi had never heard of the Mason-Dixon Line—as indolent, a place full of bigots and morbidly obese teenagers. She'd fulfilled her history requirement at school by taking a course on the early colonial period, and their instructor could not hide his preference for the proper English towns that sprang up in New England compared with the soulless, slaveholding fiefdoms of the Chesapeake. This played well at Vassar. Heidi thought that even if it was all true, it was odd for a teacher to loathe half his material. Ethan Mason, the cute but skinny junior in the back row, never said a word. Then she and Ethan started to go out, and she learned about this place, the Retreat, learned that over the centuries it had been in and out of the Mason family's hands, but always seemed to come back, and the two of them found themselves enacting scenes from William Faulkner, herself playing Shreve to Ethan's Quentin, prizing out the stories, with Ethan all but saying *I don't hate it. I don't hate it* at the end of the evening. When he invited her for the Fourth of July weekend, all she could picture, despite the Victorian hulk Ethan had been describing those nights, were white columns, something out of, yes, *Absalom, Absalom!*, which was the only book besides *Beloved* she'd ever read that took place in this swamp of American life. She'd arrived last night, with just enough light left for her to see that the house in no way rose up from the site in the manner of an antebellum edifice, but rather seemed to skulk in the dusk, as if whipped. Oh, she thought, so this is what Ethan has been telling me.

She went back to her drawing, long enough to hear the faint sound of a car, or two, drive down the lane, and from across the creek a gobbling of turkeys, and then, from the scrub of trees and grasses at the edge of the lawns, a rustling, and she wondered if it was a fox or a moose, or something dangerous, or just those dogs, which were always out prowling. With another clattering of branches, a man burst, tumbled, out onto the grass. He was short and solid, with a head of bushy black hair and a beard. "Sorry," he said, looking back at whatever on the path had tripped him. "I'm Paul."

"I'm Heidi."

"I know. Ethan's friend."

"And you're Rosalie's husband," she answered.

"Well. We have that covered." He shrugged. "I don't mean to disturb you," he said, but he approached and leaned professorially over her pad in the way that all art students both crave and dread. She had no choice but to turn it slightly toward him, wishing that her heart had not suddenly begun to thump.

"Rose mallow," he said. "This one is blooming early. Later in the month this whole bank will be in bloom."

"Gee," said Heidi. "I'll miss it."

"Marshes are kind of my hobby. Especially here, where they can go either way."

"I'm sorry?" Heidi thought she was sounding like an idiot, but what could he have meant, "go either way"?

"Right. I mean, in a mixed brackish marsh community you get this melting pot of freshwater and saltwater plants. And of course, when you have a wet spring like we just did, it favors the freshwater guys. That's what I was looking at." He pointed toward the slightly mashed opening he had just plowed through.

Heidi waited for a few seconds in the final hope that he would now comment, favorably, on her drawing, and he, so experienced with the desires of those of college age, did not miss it. "You know, in my field, we are always looking for good illustrators."

He said this through his sinuses, as if flushed with emotion, and Heidi, just as savvy about professors as he was about students, knew he thought he was nurturing her, paying her a fine compliment, just the thing to end the office-hour session. But she could not help snapping the cardboard cover closed on her portfolio, getting to her feet, and saying, "I have no desire to be anyone's illustrator."

Paul tried to backpedal—but of course, he just meant as a sort of paying gig, a day job, because of the detail and precision of this *fine* drawing; it's so hard to get people to *see*; seeing is what people can't seem do anymore, opening your damn eyes and noticing what is staring us in the face like, well, the rise of sea levels or the changes in migrations—and she pretended to be appeased. Maybe she really was. She seemed the sort of girl who was happy to land a punch but did not want to pick a fight, which, of course, meant that if she were still offended, she wouldn't say so.

"Well, I'd better go weigh in, the fish thing," Heidi said.

"This happens every year. Those of us on the periphery have no role in it."

"I'm sure you're right."

"I'm very fond of Kate," he said. Meaning, well, meaning he was sorry to have been disagreeable this morning to Rosalie and, by extension, to Kate, not to mention to Harry. He'd already pissed Ethan off with that crack about the salmon, and now he had mortally offended his girlfriend; *That guy is such a douche!* he could hear her saying. So yes, fondness was in order. "If she lets you help her, you'll have fun. She's always been candid, and now . . ." he said, not sure he should continue, having already bombed, "and now, with her illness . . ." This was getting impossible, but needed to be concluded. "Well, you know where you stand."

Paul watched her climb the terraces back to what this family still called the Mansion House. From down here at the edge of the water, the wraparound porch looked like a huge, insane grin;

what he pictured, hallucinated, was Chief Wahoo, the Cleveland Indians mascot of his youth, now replaced on the caps with the letter *C*, possibly, he thought, the most anodyne letter in the alphabet. When Heidi finally reached the house and opened the screen door, she disappeared as if gulped. Rose mallow, he mouthed as if completing the lecture, *Hibiscus moscheutos*.

Paul turned again to face his brackish marsh, as if seeking consolation from a nonjudgmental pet. "You still love me," he said. And it was so beautiful, so glorious, this ancient system of the estuary, a seesaw balanced on a fulcrum of salt. Everyone and everything with its own tolerations; wild rice to bulrush to cordgrass; marsh duck, bay duck, sea duck. The Bay seethed with its life cycles, the flood of the alewife and the shad swimming north to spawn in the fresh water of the Susquehanna River; the rockfish, preferring a touch of brackishness for their reproduction, convening at mid-Bay and then departing for the Atlantic, where they're known as striped bass; the perch and the blue crabs living out their lives in the basin. And let's not forget the croakers and menhaden that spawn in the Atlantic, their larvae carried into the Bay by the deepwater currents. Simply fabulous! Paul's spirits were picking up. And all of it, or mostly all, because of the marshes, the vital organs of the Bay, and the marshes are there because of the low-sloping shores, and the more the shores wash away, the more the marshes thrive, and in this rather climactic manner the Chesapeake Bay is eating itself alive. Which may not be good news if one happens to be a landowner.

When Paul met Rosalie, he'd been studying geomorphology, earth surfaces and landforms in response to the ages, the Holocene and the Pleistocene, to quaternary environmental change. The big stuff, the planetary surface, glaciers and canyons, coasts. That's what he still taught today, the lecture and the lab. When he started graduate school, he'd shunned the "birds and bunnies" end of the discipline even though, as the years went by, he was aware that he was becoming more interested in what flora and fauna inhabited these rocks, rills, and valleys, rather than just how they came to be. Then he met Rosalie—they were in Ann Arbor—and she brought him here to meet her parents, just as Ethan was doing with this girl Paul had mortally dissed, and everything he had been studying and thinking made sense, a whole of being, a unity. The Chesapeake Bay, a sort of eternity in a bottle, the myriad responses of a place to time. The same was true about the humans who gathered around it. This gathering, for instance, of direct descendants of those who first displaced the Indians and then enslaved the Africans. Well, different place, different time. Paul hoped that was good enough, since he had married into it; all this history was like oobleck: how it behaved depended on how hard you punched it.

But enough. He followed Heidi's path up into the house. It was time for the brunch, the traditional Mason Fourth of July Brunch. He was hungry, Daniel would be waking from an early nap, the day would begin. Conversations would be had. Where were the dogs, Paul wondered, not because he wanted to see them but because he dreaded that moment when they were invited to join the fun. *Bring in the hounds*, Harry would yell. He walked through the massive hall—the hall was the one space in the house that seemed as vast on the inside as one might imagine from the outside—and wound his way back to the kitchen. There was a large, battered farm table in the middle of the room, an expanse of stained chestnut that served as either the origin or the destiny of almost any activity in the house. Over the years, Paul had seen everything on this surface, from the split half of a pig to a hundred years of *National Geographic* magazines (don't ask), to the guts of Ethan's moped (no one was amused at that), and now a brunch was being assembled. Heidi had been given a job slicing tomatoes and looked happy enough; Eleanor had apparently made her way back from the rivershore and was sent out to pick dill and basil from the herb garden. Rosalie and Ethan had returned from the Food Lion with things that had been forgotten—lemons, mayonnaise, capers, toilet paper—and Rosalie, Paul assumed, was upstairs rousing Daniel lest he sleep into the afternoon and make everyone miserable for the rest of the day. And then there was a man Paul had never seen before, someone maybe about forty or older, a gaunt figure standing in the middle of this bustle uselessly and in the way, and people were moving him here and there like a dog or a step stool, but no one seemed to mind.

"Well," said Kate. "This should do it." She pushed her bandanna a little higher on her forehead with the back of a wet hand, then patted down the front of her overalls. The truth was that her hair had actually recovered enough not to give anyone that much pause, had grown back enough to look punk, heedless of youth and beauty, not to look like someone clawing for life as a cancer survivor, but she had grown to like the feeling of the bandanna. "Come and get it."

"Where's Dad?" said Eleanor, who had returned with the herbs.

"Where is Dad. Ever?" said Kate.

"Mom."

"He's picking up Pop."

Rosalie returned with Daniel in her arms. "Did you set a place for Daniel?" she asked.

"We're not setting places for anyone. This is just buffet. Or, as we say in America, 'boofaay.'" She smiled, as if she had made a mean joke. "Did you say hello to Francis?"

Oh, thought Paul, so *that's* who he is; he thought it might be. Francis Handy, the adopted son of a couple who had worked their whole lives on the Retreat. He lived there now, with his father, Bo, in a house at the end of the farm, under an enormous white oak reputed to be, after the demise of the locally famous Wye Oak, the largest in Maryland. Francis had been a spacey kid apparently, a farm boy who early on had loved to draw and paint and take photographs and had dreamed of going to France and becoming an artist, a sensibility that perplexed his otherwise loyal parents. Francis did a year or so at the community college and since then just worked around, at the hardware store, at Walgreens, for the county, even as he skirted just barely above the law, drugs, being led astray by the wrong people, all that. But he had never stopped being a photographer, with an eye for the marginal places and people at the edges of the Eastern Shore, and Kate had taken him under her wing, set him up with wedding shoots when she could, even arranged a show at a gallery in Annapolis of a study he'd done of "lady" bodybuilders posing in the horse barn at the Retreat. She believed he had a book in him.

"Hello, Francis," said Rosalie. She used to complain about the way he stared at her.

"Hello, Rose," he said.

Yes, thought Rosalie. Two people in the world call me "Rose": my father and Francis. And two people in the world call Eleanor "El": their father and Francis. And really, how could she mind: Bo and Francis (and, until her death, Bo's wife, Velma) had lived there through every change of ownership, knew more about the history, the white families, the Black families, than anyone in the county. The Handys were the conscience of the place. Bo himself spoke from the time, as they say, Before the Bridge; he spoke the languages of the land *and* the water. In fact, Rosalie, when out of practice, could understand almost nothing of what he said; she just nodded and smiled like any other rich DC interloper. So Francis calling them Rose and El was in no way an impertinence; it was rather, she thought, an anointing, an offer of protection. He had never called Ethan "Ethie" the way they all once did; Ethan seemed to make him nervous, skittish, fumbling his fingers. Rosalie didn't know why. Who in the *world* would be afraid of Ethie?

"Sit down, everybody," said Kate, and here was the best part of the day, any day really, sitting randomly around this epochal table with the boys and girls of her life in front of platters of scrambled eggs, beautiful ripe tomatoes, chicken salad with the crunch of walnuts and chewiness of dried cranberries, gorgeous early peaches, bread from a new bakery on Kent Island, and two bottles of rosé, from which Kate had already poured herself a small glass. Well, two very small glasses. In the past she might not have found this moment so fulfilling, and in the future, if she had one, she might not either, but right now, yes. And yes, a little sip of wine despite Eleanor's disapproval; a stage-four cancer diagnosis will inure one to the censures of children. Yes, this made her feel good, this interlude, even though what awaited her was that fucking fish. How long do you poach a thirteen-pound salmon? Kate was getting tired of this hyper-mindfulness, where every thought, memory, emotion, every trivial token of her own soul, seemed to shout at her, bellow in her ear; it seemed to have arrived either with her illness or with the treatment. But this was good, this moment. As she expected, Francis claimed he had already eaten and sat instead at the far end of the table, looking awkward but not uncomfortable; she'd never seen him eat anything and suspected that it was more because of his teeth than any other hesitation. An eating disorder seemed unlikely.

"So what's the plan?" asked Ethan. He and Heidi had settled off somewhat apart from the group, a family of their own; a table of this size allowed it. If one wanted to cram a bit, twenty people could sit here. The sun poured in behind them and gave the blessed young couple a bit of an aura. They were sharing a plate, which heartened Kate but struck both Rosalie and Eleanor as too cutesy by half, or three-quarters.

"Well," said Kate. "What is ever the plan for these days?" Time, uncounted and unnoted, was precious for her. "When the French get here, Dad's going to give them the tour. They want to see Tuckertown."

The name of this enclave, this once-bustling Free Black village at the edge of the Retreat, brought Francis out of his usual silence in the presence of a large gathering of the family; whenever he did this, considering how difficult it was for him to come forward, it was because something said had struck a lever or bumper in his brain. Francis had no interest in small talk or, perhaps more accurately, no interest in contributing to small talk, but he seemed to enjoy listening to it, like a radio show on low volume, like the police scanner Bo listened to in their house. "Why Tuckertown?" he asked, and Kate explained to him: Julien Bayly, visiting from France, wanting to see where his great-grandmother Beal grew up, the old story.

"But whatever." Kate resumed about the day ahead. "The beach. Various contemplative strolls. A boat ride, if the outboard starts. Liberty Hall."

"Right," said Eleanor. "Rosalie is going to kayak to Wilmington, and—"

"Wilmington?" Rosalie interrupted. She had been so focused on managing Daniel's lunch—managing a real estate office was what she did in real life—that Eleanor didn't even think she'd heard what she said. "Wrong bay, dear."

"Isn't that what that canal is all about?" Eleanor asked.

"And you're going to work on"—a pause—"the novel."

Oh dear, thought Kate. *Your* novel, timed in that way, would have been bad enough, but this "*the* novel." This took the tone into an entirely different register. So much loaded into it: Rosalie's disdain for what she saw as Eleanor's fecklessness, a genetic schism that Kate and Harry were responsible for—her literature, her art; Harry's preference for the concrete, the quantifiable— all played out in their daughters. Kate wouldn't argue for one over the other, for one in the place of the other, but "*the novel*" was aggressive and mean, and why had Rosalie been mostly disagreeable since she got here? Was there trouble between her and Paul? Had she had a miscarriage, or was she still being harassed by that man at work? They never should have bought that house in Chevy Chase; they knew it was too expensive and too big for them when they did it. And, by the way, what had Paul done to upset Heidi, if indeed Kate had overheard correctly?

"She let me read the opening, about Mary Foxley coming here, and I thought it was good," said Ethan.

Ethan's intention was to defend Eleanor—*anyone* in the family being attacked, even Dad's dogs, could depend on him—but as Kate watched the pallor of deep hurt wash over Rosalie's face, she realized that he had scored a deeper blow than he understood. In fact, even Kate could not deny that she felt a raw scrape: Had Eleanor also shown it to Harry, and not to her?

"No one knows anything about her," said Rosalie.

"That's the point, *dear*," said Eleanor, firing back. "Trying to reconstruct the story. Some of us care where this place came from."

"Some of us might think more about where it is going."

There was an unfortunate pause until Heidi said, "I think it sounds really interesting. No one cared about what the women did back then. No one ever asks what it was like for them." When she asserted this, she did, in fact, raise her tone into a question at the end of the sentence, and in truth, Eleanor's great theme didn't sound like much spoken so plainly by a college girl, but for the moment, Eleanor would not complain.

"Thanks, guys," she said. She had a nice peach in her hand and she debated whether to throw it at Rosalie with all her might. The problem was that she'd probably miss and hit Daniel; alternatively, if Rosalie threw a peach at her, she'd drill her right between the eyes. Instead, she glared at Rosalie, and everyone went back to their lunches a little wounded, chatting about stink bugs and the prospect for a third span of the Bay Bridge.

Out of this nattering Francis spoke again; his mind was always churning. "I like stories," he said. "Once they're told, they last forever."

Into the momentary pleasing silence, Kate jumped in. "Like your photographs," she said with an encouraging tip of her head toward one of his shots of the farm, framed and hanging behind Rosalie. "So narrative."

"No," Francis said. "A photograph only lasts as long as the shutter is open. Maybe a hundredth of a second."

"Oh. That's so awesome." Heidi lunged for her phone, and her thumbs flew, presumably recording what Francis had said.

And Paul thought, We all have our own clocks. Our moments have their own duration. We all believe time passes at a certain rate. How we live life depends on how we think time passes.

"Then," said Kate, "the print isn't the photograph?"

"No," said Francis. "Anyone can do the print. Anytime." These thoughts had just popped out, but they were deeply felt. They'd been arrived at during nights that lasted longer than any art student ever invented could possibly imagine, but now this attention rattled him. "I'm just saying what I feel," he said. "Stories are harder to make than photographs."

Eleanor did not want to hear about the challenges of writing fiction; on the other hand, over the years, random people like cabdrivers and hairdressers had said such things to her as "Stories are about change, right?" and "My favorite part of a story is when we learn the truth at the end," and she always nodded as if it were obviously so and then rushed home to scribble it down. *It's about change, Stupid!* said a Post-it on her bulletin board, alongside the one that said *Recognition or Revelation!*

"Of course," said Kate, though what she was assenting to was not clear, and Eleanor wished to hell that her mother would let it drop and let Francis simply take pleasure that in this moment, when he had spoken from the heart, everyone listened. In a few more seconds her mother did let the moment pass, saying she hoped Francis would stay with them for the afternoon and take pictures of the gathering. Kate thought she must remember to set a place for him at dinner, but of course that was ridiculous: he'd never sit down with them at the table, though if he were still around by then, he'd probably be willing to pull up a chair on a corner beside her.

"Okay," Kate said. "Let's say this cleanup is Paul and Rosalie's, as long as Daniel seems to be behaving so nicely."

Rosalie decided not to take this as a jab—although it was, she thought. Everyone but Francis filed out, though Heidi lingered as if she wanted to query him further; behind her glasses her eyes had narrowed and sharpened as if she might impale him. But then—smart kid, thought Rosalie—she dropped it and followed Ethan out the door. Rosalie let her mother put the leftovers in those plastic food-storage containers she loved so much. "Thanks, Ma," she said, being sweet. "A really lovely brunch. And I didn't mean anything about, you know, Eleanor. I thought we were just kidding around."

"Eleanor was, sort of. You weren't at all."

"Maybe I am a little tired of this family being held captive by Eleanor's damn novel. And, well, what good is all this history? For her, really. That's what I was trying to say. We've all got lives too, you know. Like, in the present?"

Rosalie had loaded such a mirepoix of sibling complaint—which, of course, is often indistinguishable from sisterly love—into this that Kate could only nod at her. "I'll take Daniel," she said. "Daniel, let's go play hopscotch on the gravestones." When his protectress left, Francis, who felt no discomfort at being present for a family spat, disappeared. At least that was how it seemed to Paul: disappeared, evaporated, once there, then not there.

"So that's Francis," he said, scraping the dishes into the sink tidy after Kate had left. He'd never heard of a "sink tidy" until he met Rosalie; it was something WASPs did, tidying a sink, but now, yes, the world had caught up to the idea of compostables, and sink tidies had a new life.

"You've never met him before? That's odd, I think." But maybe it wasn't. Men were a problem for Francis, especially Harry, his landlord, sort of, not that Bo would ever be asked to pay rent on a house that would forever be known as the Handy House. Fifty years of labor had earned him that, but after Bo died, there might be an awkward question about what exactly was owed to his son. But that was for another day.

"I was surprised," said Paul.

"By that comment about his photographs?"

"Yes. About stories lasting forever and the photographs lasting an instant. For him the photograph *is* that physical act. Only that tiny speck of time."

"Not everyone thinks in eons."

Paul took this as lightly affectionate. The problem—his professional, academic problem—was that he didn't think in eons quite the way he used to; he'd become more interested in seasons. "I don't know that I really agree with him, but so what."

"I've never said I thought Francis was stupid," Rosalie said. "Imagine what the world looks like to him. His parents were the kindest people in the world, but they were quite old when they adopted him, and they were from another century. When I see those Dorothea Lange and Walker Evans photographs, I think of Bo and Velma."

Paul put this bit of history aside. "I thought Heidi was going to spring out of her chair," he said.

"The lovebirds. They're probably heading to the hayloft."

Paul wished that the idea, the picture that came to mind, did not thrill him quite as much as it did. To be barely out of your teens and able to fuck in the hay, heedlessly down the path to a moment of bliss. And not according to a schedule on a calendar, to rises and falls of body temperature. But then he thought, Sex is sex, no matter the occasion. "Sounds good to me," said Paul. "Aren't we supposed to be getting at it about now?"

"I still want to wait. I'm just not ready to try again. You understand."

"Ready for the tour?" called Ethan up the narrow stairs to the "maids' rooms" on the third floor. In the hundred years, at least, since servants had lived there, nothing in these rooms had been altered—the lumpy mattresses, the washstands, the claw-foot bathtub. The air under the eaves stayed hot and papery, as if the final exhalations of the last chambermaid were still in the mix, as if her dying groan had likewise been preserved. Heidi had slept fitfully; she had dreams of being lost in a decaying mansion, but then in half consciousness she realized it wasn't a dream at all. When she finally woke, Ethan had already left to beg off his silly job at the marina fuel dock, something he'd done for years. "The tips are great," he'd said.

"In a minute," she yelled back. "I'm just changing."

Ethan listened for the sounds of belts and zippers, and what he hoped above all else was that in a few minutes he would be undoing all these efforts. Hurry *up*, he thought, and when she clumped down, he knew why. Heidi was just so *cool*, her big glasses and pointy little jaw, her incredibly—his word—thick brown hair and thin waist, and the way she let it all hang out. Her parents were potters, not just hippies but second-generation hippies. Ethan was still amazed that she was into him, but here she was, at the Retreat, perhaps making more of a statement to him than she realized. He followed her down the main stairs, and over her shoulder he saw the portraits of the founders who had started this all, Richard, and Eleanor's Mary Foxley; Mary Foxley was, well, kind of foxy, even in her seventeenth-century getup.

Yes, at Vassar, Ethan had told Heidi all the stories he knew. About the time his great-grandparents lived here for a year or two at the end of the Depression after Edward Mason went bust in England; about the boy who would have been his great-uncle drowning just before they went back to England at the outbreak of the war. About Pop selling the place and Ethan's father buying it back in 1998, the year before Ethan was born. And the stories, most of which he'd heard from Bo, that went further back, to when the place had been a fruit orchard—about a young Black man's body being found in one of their barns, and about another Black man, a World War I veteran called Robert Baby, who lived like a hermit in a shack in the woods; even back to slavery on the place.

"You're kidding," Heidi said. "You live where there were slaves? Your family?"

"Slavery was at the heart of the American project from the beginning," he said, "my family as much as your family. No American is unimplicated." He was quoting—they'd both read the same texts in their course on Colonial America—Howard Zinn, he thought.

"No. *My* family does not live in a place that was built with slave labor," she said.

Ethan had no idea why he lost his temper as much as he did, as much as he ever had in his life, but he fired back. "Your parents, whoever they are"—more on *this* later—"don't know shit from Shinola. Up there in blameless New England. Guess what? New England got rich on slave labor, on tobacco, on cotton and sugar. You want to know how the New England textile mills got their start? Making what they called 'Negro cloth.' Also called 'Lowell cloth.' To clothe guess who. Monks in hair shirts had it easy compared to that stuff." He'd made his point, should have stopped there, but the skinny boy who sat silently in the back row of the classroom while New England was being lionized as the greatest society since Athens was licking more wounds than he had realized until, perhaps, this moment. "Your parents pandering their pots to hedge fund billionaires with third or fourth wives and third or fourth homes in Woodstock," he continued. "All paid for by ripping off the American worker. This isn't two hundred years ago. This is today. Vermont! We're a lot of things in the South, but we're not smug about the past. We know what we came from, we know how our bills got paid."

Heidi was stunned by this; she'd had no idea that this rage was in Ethan. All she could say was "Maryland isn't in the South."

"Oh," he'd said, still swaggering and slashing. "I'm not talking about Bethesda. You come down and see *my* Maryland, and maybe you'll think differently." This was far from an invitation, but it was the first time the thought that this girl might see the Retreat came into his mind. But still, quietly, coolly, she told him he'd better go back to his own place for the night. She refused to see him for a week, but then almost inexplicably relented. As if—no, not as if, but in fact—admitting there was some truth to what he said. Ethan was frantic by that time, sure he'd never see her again; he would have disavowed every word of his outburst except for the memory of how good it felt saying those forbidden things.

When they came out of the house, the dogs, waiting for Dad to return with Pop, jumped up with delight and dutifully fell in line; Ethan was the only human besides Harry that they'd follow. The group headed down the lane, past the last appendage to the Mansion House, the brick smokehouse—"Filled with snakes," said Ethan. "A regular knot of vipers"—and the icehouse, an A-frame roof over a ten-foot cellar. They pried open the door and peered into the hole. "More snakes," said Ethan.

"So far this has been a great tour," she said. She was carrying her sketchbook. Ethan hoped she didn't decide to stop to draw something. If she did, he'd have to stand loyally at her side and watch her pencil move. Excruciating, and each time she erased something in order to do it over, he wanted to scream.

At the bottom of the Mansion House lane stood the stable, a building that was half designed for horses, with stalls and a roomful of carriages—"Filled with snakes, I suppose," said Heidi—and half for automobiles, three bays with grease pits and a chain hoist. In one of them was a Model T, in another, a Studebaker Avanti. "That's Pop's," said Ethan. "He had it shipped from California when he moved here. I don't know if it runs."

"When your Accord finally dies, you can move it in here," she said, pointing to the third bay. "It would fit right in."

They skirted the gulley that separated the Mansion House grounds from the farm and went into the "hospital barn." The white tile walls and terra-cotta floors still gleamed, at least in places where the woodchucks hadn't deposited mounds of dirt excavated from their burrows. "I don't think we should go upstairs," he said.

"Snakes?"

"No. Bees."

Across from the hospital barn was the main complex of the farm, seven gables in a line, with a machinery shed at one end and a granary at the other, corncribs next to each, and then, in the center, the three gables of the horse barn. It was in this building, all these years ago, that the body of a young man, a young Black man, was found in the hay, stabbed to death. His killer was never found, a mystery no one ever bothered to solve. There the body would lie, and there it remained for Ethan, who had told Heidi what little he knew late one night in her dorm, the open window bringing in the freezing northeastern air—this was why the *Absalom, Absalom!* thing came to mind; he couldn't remember whether this was before or after the revelations about the past history of slaveholding, but at that point he still figured that even if they lasted as a couple into the summer, she'd never agree to set foot on the place. She'd wonder why, with the four points of the globe to choose from, choose to be *around* all that? Why assume the burden so willingly? Place was just a choice for her, as was history. Why not pretend it had never happened? Why put yourself in the unwinnable nexus between the blamelessness of ignorance and the presumption of guilt that is supposed to come from opening your eyes? If there was any room in there, in the middle, Ethan hadn't found it yet. All he knew was that he didn't like anybody at either end.

But here they were, on this fine July Fourth day, pulling open a small side door of this same building and stepping carefully in the dark out onto the main floor, where the shafts of sun coming through cracks and gaps in the siding made the place feel like a cathedral, and a very slight breeze and the pleasant cooing of pigeons provided their own meditative, perhaps timeless air. There was a peacefulness to it, a hush, a very private sort of communion. The dogs sniffed happily at the detritus piled here and there, the junk, cast-offs, and has-beens. At one end was a stack of hay bales, though Ethan didn't know why they were there or how long they had been there; there hadn't been livestock on the farm for many years. So this was old hay, but not ancient enough to be where the body had been found.

"Gee," said Heidi. Ethan thought for a terrible moment that she was reaching for her sketch pad, but thankfully, she was merely setting it on a bale in order to look around, to extract a long sprig—alfalfa, it was—and chew on it farmer style. "There's something about a hayloft." She said this suggestively.

Ethan could only agree.

"I bet you've had sex in here," she said.

Ethan never had; he'd never had the opportunity. "Uh, no," he said.

"I bet you've jerked off in here."

That he had done, more than once, but he tried to duck it.

"I don't know why that's such a big deal," she said. "Why is masturbating something you're ashamed of? When I was thirteen, my mother gave me a pamphlet explaining how to do it, but I'd already figured it out on my own." At that she took off her glasses and laid them on a hay bale beside her sketch pad. To have sex was the only reason he knew of that she ever took off her glasses; he supposed she took them off normally for bed, but he'd never slept with her without making love first, so he didn't know for sure.

After the cleanup, Paul waited long enough to make sure that Daniel was happy being entertained by his grandmother and then tiptoed upstairs to their room. They were staying in the Linen Prairie Room, as it was called, because most of the space was taken up by an immense four-poster bed. Another room, the Big Room, would have given them more space to spread out Daniel's things, given them a better view, and it had a desk where Paul, he hoped, might get a little work done in an odd hour like this, but that room had been considered Eleanor's during the brief period when the Retreat had been her home of record, and she had taken it over when she arrived earlier in the week. All was precedence here at the Retreat, after all; once done, forever in stone. Except that Rosalie's Room had been turned into a bathroom. Who says things don't change around here, thought Paul with some bitterness.

Paul had never lacked for family. The founders of his family were two brothers, hatters to the business class of Cleveland; theirs was one of hundreds of establishments across the country that was ruined when JFK went bareheaded at his inauguration. Paul grew up with dozens of aunts and uncles and cousins, even if from year to year he could never remember how one was related to the other—not that anyone was reluctant to give the begats, at length. Paul's family was not about stories and legends, not about history and tradition, but about personalities, people relentlessly being themselves from decade to decade. Aunt Hannah, the loud, boisterous one who was always asking, "What did I say that was so terrible?" Aunt Thelma, immensely fat, always taking "one more little piece"—Thelma slices, the kids called them. Uncle Freddy, who was in jail: Uncle Freddy was always in jail, serving a life sentence, it seemed, even if all he had done was pass a bad check from time to time. This was never explained. *No one* wanted to talk about Freddy. And all Paul's cousins, little packs of mice scurrying around the edges, Leonard with his firecrackers and booby traps, klutzy Marcia: Had Paul ever seen Marcia without Band-Aids on her knees? His family was not about *once upon a time*; it was about *over and over*.

Not so the Masons! For one thing, there were so few of them, if you counted only the living. Harry was an only child, as was his father, Simon, at least the only survivor after his older brother drowned. Besides her cousin Lotte, Kate had a sister who lived in Texas; she had a couple of kids no one ever saw. *This is family?* as Aunt Hannah might say. For another thing, Paul's family had nothing to do with place. The immigrant family, unless the immigration happened three hundred and fifty years ago, has given up the idea of an ancestral home. As Ruth said to Naomi, "Whither thou goest, I will go, and where thou lodgest, I will lodge." And oh, did Paul's family lodge. In his academic career he had observed, with pleasure, that the most enthusiastic shout-outs at graduation always came from the Black families, except for the familial outburst at his own graduation from Michigan, and he had thought he was going to skip the event. Whither thou goest. Who needs a family seat? His parents' reaction to the Retreat after his wedding was one of bemused wonderment: Why would Rosalie's father, who apparently had had a successful career in venture capital on the West Coast, give it all up for this? As Aunt Hannah said, "With all that, they can't even afford a respectable car." A Buick, she meant.

Paul could go on. He was sitting at the little table crammed in beside Daniel's travel crib—simply depress button A and button F at the same time, then gently pull up on slot B, which required three hands! Or some magic. Swedish parents these days, it seemed, didn't bother to marry, but apparently there were always two of them available to set up a crib. Paul could go on about his wife's family, but he had other things on his mind. Like this article he was supposed to be working on, the article his chair said he absolutely had to get accepted or tenure would be very rough. Paul had just finished sweating out his third-year review, and his reward for that was to begin living in terror of the tenure decision, but then . . . Something was happening deep, very deep, in Paul's mind, some little frisson that had sparkled late one night a few months earlier, a wan little blink of lamplight in the mineshaft of his soul, from which he had quickly turned his gaze but which he did not snuff out; it flickered there now as he glanced at his desperate abstract. *You don't have to do this.* "Too cryptic," his chair had said about his research plan, but it was cryptic, enigmatic and equivocal, precisely because Paul had no desire to say anything else. Writing is writing; it is fueled by desire. Eleanor's stalled novel was a mere butterfly compared with the crushing wheel of Paul's article on . . . oh, who cared what it was supposed to be on. Yes, Paul had not given a name to that little flicker of light, but he knew what it meant. It meant, simply, that he could take his academic career and shove it. Be done with all the students who took his introductory lecture course on geoscience because they thought it was a gut way to discharge the lab science requirement; be done with road rage incidents between tenured professors over parking spaces; be done with the constant required online human resources tutorials that purported to make him a better person.

And then what? Not what would he do: Paul had a thousand alternatives to his deathless academic career; at any hour of the night or day the image of some new calling would pop voluptuously into his head, rather like that unbidden tweak from the groin that could come on without the slightest pretext. Paul didn't allow himself to fantasize about a career as an NPR science reporter or a Grand Canyon river guide any more than he would allow himself to imagine sex with his sister-in-law. What about the mortgage, Daniel's preschool, this hope for a second child that was causing so much pain to Rosalie. So much . . . disruption to their routines, beginning with their sex life. Rosalie's salary would be more than enough to sustain them during some kind of career change, or it would have been if they hadn't bought the palace in Chevy Chase. Aunt Hannah had it right: so big that house.

So big *this* house. Plenty of room to live in; plenty of room to die in. How many people had died in the room he sat in now, the room that looked over the family graveyard? It was said that this was the room where Edward Mason had laid the body of his son Sebastien; in these rooms the mourning began, and once started, it continued forever. Paul could not help but feel watched here by an army of silent onlookers; sometimes he imagined this house as one huge eye with thousands of receptors, one for each soul that had been conscripted into its dominion. "*Ommatidium,*" he mouthed, just to be technical about it. Richard (1713–1786) was the rumored ghost, with sightings too numerous to list, but as Eleanor had said this morning, what could *he* have to complain about? No, she was right, there was a politics of memory, of inheritance, of generations in the spirit of this place, and the revenants we need to fear are those calling out from foreclosed lives for justice, for vengeance.

Paul had certainly allowed his mind to wander a long way from coalbed methane, if that's what he was supposed to be writing about.

So many ways to live a life. So many ways to think about what mattered and didn't matter. Sex, for example. Did sex matter? Those young people off screwing. How indecent was that, thinking about his teenage brother-in-law having sex, thinking about it and getting turned on by it. That skinny, foxy girl. An erection rose. He looked around furtively, thinking, You know what? I am just going to take care of this problem right here, and who could fault me after these weeks of "I'm not ready yet," or "It isn't the right day." But no. How pathetic would that be, a teacher with a tenure-track job at a top-twenty university sitting up here masturbating while real people with real lives went about the business of this day. Besides, in this house of eyes, nothing was private; he'd be in full view, watched by the world, as if a video camera had been left running and would continue to run until the end of time.

Eleanor sat in the small room above the kitchen that a previous inmate of the Retreat had made into an office; it had a writing table and a compact upholstered chair, and the narrow but tall window looked into the branches of a pecan tree. It had been a maid's sitting or sewing room or a butler's pantry, or something of that sort, but in any event, she had claimed it as her own writing room years ago. When she showed it to Vittorio on his one previous visit, he said, "Your novel should write itself in this room." Like, he was saying, all you're doing is just repackaging history, so what's taking so long?

It wasn't as if she had been at this for so long as all that, she told herself bitterly. Would say to Rosalie, angrily. She was barely past thirty, had been out of her MFA program only four years. "Five years is when we start looking for you guys," said one of her professors, a man to whom she would still like to give a swift gut-blasting knee to the testicles. But yes, a false start or two, and then, during one very late night of despair, she reached for material that really seemed part of her, something that had always been part of her without her being aware of it, something that wasn't just words, goddamn words, words just posing for some meaning, an affect, an invention with no purpose. Oh yes, Eleanor could list all the ways writing could be empty, because she had tried them all. This was one blisteringly hot night in August back here at the Retreat; her parents and Ethan had window air conditioners in their rooms, but in the rest of the ark, if you were just visiting, you were on your own. She was prowling in the heat in her white nightgown, quite prepared to bump into any other restless souls, living or dead, and to her surprise, she'd found Mary Foxley, staring at her, calling out to her from an oval portrait hung on a wall, eager to give testimony of a forgotten life.

Well, what *was* taking her so long? She'd brought the question onto herself by announcing, a year ago, that as Stendhal had done with his great novels, she had the complete work in her head and—ventriloquizing like this was one way to survive a writer's apprenticeship—all she had to do was transcribe it. What she meant was that in the ten days after this initial visitation from Mary Foxley, in a furious burst of inspiration and productivity, having done almost no historical research whatsoever, she had written a complete novella on the subject, and all that was required now was to bone up on the facts and terms—for example, the word "boat" was too generic to be used in a maritime world— expand the scenes to show, not tell, and voilà, a novel for the ages.

Eleanor glanced through the pages on her screen. A minute earlier, out of either boredom or desperation or both, she had changed the typeface on her manuscript—from the classic Century to something called Waldbaum Display—a sort of writer's geographical cure. But still, however serifed and glyphed, just words on a page. Words. These sections of the novella: she had pumped them up—with what? well, with words—like balloons ready to explode in her face, but still, she faced the terrifying prospect that in those ten days she had exhausted the subject, said everything that mattered to her, had come to the end, when all she thought she was doing was writing an outline. For inspiration she reached out and brushed her fingertips on the lineup of sources arranged between bookends on the corner of her table. This little library accompanied her wherever she went, like a traveling priest's Mass kit: Middleton's *Tobacco Coast* as her chalice, James Horn's *Adapting to a New World* her paten, Jean and Elliott Russo's *Planting an Empire* her pyx, and her flask of holy water was a collection of essays called *Colonial Chesapeake Society*. Not to forget Rountree and Davidson's *Eastern Shore Indians*, for some sections her Bible. Talk about "being replaced." Then a few, as they might be called, codices: the old warhorse *Rivers of the Eastern Shore*, with the drawing of Mary Foxley's husband in a batteau on the Chester being "rowed by his slaves," which was probably wrong, of course; indentured servants, to be sure, but it was not until the last quarter of the century in the Upper Bay that these English men and women were replaced by African slaves. A mere technicality perhaps. Eleanor did not keep on her table any of the few previous works of fiction set in the region, not *The Lord's Oysters*, not Michener's *Chesapeake*—God, how many times had people thrust *that* on her!—not even one of John Barth's novels, as distinguished company as any one of them might be.

But what was it like for Mary Foxley, a woman on her own from the day she came ashore to the day she was widowed, to the day, twenty-five years later, that she died? Could these books answer that for Eleanor? Could this little writing space tell her? Maybe, by the time everything had been brought ashore and settled; by the time the four-room—house? cabin? shack? dwelling? yes, dwelling—that Mary Foxley's husband brought her to that first night had been doubled in size, with the first brick chimney built north of St. Mary's, with a lean-to for a summer kitchen; by the time the Indian clearings had been taken over for grain and enough trees felled so that tobacco could be planted around the stumps and the first hogsheads packed and sold; by the time the hastily assembled palisade designed for protection against native attacks had been converted to livestock pens—by then there might have been thirty immigrants huddled onto the land. Enough for a village, maybe, but in no way would more than two or three of them be women. The girls they rounded up in London or in Bristol and sent to Virginia mostly ended up working in the households in Kecoughtan—or Hampton, as Eleanor believed they had started calling it by then—and in the plantations on the James and the Rappahannock; this Upper Chesapeake adventure began as an enterprise of men. What women came with Mary Foxley way up here to the Chester, on the right-hand shore of the Bay? Was that a problem for her? Maybe women back then didn't think about, even place value upon, the companionship of other women, but this didn't mean that in England they did not spend their lives in the company of women. Who, when the morning rush of chores was over, when the laundry water had been put on the fire to heat, when the boy had been sent to the garden to pick beans and the husbandman was busy selecting a goose for dinner—who did Mary Foxley sit down with for ten minutes of peace? Who attended her births, which kept on coming? And what about the wives of the other planters, the Lloyds to the south, the Wrights and Earles to the north, who would, as the inscriptions on the graves made clear, be the mothers of the children whom Mary Foxley's sons and daughters—those who survived—would end up marrying. Who were they, really? And how did they come to be part of this enterprise of men and, ultimately, to take it over after they died?

There was a tapping on the door, a respectful, sorry-to-disturb-the-great-project kind of scratching, as if it could be ignored with no offense. "Nellie?" said Rosalie. This "Nellie" was going way, way back; way back to nights huddled under a quilt in the same bed while their parents argued in the kitchen below; this "Nellie" was the whitest flag, a meeting place where nothing outside could be allowed to intrude, something that could not be ignored, ever.

"Yes."

"May I come in?"

"Oh, for God's sake. Of course you can come in."

Rosalie entered, squeezed past Eleanor at the desk, and sat in the tiny wingback chair. Women were small then, their mother had said once. "I'm—" she started.

Eleanor interrupted. "You don't have to say anything. You can't say or think anything bad about my novel that I haven't said to myself."

"Well, I'm sorry anyway."

Eleanor gave her a bare nod.

"And I don't want you to say mean things to yourself. That's just as bad. Look at all you are doing." She pointed at the line of texts.

"They're just history." Eleanor waved at her computer screen. "I was just rereading a section about growing tobacco. About the great tobacco bust of 1670. Do you think anyone, any reader today, will care about how tobacco was grown, about how much it was worth in 1670?"

"Well," said Rosalie, "your character does, right? It was her life. It mattered to *her*. So what's wrong with that? You're trying to replace stupid myths with a story based on fact."

"Because history trumps plot," Eleanor answered. "The characters have no choices, just realities. Choices are what we expect in a novel. A fact is not a choice. Mere circumstance overcomes desire." Rosalie would have no way of knowing this, but every pithy phrase—nostrum, shibboleth, catholicon—she had just uttered had been spoken in at least one of her MFA workshops; scenes from Columbia flittered in front of Eleanor's eyes like last night's party streamers. Useless to her now.

"Sounds like things people must say to each other in writing workshops," said Rosalie.

"Oh," said Eleanor with a small flicker of pleasure. She laughed. "Yes. I'm busted."

"I just don't see what the difference would be between fiction and history. Whether a reader would know the difference, I mean."

"I don't know if one would. How about you?" asked Eleanor.

"About me what?"

"About reading my novel. I haven't asked you, because I know how much is going on in your life these days, but would you?"

Rosalie hesitated for a moment, wondering whether she ought to play this cool, to say, *Sure, I might have time if it would be helpful to you*, but that wasn't the sort of game she played with her sister. The rivalries were of a different sort, precisely the kind of elbowing and jostling they had both just engaged in at brunch; here, face-to-face, heart-to-heart, only the truth could be spoken. "Are you kidding? Of course I would. I was hurt that you didn't ask me, that you showed it to Ethan before you showed it to me."

"At graduate school we were told that asking someone to read your manuscript was like asking someone to bear your surrogate child."

"Ick. Who said that?"

"An asshole named Alexander Braithwaite. Whose last novel was published, can we say, over thirty years ago. The idea that any of his students might actually have a manuscript completed was offensive to him. There's nothing more pathetic than a creative writing teacher who isn't writing." Take that, Braithwaite, thought Eleanor. In the meantime she was reaching into her satchel for the printout she had brought for just this reason, to give to Rosalie. It was about 160 pages, maybe fifty thousand words, almost enough. She shuffled through it, took out about fifteen pages, and handed them to Rosalie. "Here," she said. "I don't want to overload you, but here are some pages on the contact with the Indians."

Rosalie took the sheaf, dropped it into her lap, and riffled through a few pages. *It is not my purpose to speak of the pleasures of residing on our Tobacco Coast*, she read. "What's the Tobacco Coast?"

"It's here. The Bay in the seventeenth century. A modern historian called it that. I like it, so I let Mary Foxley use it." She pointed to Middleton's volume in her library. She let the moment settle before she lowered the screen of her laptop—no more of this. "So," she said. "What's up?"

"Dad is back with Pop. He looks cadaverous. Rowdy is devouring a woodchuck on the back lawn. Mom is playing with Daniel. Paul is having a quick nap, I think. We'll be headed out to the rivershore."

"Sounds about right."

"Can you help Paul with getting Daniel to the beach? I want to row around. I promise I won't head off for Wilmington."

"Sure," she said.

"Oh, and Heidi lost her glasses," said Rosalie.

"What?"

"Exactly. They went for a stroll around the farm and she lost her glasses along the way. Seems an odd thing to misplace."

"I'll say," said Eleanor.

The sisters looked at each other and then started to laugh. They did not need to discuss why she might have taken them off.

"She has some prescription sunglasses. It's funny how much they change her looks. Much less pretty. I almost introduced myself to her all over again."

3

"Y ou go out, and I'll bring you some lemonade," said Kate, meeting Harry and his father, Simon, at the top of the landing. They had returned late enough for her to worry that they had stopped at what Simon called "the pub," otherwise known as Ruby Tuesday. It was frequently Simon's first stop after being liberated from "the stir," otherwise known as Osprey Neck Retirement Village.

"Some difficulties getting off," said Harry cryptically. He nodded toward his father, who was taking his first tentative steps into the hall, peering sharply, nervously, as if pecking at things. Harry watched him poke his head into the study, where Simon's own father, Edward Mason, had once run his English business in exile before the war. The same desk, the same bookshelves of musty nineteenth-century classics; in Harry's mind, Edward Mason, all noise and clumsiness, was too big for the room, too big for this immense house. A Gargantua caged among the bric-a-brac. When Simon sold the house, he'd left most of this clutter—books, objets d'art, engravings of foxhunting and bird shooting—as an inducement for buyers interested in assuming the manor from top to bottom, and here it had all remained through two feckless owners, as if it had been waiting for the Masons to return. Difficult to imagine this happening with any other piece of real estate, but there were forces in the house that resisted change. Even interlopers felt this; the house had never even been burgled. "Unlucky charms, perhaps," Kate had quoted upon entering the house for the first time after Harry bought it back. The rest of the contents, the stuff Simon deemed valuable, like portraits, furniture, and other relics, he had put into storage. He had always planned to sell them, dispense with a choice piece or two from time to time as needed, but his heart—and Harry's contributions to his livelihood—held him back, and by the time he got around to having the stuff appraised, things brown, silver, and porcelain had begun to lose their cachet. Besides, none of it was all that good: the best of the Mason trappings had burned, presumably, in a fire that destroyed half the house in the 1840s; the Mason portraits had mostly survived, been rescued—which might offer some evidence about what was most valued by a family intent upon preserving its legacy. So back it all came when Harry bought the place, the veneers peeling, the silverfish still munching away, tarnish as thick as barnacles, like cannons brought up from ancient shipwrecks. The portrait of Oswald returned to its spot above the dining room hearth; a sideboard, as big as an ocean liner and filled mostly with dead light bulbs, incomplete jigsaw puzzles, mouse nests, and stained linen, resumed its mooring in the hall. The overdue storage bill for all this stuff, in units maintained by a local family-owned lumberyard, was over ten thousand dollars. When Harry paid it up, the son of the family said, "We were just waiting for your father to die before we auctioned it off."

"Hmmm," said Simon, squinting birdlike into the spaces.

It was meant as a statement of mild discomfort or displeasure, though what exactly had caused it was not clear; Simon in this place, where his older brother drowned eighty years ago, was *the* moth to *the* candle. Mason's Retreat was his life sore, the part of his body he could not stop himself from touching. In return, the house itself seemed to stir when he entered; unfinished business perhaps, for both of them. Harry had bought it back for his father's sake, a gesture he hoped would redress some of the sadness of Sebastien's death, relieve the shame of selling off a family heirloom, redeem a lifetime of mistakes. He would have done anything within his means to heal the broken bones in his father's life, and at that time, anyway, Harry's means were considerable. Kate almost divorced him. "Why, Harry? That place has caused nothing but misery. What crime against humanity did your family *not* commit on that land, displacing Indians, enslaving Africans, exploiting workers?" At the time, Harry had no answer to history; for him, all was personal. "I'm doing it for Pop," he said. "You are not," she answered. "Pop had the sense to get rid of it. You're doing it through some twisted logic of your own. To atone."

To atone. Not for the family's crimes, but for his own years of drinking, of working too long, of wasting so much of his time, her time, their time, of inflicting so much dull malaise on his family. One day he was driving up to his office on Sand Hill Road, and some synapse clicked somewhere, and before he knew it, he was screeching onto the shoulder; the dust and gravel settled, and he looked inside and saw no soul. But he had mostly quit drinking by then, and with this new clarity he saw not simply a path out of the pit but a rainbow of ways to save himself, each one more unlikely yet more obvious than the last. Like buying the old family seat. So yes, Kate was not wrong about atonement; he bought the Retreat for Pop but also to affirm to himself that things endure despite the hash we make of them. It remained difficult for Harry, even now, to say exactly why buying this blighted family relic was atoning for the years when he'd refused to confront his alcoholism, but the truth was that his life, and their marriage, had turned around from that point on. The gamble had paid off. Harry got sober, quit his venture capital firm in Menlo Park, and—still atoning—joined a partnership in New York that did "socially responsible"—later, "sustainable"—investing. Kate got pregnant unexpectedly. A few years later, with Eleanor off to college, they spent a summer at the Retreat—"We own the damn thing," said Kate, "so we might as well populate it"—and never left. Ethan was seven, a slightly withdrawn and nonverbal child who had blossomed that summer on the farm, which had something to do with their decision. To this day Harry continued his practice part-time from a charming little office on Lawyer's Row in town. Kate reconnected with some of her Berkeley Ph.D. program mates and with their encouragement began a book blog on fiction in translation; European and American publishers swamped her mailbox. Literary programs at some of the embassies in Washington began to invite her to talk, to introduce their latest stars to American readers. She had been invited to give a paper on translation theory at the MLA convention on a panel called World Literary Spaces: Boldly Going (in English). Then she got sick.

"Oh," said Simon, settling into the chair that looked directly down the allée of boxbush to the parting of the grasses on the way to the dock. "Oh"—as if surprised to be seeing this view for the first time in many years. Through this opening, in August 1939, he had seen his father emerge with the body of Sebastien in his arms, though when he first saw them, he thought that the tragedy had been averted, that Sebastien had been found safe, that all was well. "Ah," he said as a way of passing on from that memory. He did this every time he came here, every time he took his seat in the chair on the porch he called "the position," a place to spend an afternoon. "So where are the young?"

"Rosalie and Paul and Daniel are off doing some project, I suppose."

"Daniel?"

"Your great-grandson."

"Oh yes."

"Eleanor, I think, is working on her novel."

"The one about Mary Foxley? Still that?" He did not wait for confirmation. "The Masons are a rabbit hole from which no human can escape. They go in as humans and come out as rabbits. I've told her that. I've told her that researching this family's history is like being bricked alive in a mausoleum along with Attila the Hun and Typhoid Mary."

"Yes," said Harry, pushing on. "Ethan has a girlfriend here. She's very cute. But from the sounds coming from the third floor, something seems amiss."

"Trouble in paradise?"

"No. I think they lost something on a walk. Ethan is saying he'll retrace their steps."

"Then all is well."

"Yes, Pop. All is well." As well as it could be for his father, thought Harry, at ninety years old. Considering the scrapes, the low points, the periods when Simon was little more than a con man one stunt away from going to jail, the fact that he was sitting on this porch with this ease was a marvel. Or perhaps a scandal. Nothing in this place was ethically one-sided; there was no ambivalence here, just a contest for the last word.

"And Alice Howe. Is she still alive?"

"Yes. She's coming for dinner, and fortunately, she's still alive."

Simon laughed at this, a little. Almost nothing from the outside, almost nothing anyone said or did ever seemed to fully get his attention, but Harry never quit trying to jolly him.

"And Thomas and Beal?" said Simon.

"Well. They *are* dead."

"So I heard. I meant some descendants of theirs. Weren't some French descendants of theirs floated as *divertissements*?"

"Yes," said Harry. "A great-grandson, and I think his son or daughter. They've been in California, in Napa," he said. The family owned a winery in France and, apparently, a number of vineyards in the U.S."

"Ah. Home."

Harry had heedlessly mentioned California, knowing instantly that he had made a mistake.

"I've been miserable ever since you brought me here," Simon said. "Why did you do that?"

"To be with your family."

"The ghosts of my family are always with me. My father as a voice. My mother as silence. My brother as an absence."

"Oh, Pop. Come on. You'll have fun," said Harry, thinking it was certain that his father *would* have fun, was even now having fun with these shows of pique and self-pity and impertinence. His posh retirement community was populated by courtly old WASPs and earnest moderate Republicans, whatever they were, and God knew what they thought of him and the resort wear he had brought with him from Malibu. He was never caught unguarded. He failed rarely because he attempted very little. He was always looking for a crease, a wormhole, a passage through the moment that required a certain nimbleness but no particular effort. It worked, as long as Harry was there to enable it, which enraged Harry even as he knew he would never stop. Harry's mood was turning a bit, but fortunately, Kate arrived just then with the lemonade.

Simon took a sip. "No rammer in here?" he said.

"No, Simon. Just lemonade. It's going to be long day for you." Kate felt like a nurse saying this, and indeed Simon took it meekly, like a patient. Kate knew all about it: aides, barely out of their teens, nurses, doctors just out of their residencies. Trying to please them, trying to make them like her and her miserable diseased body, as if it would influence her diagnosis, win her better care, or at least make them grieve for her when she was gone. As if to make up for all this obsequiousness, to reestablish some sense of power, she'd taken to snapping at all the other young people—young women—in her daily life, grocery store checkout girls, bank tellers, waitresses. It had been Ethan, actually, who brought that little piece of mind trash to her attention: "Why were you being such a bitch to that girl?" he asked one day. "You should see the looks they gave you on the way out."

It still stung, to be called a bitch by her son. Really! One of her least favorite words—but this was not the sort of thing she wanted to be thinking about today. Behind her, the household was stirring: Rosalie had reclaimed Daniel, and the family was dribbling back into the kitchen to plan the trip to the beach. She wondered whether Daniel would get stung by a jellyfish. As the amenities for the outing were staged in the hall, new colors took over the day: the red of the coolers, the purple and orange of the towels and paddleboards, the deep French blue of the market umbrella. Eleanor would undoubtedly be wearing her black maillot, but also that violent pink floppy hat; the ensemble made her look like an especially lethal tropical flower. Rosalie looked like an Olympic discus thrower no matter what she wore. Would Ethan's still adolescent body ever put on weight? His arms were just little sticks. "'From my study I see in the lamplight,'" Kate quoted to herself, "'Descending the broad hall stair, / Grave Alice, and laughing Allegra, / And Edith with golden hair.'" Yes, it was the children's hour, the hour of the young; later in the day the median age would shoot up, led by Alice Howe's ninety-six years, but for now those who would follow were in charge, those who were healthy, those whose cells were not feasting on each other, young, liquescent bodies slipping into bathing suits. Rosalie and Eleanor had apparently made up; Ethan's girlfriend—Heidi, Kate reminded herself—did look strangely buglike in those dark glasses, but at least she could see. The day had so far remained clear and dry, but the buzzing of the locusts told her the temperature was reaching ninety degrees; the humidity would follow along soon enough.

"Are you going with the kids?" Harry asked.

"No. But why don't you?"

Harry considered twisting her arm a little: spending time on the beach, the narrow little band on the shore of the Chester River or the white expanse of Santa Monica, had always been something Kate loved to do. She was a fine swimmer, a powerful, athletic, out-far-beyond-the-surf kind of swimmer; she'd become a speck, shark meat, and Harry didn't even like to get wet. But he knew well enough why she would resist now: her body in a bathing suit—not that she couldn't go there perfectly happily in her overalls; Harry used to sit at waterside in a coat and tie, watching Ethan swim. That's what she would be thinking about, and the horror of it, Harry knew as well as Kate did, was that the girls, Rosalie especially, would be nervously wondering the same thing. "How does Mom look?" had been, from the first diagnosis, the way Rosalie asked for the news, the updates, and it was *so Rosalie* to think this way, not because she cared all that much about physical appearance and style—this was Eleanor's realm— but because she was simply a person who focused on observable fact. That's what made her successful in her business.

So how does Mom look? Harry asked himself in this second

or two while making up his mind that yes, he would go out to the beach with the kids; yes, it would be fun to see Daniel splash in these benign waters. Mom looks okay, he thought, pretty good; the grad student he fell in love with was still there. She'd gained back several pounds, lost that pallor, her gray hair was coming back under her bandanna, and her chest, well, she'd never dressed to reveal or emphasize her breasts; she had no interest at all in reconstruction "at this point in my life" and that was fine, except all of it, whatever she did or didn't do, was writ large in a bathing suit. The flatness of her chest would be alarming to the kids; the little prosthetic bumps sewn into her suit would be embarrassing.

"Sure," he said, and went off to change.

Kate had not intended to, but rather than have them both abandon Simon at once, she sat down to chat for a moment with him. The Simon she did not like was the one when Harry was in the room. She didn't much like that Harry either. She couldn't, wouldn't criticize them: nothing about either one of them was untouched by the other. They were like Dog and Owner, though she couldn't decide who was Dog and who Owner. She had never known, never imagined, an adult so powerfully yoked in mind and spirit as her husband was to his father, some kind of survivor's guilt, she thought. Harry's mother had split when he was an infant; she was still alive, Kate thought, but Harry had nothing to do with her. In her absence, Simon and Harry had grown up almost like twins: they had their own language, their own rituals, which, simply described, usually amounted to Simon getting more and more sullen and unpleasant as Harry tried harder and harder to humor him. The thought of these conversations made Kate put her hands over her ears. But Simon alone and reflective, not drunk but in the relaxed glow of a cocktail: that person she liked so much that she picked up his lemonade glass, went to the kitchen and gave it a tiny squirt of vodka, poured herself another half glass of rosé, and returned. The beach party, Daniel screaming at the top of his small lungs, was just then departing in a caravan of cars, Harry leading the way in his jaunty electric utility cart with the two dogs in the back. In a moment they would be turning onto the tractor ruts across the corn fields, the welcoming, eternal strip of water in the distance. Rosalie seemed not to be joining them; perhaps she was planning to kayak around the point to meet them.

"They're off," she said as she sat down.

Simon took a sip, brightened, and pressed the glass against his upper lip in order to sniff in the glorious fumes. Finally he put down the glass and, as if this elixir had thrown a switch in his head, he said, "So. How are you? I don't want to keep asking, but Harry tells me nothing, and I hate not knowing. That's what all the inmates at the stir do, just pretend all is well, and then one morning the hearse arrives and you think, Wait a minute! I was supposed to play tennis with that guy today."

Kate laughed; she understood the consolations of gallows humor. At this unique distance, death could be funny. "Well, I'm in remission, pretty much. I think. I hope. It's a rather provisional existence. I live my life in three-month increments between scans. I'm tired of living this way, actually. But thank you for asking. It's kind of you."

He took the gratitude but waved off the kindness. "I'm sorry. You've borne a lot in your life. Harry is a good man, a kind man, as you might say, but weak. The fatal combination. You don't deserve this unlucky turn."

Kate ignored the comment about Harry; insulting the other was in line with the game they played, that they never stopped playing. "I am not sure health is about being deserving or not."

"Perhaps. You would never be able to persuade me I deserve my good health, but it makes me appreciate it all the more, knowing that I don't."

Kate raised her glass and gave a dry toast to his good health.

They sat peacefully. Through the trees she saw Rosalie dart by in her orange kayak; doing what was right, doing what was healthy and good, came naturally to her. Temptations were not a problem for Rosalie: the choices she made simply happened to be the more estimable options: brown rice, walking tours, the hard truths of science. Childhood had been easy for her. As Eleanor had struggled with what were finally diagnosed as attention issues, as weekends for Eleanor became an unbearable drama of promises and procrastination and tears, there was Rosalie with her completed homework already transferred from a folder marked "Homework Not Done" to a folder marked "Homework Done." In many ways Rosalie was the child to whom Kate had been least attached, but she would die easier knowing she had put this sort of person into the world, that she would be there for her brother and sister to the end.

"Rosalie," said Simon, amused, hip to everything Kate had just considered. That was all he needed to say, and anyway, he was speaking to himself. It had taken Kate at least ten years to figure out that her father-in-law's silences, his vacancies, were sometimes the kind of tuning out that would make one suspect he was drunk, and sometimes they were precisely that, but sometimes not. That a man whose lifetime ambition was to be an actor was really, more than anything, an observer of others, perhaps made sense. Perhaps it was a cliché about acting, Kate mused. But when Simon latched on to something, he kept at it.

"This thing Eleanor is doing—" he said.

"Her *novel*," Kate interjected. How hard it must be for writers—prose writers, she meant—to brand a piece of writing in progress as a form or genre, a play, a novel. What kind of art takes so long to create, and when finished, what art form takes so long to experience? A lyric poem, one of those majestic curiosities of language and inference—well, it takes longer for the eye to range over a large canvas than it does to read an entire Paul Celan poem. Prose writing can be a slog; the work can be a beast, and at this moment she was tired of Eleanor's hard work being treated as a character flaw. "It's not a thing."

"Yes, but it's not really a story, either. It's a confrontation with this family. It's like playing Hamlet"—the thwarted actor—"and I worry that it's too big a part for her at this point. It didn't turn out well for Hamlet. The specter of his father made sure of that."

"Certainly not. His time was out of joint. But maybe what Eleanor is doing is the sort of thing we all should be doing more of. These days."

"Sure, sure, sure," said Simon impatiently; the politics of "these days" was not something, had never been something, he had time for. "This is closer to home. This is her *patrimoine*, as you French say. This is in her DNA."

The thing about the French was a joke; he had always been wildly impressed with her languages, especially because he knew that if he had applied himself at all in those earlier days, he could have matched her tongue for tongue. Kate said, "Of all the ways to practice history, the family version, genealogy, is the worst—"

Simon interrupted. "Come up to Osprey Neck Retirement Spa and Village"—he gave the word "vill*age*" a French slant—"if you want to see the horror of it. There are chapters of the Daughters of the American Revolution and the United Daughters of the Confederacy, and they meet daily."

"—but here we are." She waved her hand around, wagging at the wrist. "Your father brought you here; Harry brought me here. It's hard to ignore, which is what I would prefer to do. Honestly."

"Eleanor is having trouble because she has to confront history on two levels: the original sin and"—he perfectly mimicked

Kate's hand gesture—"this. She thinks she can remake Mary Foxley by redrafting the narrative, as you young people say."

"Simon," said Kate sharply, "I have watched Eleanor struggle with this for the past two years, and I can tell you that remaking the narrative is not her intent. There wasn't any narrative to begin with. That's unfair to Eleanor."

"Sorry," he said. "You know how much I love Eleanor. You know she is the favorite of my issue. I plan to favor her unfairly in my will."

"So you have said several times."

"Oh. I have? Well, the next time I think of warning you about it, one of us may have died. Very likely me."

"Very funny," said Kate absently. She was getting ready to move on, but Simon still seemed to have something he wanted to say.

"From what little anyone knows about Mary Foxley, she must have been an iron maiden."

"Iron maiden?" Kate asked.

"Am I being politically incorrect?"

"Don't you mean Iron Lady?"

"Oh, yes. Margaret Thatcher. But that's right. Imagine what it took for Mary Foxley to survive here."

"Well. That's Eleanor's point, I think. To dramatize her role. To look at what it cost her . . . and all the women here."

"She's right about that," he said, loudly slurping his glass dry in hopes that Kate would refill it. "The women all paid more than their due. But they have always played the most interesting roles, wouldn't you agree? That old battle-ax who gave the place to my father. Mary Bayly? The original Iron Lady. I've seen a photograph of her sitting on this porch in this very spot with that Miss Whatever-Her-Name-Was, the companion no one was allowed to talk about, the companion no one even *knew* about until twenty years after she died."

"I suspect that if you look at the history, you'll see that women were allowed to play no real roles at all."

Simon ignored this last comment, and in truth, Kate didn't believe it; she was just trying to extricate herself from Simon's web. But yes, Simon was right, she had often reflected on the fact that for large swaths of time, the Retreat had been held together by forsaken wives, widows, and spinsters. Occasionally, on her first weeks and months here, when Harry was still largely commuting from New York, she would go out to the graveyard and talk to those Annas and Elizabeths and Marys who had gone before her, but at that time they kept their discontents to themselves. The men go off and do what they do, die in foolish quests or, in later times, fuck their secretaries; the women stay here on the farm and live their lives. Which was more interesting, at least to her, these days?

Simon was still talking, though Kate had lost the drift. "And yes," he concluded, reluctantly surrendering his glass. "Eleanor is looking for power, for *agency*"—another slur on the young, but what did amaze Kate about her father-in-law was how current he remained, how he was able to keep updating his store of critiques—"but what she may find is blame."

Time to move on to the fish, thought Kate.

She cleared the final residue of the brunch, turned on the dishwasher, put, as she thought of them, *les nécessaires* back in the refrigerator. She preferred this piece of French to the aseptic word "condiment." She'd heard a suave Frenchman say this angrily to a waiter in a restaurant in Nice in 1976: "*Où sont les nécessaires?*"

The man had ordered steak tartare, wanted his minced onions, capers, cornichons, spritz of Maggi sauce. He was there with an American woman, with a tiny poodle drawn up in a third chair; the man spoke no English, she spoke no French, it was all impossibly sordid. Why would one remember such a thing, besides the shocking sadness of such a pathetic attempt to buy fun? Why, ever since then, for more than forty years, why did she say to herself *Où sont les nécessaires* every time she wanted ketchup or mustard, or indeed, onions and capers. At McDonald's, with the kids' Happy Meals, "*Où sont les nécessaires?*"; sometimes she mouthed this to the lady behind the counter. At the Crab Deck on Kent Island, waiting for her tartar sauce, the phrase returned unbidden, again, back to Nice in 1976. Considering how forgetful she was becoming, it seemed wasteful to her that mental froth was occupying a greater and greater portion of her recoverable memory, not just the words, but whole episodes, like herself at seventeen being taken by her AFS host family to the restaurant at the splashy Hotel Negresco on the Promenade des Anglais, all tricked out in Belle Époque, a small orchestra playing de Falla, Strauss, Chabrier, the gaiety of it, her heart thumping behind her small teenage breast, her mind saying, Yes, I will have this in my life, I will work harder on my French, there is no going back for me. And later, reading Henry James in college, she'd picture Daisy Miller or Milly Theale or Maggie Verver as herself during that summer, the American naïf.

In such a way, she reflected, a person is born—these little moments, whether perceived as momentous or trivial at the time, arranging themselves in her soul like bits of DNA on the double helix. "From the thousand responses of my heart never to cease, / From the myriad thence-arous'd words." Yes, as usual, as always, Whitman had it right. Kate was glad for her "thence-arous'd words" (in four languages!), even those elicited from the bad moments that came to her at other times in similar detail—like the sound of ice clinking in a glass somewhere in the house on Saturday morning (please, dear brain, don't go *there*). She had not become Käthe Lorenz, the global literary theorist, but as Kate Mason, she had not done nothing. And yes, she forgave Harry for those years; she forgave him with all her heart, because he deserved to be forgiven. That was her choice and her privilege: "I, chanter of pains and joys, uniter of here and hereafter."

She clunked the refrigerator door shut, though not before she and the fish, which was splayed out across an entire shelf, eyed each other. So Kate imagined, though this poor salmon, which had been swimming happily off Alaska two days ago—so she was assured, with a price tag to match—didn't have much choice in the matter. "Just about thirteen pounds," the fishmonger in Annapolis had said; "you'll probably need to cut off the head and tail to get it into your pan." Well, he didn't know about the wonders of the pantry at the Retreat, including a fish poacher more than two feet long. Fish were fish, back then. Eleanor had told her that a single sturgeon, over ten feet long, had fed the entire settlement in St. Mary's for two weeks in 1640. Kate assumed that the sturgeon was not poached in court bouillon—white wine, mirepoix—or glazed with egg whites and gelatin, a few fennel fronds for garnish. She assumed they lacked *les nécessaires*, *sauce verte* and all.

Kate had thought a lot about her life, through the haze and nausea of chemo, through the falling asleep with two breasts and waking up with none, through the terrors. Yes, "I, chanter of pains and joys," she quoted once more to herself, standing in the middle of the kitchen, wondering exactly what she would do for the next blissfully solitary two hours. The cook's privilege. She had been thinking about her other privileges, beginning with the best medical care that money—cash money, checks written—could buy. This place was a temple of privilege, which, with each passing day, seemed less and less hers. Was she leaving it, or was it leaving her? It was typical, she supposed, that one married into a family without ever becoming part of it, like a relatively harmless parasite hooking a ride on an unknowing host. What was this annual occasion for her family and for the nation—not a remembrance, but a recommitment to *forget* how it all came to be? (Yes, at Berkeley, fall of 1983: terrible menstrual cramps, curled up with *Imagined Communities* on a ratty orange sofa.) Sometimes Kate wished she were less educated, or stupider; to know history is to be a hypocrite. It's not as if there weren't other models, the Buddha renouncing his wealth. "Easier for a camel to go through the eye of a needle," Kate reminded herself. Yet what an empty gesture it would it be if, this evening, with fifteen—is it fifteen; am I counting Daniel?—people seated around a table that, with leaves inserted, could easily accommodate more, Kate stood up and said, *It is time to remember those whose lives were destroyed in order to make this moment happen for us.*

Kate leaned out onto the porch and, as she had expected, found Simon fast asleep, his skinny, skeletal head propped back against the shutters of the French door, mouth open. She went upstairs thinking perhaps she should take the tablecloth and napkins out of the dryer—well, she should do it before they got completely wrinkled—but on the way to the laundry she passed Eleanor's little study, and there, on her table, cracked open licentiously, was her laptop, a secret door like C. S. Lewis's wardrobe, an *invitation au voyage.* Harry would never, in a million years, violate the privacy of an open laptop; if it were Donald Trump's private emails to Vladimir Putin, Harry would consider it dishonorable to read them, but Kate had never felt such scruples. Her daughters' diaries, her son's emails and Facebook posts, previously opened letters in their envelopes: all were fair game. And yes, without such willingness to snoop, she and Harry never would have dreamed that Eleanor and some friends from school were dabbling with snorting heroin; once a parent has looked into that kind of abyss in a child's life, she remains vigilant. Keep your friends close, your enemies closer, and your children under lock and key. So she sat down and was relieved, pleased, delighted to see that the open document was Eleanor's novel. She scanned through a few pages:

We were twenty souls at that point, huddled onto the higher land to the north of the creek that now bore my husband's name. Our indentures, mostly men and boys, lived in huts around the barns and around the house Lewis had built for us. In his instructions to the colonists written many years before our arrival, Lord Baltimore had directed that houses be built in a decent and uniform manner and that they be placed in rows along the idea of streets that would soon form the center of a fine town. This was not my husband's way, and despite Lewis's preference for such order—who is this Lewis? wondered Kate, scrolling back to discover that he was a carpenter, an indenture who came with his family and with a reduced period of service on account of his skills—*there had been no plan for the placement of dwellings, but rather an arrangement of whims, the breeze on a slight rise for a few, the shelter of a gigantic oak for a few more. My husband did not dictate who was to go where; he was a social man, not a master; for all its privations, he had never minded the close quarters of the navy and took comfort in the density of the village he had created in the wild. After Mr. Evans*—i.e., Lewis—*died, his widow and her children lived several hundred yards away in the tidy little cottage he was building for them before he could no longer continue, and they remained there even after she had married Mr. Lillingston. Mr. Lillingston came with two children of his own and a son of his late wife and her late husband, and after he died, Mrs. Evans*—*as she remained in my heart*—*married no more and raised the five children on the Haven. I had four children to raise, my*

William and the three born in Maryland, and when I gave birth to my last, at age forty-two, we named him Richard, after his father, because it was now plain that my husband would not live for many more of a year. And he did not, and as a widow, I went forward, as did Mrs. Evans, and as did Henrietta Maria at Wye, and Elizabeth at My Lord's Gift. We women died young in Maryland, or we died old, and all our husbands died in between.

Kate paused there; that was a pretty good line and, indeed, a statement borne out by the evidence in the graveyard. Her interest quickened with this theme, but instead Eleanor's narrative continued with descriptions of the buildings. Kate's eyes flickered impatiently—well, ever since she got sick, she had lost the desire to give narrative the time it needs to unfold. Kate had *no* interest in *delay* and *suspension*. Get on with it! A few weeks ago, trying to reread Dickens, she thought, I am running out of time! But this wasn't Dickens, it was her daughter, so she tried harder to at least skim from line to line:

Our house stood in a locust grove at the highest point above the water, and the few breezes in the summer passed unimpeded through our windows . . . At night, as my husband tossed and turned fitfully, I thought of those healthful breezes as spirits, angels sent by God to calm his anxieties and to give us hope for the coming day . . . When I landed, our house had three rooms on the first floor, an entrance hall in the center, and dining and living chambers at either end, each with a fireplace; bedchambers on the second floor, each with a dormer looking over the creek. The kitchen hut was twenty feet away, with a dirt floor and storage space above . . . survived the Great Hurry Cane a few years later—hmmm, reflected Kate: Hurry Cane, that's quite pretty, actually—*without significant damage would have pleased him . . . The hall was furnished with leather chairs my husband had brought with him and a table Lewis made out of oak; hanging on the walls were portraits of my husband's father and mother, Oswald and*

*Elizabeth, and my husband's sword, of which he was proud . . . The
entrance hall remained the center of our lives, our place of business in
tobacco and livestock, and was where, after I began to conduct trade in
goods brought from England, I met my customers . . .*

Customers? thought Kate. Would they have used that word?
She moved on from more buildings—so-and-so's hut, the
granary—and found herself in the heart, she supposed, of Eleanor's project:

*. . . and the servants' huts had one room for all seasons, and chim-
neys made of wattle and daub, and they slept at night where they
might have stood in the day, but our comforts and our labors were not
much different. These two, like so many of our servants, were starting
over, orphans, or young people whose lives had lost any prospect, or
women who had lost their husbands. I believed the girls were safer
with us than on their own at home. I was starting anew every bit
as much as they were. On those days when I awoke with dread and
fear and loneliness, I knew they did too; on those evenings, after a
day of honest work and simple satisfactions, when I marveled at the
great dome of the heavens and the red sky, I knew they did too. My
husband and I had more, but we did not have so much better; we did
not waste our time with luxuries. We ate the same food, which we had
in abundance. The game was plentiful; the flocks of pigeons and wa-
terfowl filled the skies and turned our creek into a solid mass of birds,
and their filth. In leaner years we were sustained by devouring oysters
and terrapin, and in time we learned to construct Indian fish weirs,
which seemed to divert the full bounty of the rivers right onto our
hearths. We worked six days a week side by side, and on the seventh
day we took our rest; and when we died—even the meanest, sickliest,
most newly arrived orphan boy, even the newborn that never took a
breath—we gathered at their graves as one and mourned their loss.
I believed that this whole enterprise, the New World and our tiny
portion of it, was giving those who had come with us chances at good*

fortune that they never would have enjoyed at home, especially the women, and I realized, in time, that the same was true for me.

Kate paused again, glanced over at Eleanor's line of secondary sources, and she wondered if this was true, that all was quite so rosy for the indentures as Eleanor was portraying it. It would be a relief to think so, and in fact, it seemed a reasonable inference given the general brutishness of seventeenth-century life, but would Mary Foxley even have had the perspective to comment? Was Eleanor trying too hard to give Mary Foxley credit, or was she according Mary Foxley the simple fact of her own humanity, her capacity for pity, her desire to feel love? Some combination, perhaps. Isn't that what history is, a story concocted in the present out of selected facts from the past? Kate reflected on these in-dentured men and women who had lived in this very spot, in this ragtag assemblage of huts and hovels, and wished that they could speak, that they could give their own testimony, but she did not hear them; in Eleanor's text, they always fell silent when Mary Foxley approached.

There followed a rather too-detailed description, pages and pages, of tobacco planting, of harvesting, "prizing" into hogs-heads, rolling the hogsheads down the lawn—or at least, the in-cline toward the creek that was now the lawn—and onto waiting "flat-bottomed skiffs." Hmmm. Page Down, Page Down, Page Down, went Kate; yes, she supposed that providing this infor-mation, with attendant redolent terms, was the proof of a his-torical novelist's bona fides, but maybe that's why she had never liked historical fiction. An "unwinnable game," a critic had once remarked. The reader could "smell the oil," as Trollope famously described storytelling that worked too hard. Still, Kate understood that tobacco was their life and their future, and any real reader settling down to be educated—as opposed to a mother snooping in her child's computer—would require such detail, especially in light of the devastation that plant had wreaked upon the land, the soils, the native cultures, its ruthless need for labor, willing and unwilling.

So it was, as the years began to pass, that our lives took shape. If I had once feared the fates suffered by the first colonists at James City, I did no longer. I did not fear starvation or lack of shelter. I did not fear the native peoples. Though we were all ill from time to time, and many of our servants, most of which had been raised in poverty, died in their first year or two here, I did not fear illness any more than I feared childbirth, though either could have carried me away at any time.

I did fear death for my children, and each time it happened—of my six, only two, Rebecca and Richard, are alive as I write—the grief I felt for that lost soul was deeper than the last; there is a beautiful chorus of song from the lips of my lost children, but I cannot hear it.

I did not fear loneliness or hardship or lack of comforts, or, after my husband's death, the loss of male companionship. I did not fear the summer heat or the winter cold, the summer squalls that came up the Bay or the blizzards that came down from the north, far above the headwaters of the Susquehanna.

What I did fear, what I knew could ruin us, was the price of leaf.

Kate glanced at her watch. Time to start cooking? But this last phrase, "the price of leaf." How marvelous, how succinct. She could feel it seeping into her consciousness, one of those lyrics that says so little and means so much, *the price of leaf,* a new measure of the days, a way to assess the challenges before us, an invitation to place value on the choices we have made.

4

Rosalie dropped her kayak into the water. A sit-on-top, which she generally disapproved of, but it was the right choice for an afternoon of splashing about. In the back of their new house—so what if her mother thought they were spending too much?—she had a carport full of kayaks to choose from, for calm lake waters, for the open sea, a tandem that Paul was at least willing to try from time to time. She could still hear Daniel's wails, or was it simply the wind in the trees? Could the cry of her child join the chorus on this place? This clinging to her was new, and who could fault him, with all the different day-care solutions they had cycled through in the past few months. Paul seemed to elicit the worst behavior of all. What did that mean? Did Daniel sense something? Exhausting. That was a word she had never before used to describe her life, or to describe her life negatively; in previous years, with plenty of slack in the margins, being exhausted, spent, all in, and used up was a good thing.

She climbed on top, poled off, and took her first full stroke, the strain radiating from her wrists and forearms to her triceps and deltoids, up to her rotator cuffs. Like a person encountering old friends, she counted off the names of the body parts engaged in this motion. "Subscapularis," she said fondly, leaning into the next stroke, feeling the electric ripple move from her upper arm to her shoulder. "Supraspinatus, infraspinatus, teres minor," she said with each stroke as the water began to ripple under the boat and the heat flowed through her upper body. So effortless, in her way of thinking, by which she would mean that no effort was wasted in a kayak: it was almost flying, just a few molecules connecting her to the surface of the earth. Isaac Newton had never been in a kayak; otherwise, he'd have had to rethink his laws of motion. Paddle all the way to Wilmington? Yes, please, dear Eleanor. May I? Up the Bay and through the Chesapeake and Delaware Canal. Will take about a week. Can you watch Daniel while I'm gone?

"No," she said out loud, a general defiance. Her strokes began to accompany her angry inner chatter, punctuating the key words like a work song: things are *not* all great with Paul; the *miscarriage* has messed up my mind; maybe he could *help me* a whole lot more. She looked up and saw the Mansion House flashing through the beech and pecan trees on the lawn; she hoped she hadn't been shouting. But there was no danger of being overheard. Paul would be going to the beach, wouldn't miss seeing that sexy little Heidi, and indeed—indeed!—Eleanor, in their bathing suits. Everything Paul did these days was wrong, even when he was trying to be supportive. Talking about the miscarriage when he felt guilty. *Wrong.* Not talking about the miscarriage when he wanted sex. *Wrong.* Buying scones as a treat when he knew she was trying to lose weight. *Wrong.* Working at night so she could have some time to herself. *Wrong.* The strokes on each "wrong" got the boat going so fast it was singing. He was wrong so consistently, so one-hundred-percent wrong, that she could only believe that he, a man so extraordinarily fine-tuned, was doing it deliberately. But why? Was he angry at her because she wanted another child, or because she had lost the one they thought they had?

She stopped stroking and let the boat glide. She was halfway up the creek, with the broad basin of the river ahead—such a familiar landscape, but in no way a timeless landscape. Wasn't that, as one might say, "rather unique"? Wasn't a landscape supposed to be like Yosemite or the Alps, a vista dotted with recognizable landmarks, permanent features in human time? Not this landscape. But that's why Rosalie had always been reassured by Paul's scholarship: for a person who studied change on a planetary scale, he still believed in permanence. If things changed so much around here, he would ask, why did they still *feel* the same? And yes, just to her right was what they had called the Point Beach, which in years past had been a surprising deposit, almost a dune, of fine sand, and because the channel ran right along this beach, one could dive in, as into a pool. That beach was all but gone now, just a marshy spit; the channel ran along the opposite side of the creek. But in her eye, the beach was still there. She had been twelve that first summer visit after her father bought the place. Which was the second time she had been here, if one counted that weird afternoon drive-through a few years earlier; God, the silence between her two parents in that car was something she never wanted to hear again in her life. At their worst, Paul and she were several hundred decibels removed from that sort of aural absolute zero. But yes, the Point Beach back then was almost enough of a beach to make her proud that her family owned it, a private beach! And the first time she dove in—this was in late August—she got a face full of jellyfish tentacles; it was a miracle that she ever again waded in that water above the ankles.

She started to paddle again and nosed out into the river. Here the air was heavier, fuller, robust with the scents of the sea, unlike the moldy ethers of the creek. The parade of power boats was underway in the channel. Eleanor—and Paul, Rosalie assumed—would latch on to the appearance of the Trump flags, and it *was* chilling to think that this deranged fool could be reelected, but when one lived in DC in these times, when everything hung in the balance, one had to look past the horrors or live in terror. She'd be glad to move anywhere, on either coast, but this was where Paul's job was, and she was doing pretty well herself. Life happens, she thought. It happens, and then it's over. Or it doesn't happen, like the life of the child she had lost. She grieved over this for a second, then banished the thought by settling into a rhythm, and the next thing she knew, she was far out into the basin of the river, in the center, a mile from either bank. She looked back at the low band of the Retreat, so much fuss for something no broader than a pencil line. The channel was now clogged with enormous stinkpots, but in the past this was where the commerce happened; this was a waterway turned into a way to exploit resources, and Rosalie knew she was supposed to decry that, but why? Making money was how this place survived. There were good ways to make money and bad ways to make money, but the fact that the Chesapeake Bay was no longer a majestic Eden, with oysters virtually throwing themselves onto the beach to be eaten, well, let him who does not want a house and a car and the comforts of the American economy cast the first stone. Rosalie was sure that Eleanor's novel was headed toward an indictment of the whole project, but in the five minutes she had taken to assess the manuscript, her eyes had only alighted on a scene of Mary Foxley picking spring greens alongside a band of Indian women.

Rosalie headed upriver. She wondered why, or at least noticed that her thoughts while kayaking these days tended to bitterness. In the old days she could spend an entire afternoon engrossed in technique—the style, the functioning of her body. When she got home, she would all but tear her clothes off with her first boyfriend, Sean, and, subsequently, with Paul, and this was the best sex of her life, which was probably why neither one of those men ever objected, in those earlier days, to her hobby. Then time passed, the physical motions became automatic, and her mind would run to practical things, pros and cons of marrying Paul, buying a house. Important decisions about her work often became clear on the water, and for a while she put off confronting difficult questions until she could do it in a boat. But now, at home, just looking at her kayaks under the carport, a strange kind of stifled bile, full of affront and defensiveness, would rise up, and by the time she got to the water's edge, she was in a rage against the world.

Two Jet Skis passed, feet away on either side; the usual shit, the old insecurity about the athletic female. Rosalie had been deliberately run off the road on her bicycle, tripped while running in Rock Creek Park, harassed in the free-weight room at the gym: she'd seen it all. Assholes, she thought; in twenty years you'll be too fat and too diabetic and too useless to get off your couch. She was tempted to give the jet skiers the finger, but they were gone now, far upriver. Actually, this little contretemps had been liberating; it helped redirect her anger to strangers. She turned her boat so she could search the beach, and yes, she could discern the glint of a windshield in the field, and in front, on the beach, the dark forms of her family lounging and wading. She was ready to return to them, emotionally presentable. On her trip she had seen no jellyfish; Daniel would be spared that treat for another day.

The encampment on the beach came into plainer view: the groupings of chairs, the large blue beach umbrella, the coolers arrayed in the sand. Her father was in the middle in his Washington Redskins beach chair—an ironic gift from Ethan. Harry was a heedless patriarch, unwilling to assume the role but also unwilling to relinquish it. Rosalie wasn't sure what she thought of this, or what his own feelings might be, but in many ways it made sense: he had been a feckless parent. He offered multiple principles but very few lessons. Growing up, they faced few restrictions from him on behavior, on simple issues of safety; there was nothing with even an implied "or else." But now, as if to make up for this lax attitude, he had become as vigilant as an OSHA inspector. Maybe, thought Rosalie, it was having a child a little later in life that had awakened his fears, or maybe there was something more perverse about having a male child, the heir, but there he sat stiffly, in the middle of things, as relaxed as a lifeguard on duty, and when he finally spotted Rosalie coming closer, he stood up and waved sharply, ready to scold her for going out so far.

Paul and Eleanor, naturally, were standing together at the water's edge, supposedly watching Daniel as he hauled pails of water to a pool he had dug in the sand; he was a wonderfully busy boy, laserlike in his attention, so she and Paul contended, compared with the other almost three-year-olds they encountered at day care, at the playground, compared even with the *daughters* of their friends. Imagine that. They were already worried about him socially; he seemed far more interested in his own projects than anything to do with other kids. But still, a happy, charming scene until, as she bobbed closer to shore, Paul turned to Daniel and said—not that Rosalie could hear him—"Look, there's Mommy!" and Daniel instantly began to wail. Served Paul right, she thought, so eager to foist him off on her.

Ethan and Heidi were sitting on towels on the other side, and Rosalie was surprised but pleased to see that they had been joined by another couple. She was still not close enough to make out faces all that clearly, but alas, she knew who they were instantly only because they were Black: Jeremy Terrell—Ethan's best friend from the moment he'd been deposited, kicking and screaming, at his new school on the shore—with his girlfriend, Simone, presumably. They all loved Jeremy—at the beginning, Rosalie had to admit, a little too much for the liberal cred that he earned them all, but Jeremy was a super kid, funny and goofy, a bit of a wiseass, except to their parents. Eleanor had pegged him an Eddie Haskell, but she meant it affectionately. Jeremy's father had been a deputy sheriff for years—this did come in handy in one incident concerning a corncrib that burned to the ground—and, *mirabile dictu*, had recently been elected sheriff, a Black sheriff in Trump country.

And then there were those stupid dogs, Rowdy swimming out to her, a hundred yards from shore, hacking up seawater and lashing out with his front paws as he tried to scramble onto the kayak, reeking of skunk even though mostly submerged, and with this, finally, Rosalie had to capitulate to her family responsibilities and paddle to shore without further delay.

"There's the best flag of the day," Jeremy said. He was peering at the boats through Ethan's binoculars. "'Trump 2020—Fuck Your Feelings.' What does that even mean?" he asked, lowering the binos. "'Fuck Your Feelings.'"

"It means they don't care if we're offended at being called niggers," said Simone. She was stretched out on her towel and didn't bother to look up when she spoke.

"Or maybe it's more about liberals in general," said Ethan. "You know, the old bleeding-heart liberal." Ethan had taken a seminar the previous year called The Postwar American Left: From Adlai Stevenson to Elizabeth Warren.

"I don't know about any bleeding-heart thing," Simone answered, this time pulling her head up a bit, squinting at Ethan across Jeremy's chest. "The feelings those guys want to fuck are Black feelings. That's what the flag should say. 'Fuck Black Feelings.' Just one more letter. Would fit fine."

Ethan laughed, but held to his point. "I think it's white liberals they hate the most because we show them up. Because they know a change is going to come."

Simone now sat up fully, sharply. "You can say that, but I hate it when whites get all Sam Cooke on us."

"I was thinking Bob Dylan," said Ethan, a bit taken aback, humming a little in order to see if he had the lyrics right. "'The times they are a-changin'.'"

"'End the Bullshit,'" said Jeremy.

"What?"

Jeremy was back to looking through the binoculars and had not been listening to the discussion. "That's another Trump flag. 'End the Bullshit.'"

"Is ignoring them actually a possibility?" said Heidi, accent on "ignoring," a note of impatience. She was at the end of the line, with a slight gap between the other evenly spaced towels, sitting up with her sketch pad balanced on her knees. She did not look up from her work; it seemed she simply wanted them to change the channel of the background noise.

"Maybe so, for you," snapped Simone.

Ethan tensed, and so did Jeremy, as if both of them were used to their girlfriends picking fights, which in fact they were. Ethan shot a glance at Heidi, a plea, but her sunglasses were so opaque that he could not tell if the message was received. How, he wondered, could they possibly have lost her glasses? She'd put them on the same hay bale as her sketch pad and pencils, and yes, it was kind of a production to create a comfortable spot—naked human flesh and dry alfalfa do not mix, despite what romance novels say—but when all was done, the sketch pad was there, and the pencils, but not the glasses. Ethan all but demolished the carefully stacked pile of bales, but Heidi's glasses, it seemed, had left this earth.

Heidi was still intent on her drawing, but she finally—was this pause, this lack of reaction, part of the show? Ethan wondered—answered mildly. "I just meant that they're doing this to piss us off. It would make their day to know we've been watching them. I can't stand the idea of giving them pleasure."

"It's not pleasure they're feeling," Simone said, but likewise dropping the tone a notch or two. "It's bloodlust. Every day for them is the day before Kristallnacht, and they're getting all sexed up for it."

Ethan had met Simone once before, a classmate of Jeremy's at Salisbury, double majoring in history and econ. She was planning to go to law school and would probably get into Harvard; according to Jeremy, she had gotten about eight million on her LSAT.

Heidi, at last, dropped her pencil and held up her sketch pad for them to see what she had been drawing during this whole conversation. It was her version of a cigarette boat spewing exhaust, with a large flag: "Trump 2020—Fuck the Planet."

"That works," said Simone. Jeremy asked her to hand it over to him, and Ethan could tell, even through the glasses, that Heidi was pleased. She was *so* awesome.

"Could we look at some of the others?" Jeremy asked.

Heidi told him he could, stood up, brushed sand off her butt, and moved so that she could watch Jeremy and Simone flip the pages. Ethan returned his attention to Paul and Eleanor. He had honestly never liked Paul, didn't trust him, one of those college professors who seemed all too content with being an adult among children. But maybe the problem he really had with his brother-in-law was Eleanor. Paul's too-attentive laughter at whatever Eleanor was saying as they stood ankle-deep, sort of watching Daniel, was *incredibly* annoying, like they were in high school hanging out and Paul was the nerd trying to ingratiate himself while the girl ogled the captain of the football team. Which Jeremy had been, incidentally. But, I mean, thought Ethan, Eleanor most of the time tried to be so cool, which this was not. He looked out at Rosalie, initially a tiny blip on the screen but now drawing closer, her head and shoulders steady as her arms churned, and the dogs were splashing out toward her and Daniel was following, and then Dad was the one doing the barking, snapping out that someone needed to watch Daniel before he got in over his head. The water remained shallow for at least a hundred yards, but just then Daniel did tumble headfirst, thrashing about below the surface, and at that moment everyone started to yell—Dad, the dogs. "Goddamn you, Paul," Rosalie screamed, getting ready to jump overboard. "Get him!"

"Christ!" said Jeremy, springing to his feet and getting ready to sprint, though they were dozens of yards farther away than everyone else.

It was over in a second, Paul fishing Daniel out. The boy spluttered, then wailed a bit—"I got my head wet," he yelled—but by the time Rosalie hit the beach and jumped off her boat, he was laughing. "Again," he said, trying to wriggle out of Paul's arms.

"See?" said Paul to Rosalie. "It was nothing."

"Is it really so hard to watch him for a few minutes?" she barked, which set Daniel back to wailing, and Ethan understood that this was way over the top, as far as Daniel's safety was concerned. The real target, it seemed to Ethan, was Eleanor, and as he saw it, she had it coming.

In all this, Eleanor, paralyzed with alarm and guilt, had not moved an inch, as if the ankle-high water would not release her. Rosalie had every right to be mad at her. She knew she had been crossing a line a bit with her brother-in-law, and it was all that asshole Vittorio's fault. On the way through the fields to the river-shore, she had gotten a text from him that she assumed, before she began to read it, was him saying he had left Brooklyn, was somewhere on the New Jersey Turnpike, and would make it to the Retreat by around five. That was the plan. But no, he hadn't left yet, in fact was not coming, car this, money that, bullshit, bullshit, bullshit. She texted back, *You can fuck anyone you like, but I want your shit out of my place before I get back.*

For the last hour, through all the getting to the beach and drinking beer and hanging out with Paul, she had been riding the adrenaline of that electronic kiss-off, but now, with Rosalie mad at her and onto her, her world landed with a thud between her shoulder blades and drove her heart through her knees. Look at me, she thought. I've got nothing. A shit job writing corporate copy. A scumbag for a boyfriend. A novel going nowhere. And this celebration of something, of maybe just family, her own fam-ily, but the *weight* of this celebration—her father's expectations, her mother's illness: it was all suddenly too much, too hard to keep everything in orbit around her. This life, no longer a peak to climb, but a crevice to fall into; despair about its pointlessness, embarrassment at its triviality, mortification at its pretensions, but what else for her, who else, where else?

"El?" Her father had come up to her side while Rosalie, Paul, and Daniel tried to work it all out. "Come sit with me," he said. She turned; she knew her eyes were full of tears. He led her by the hand back to his perch in the center, the two beach chairs under the umbrella. He was still holding on to her as they both sat, as if she might try to escape.

Harry knew. He knew her loneliness; he knew she was the

vulnerable one. It gnawed at him at night, even as Kate told him that rather than supporting her with his love and concern, he was demeaning her with his fears. "Would you like someone to think you have a sad life?" she asked. "How would that make you feel?"

"Isn't Rowdy great?" he said. The dog had just shaken muddy droplets all over Ethan and his friends, causing a ruckus.

"Oh God, Dad. No, he isn't great. He's the stupidest pet I've ever known. My turtles were smarter than your dogs."

"Gee," Harry said, only half feigning hurt and surprise.

Eleanor took her hand back. "Is this why you wanted me to sit with you? To talk about the dogs?"

"Sweetheart," he said. Oh, how to unravel, unwind, disambiguate the feelings for each of his children? Merely asking that question was one of the biggest clichés of parenthood, which is why few ever bother to try to answer it. But really, on a yellow legal pad—in his very successful career as a venture capitalist he was famous with his colleagues for his yellow legal pads, hundreds of them, the analytical tool he trusted most—he might arrange three columns in a sort of schema, with items, qualities, preferences listed on the y-axis and the three children on the x-axis. The point was not to find a favorite, but to understand what it was, precisely, that each needed most from him. Even Harry would not actually do this, but if he did add it all up, the columns would reveal that his three children each needed something very different: for Rosalie, it was thoughtfulness, willingness to be analytical, not to criticize her quantitative turn; for Ethan, still a youth—so Harry thought, though he was wrong (sometimes the yellow pads were very wrong)—it was simply approval, a rubber stamp; but for Eleanor it was the gift of time, of lingering with her past the moment, keeping the lamp on for just a minute or two longer, a sign of love she could read like a book, or a poem. She was the one who had consented to go on errands with him on Saturday mornings, a little dark force in a purple T-shirt buckled not into the approved, safer back seat, where all children must sit, but in front, beside him; she was the one whose deepest needs were thwarted by the fact that between his work and his booze, Saturday-morning errands were often not on his schedule. But so what? This was Harry's attitude toward his own past behavior; live with it and become a better person. So what, because if his daughter needed time with him then, she needed it even more now. In the column with "El" at the top, there was so much to love, so much to admire, the brittle soul of a child, really, still unformed as if, at age thirty-one, she were standing on a ridge with the valley of her life still in front of her, untraveled, intact. Harry would do anything to protect her from the world's careless disregard, from boyfriends who weren't worthy of carrying her laundry, from editors who rejected her work with no idea how much each word had cost her. From anyone.

"Sweetheart," he said again with a tiny, congested sob, "I just want to talk. I haven't seen you in months."

"Yeh," she said.

"Well? How's things?"

"Kind of shitty, if you want to know." He did want to know, and she told him pretty much what she had been saying to herself a few minutes earlier: the more her job paid her, the less she could tolerate it; her ex-boyfriend had been cheating on her since the day they met; her novel was a mess; if she simply deleted the past two years of her life, *nothing* would be lost. "What's left to feel good about?" she asked.

"Health?"

She pointed to her body; as far as she was concerned, her maillot hung off it like a sack. "People ask me if I have an eating disorder."

"Do you?"

"No. But in the summer I generally try to bulk up so people won't ask me. You know, eat pasta and drink a lot of beer."

"In years to come, you'll be grateful." He pointed to his own body, a midsection that threatened to hang over his belt a little, a general state of fleshly slackness on his torso, but all in all, acceptably trim. People remarked upon it, at his age. "I have done nothing to earn this," he said.

They said nothing for a few minutes, watched the mild waves lap, little ripples on the shore, the bite of minnows that all together would someday consume this low section of Retreat land. Harmony seemed to have been restored in the family Mason-Gottlieb, but Ethan and his friends were packing up. Jeremy and Simone came over to take their leave. "So nice to see you, Jeremy," Harry said. "I miss you hanging out at the house."

Jeremy, always polite, said he missed coming over.

"You should both come to dinner with us, unless your family has something planned. Plenty to eat. Kate is cooking her usual whale."

"A whale? You eat whale meat?" said Simone.

No, Jeremy explained, Kate always cooked a big salmon on the Fourth of July. Some kind of tradition, a "New England thing," he so accurately remembered and respectfully added. He'd been a guest at the dinner several times over the years.

"But you know, Jeremy, we're going to have some interesting visitors today, and somehow, they may be as much cousins of yours as they are of ours."

"Really? These French people E. was talking about?" The boys had known themselves thus—as E. and J.—since the beginning of high school, and for years Kate referred to them, addressed them, called them to dinner as a collective EJ. On her calendars from those years: EJ here for supper; EJ at Bonaroo; EJ to New

Carrollton. It fit the family pattern, Harry reducing the girls' names to Rose and El.

"Yes. I asked your father about this once. The mother's family name was Terrell." Jeremy seemed ready to ask the unasked question, so Harry continued. "She was African American," he said.

"Huh," said Jeremy. He was a boy of talent and grace, but also one who knew how to deflect; EJ: masters of deflection. "Thanks. Maybe we can stop by."

The young people left, and then Rosalie threw her kayak onto the roof of their car and they left, and even though it was now past three o'clock and time for all to get cracking, Harry and Eleanor remained. And the dogs, of course. "This is the best time on the beach," said Harry, any beach, when, sun-maddened and salt-encrusted, the first families begin to head for their cars, and the noisy group with the coolers and boom boxes—"Dad," said Eleanor, "*no one* has 'boom boxes' anymore"—finally depart. Suddenly you feel a oneness with the sand, the little plot of it you had earlier carved out that now seems to extend all the way to the shore, into the sea, to China. Or wherever. "The busy world is hushed, the fever of life is over, and our work is done," says the prayer.

"So," Harry said, after they had both enjoyed the stillness, "how is it a novel is a mess? How does that work, that you know it, or that you think it?"

"You know it's a mess when you put everything you've got into it and get nothing in return. That is what my professors at Columbia used to tell me, that you know you've got something when it *does* begin to give back, when it begins to teach you, when it begins to tell you where it wants to go next, but it isn't happening for me."

"It seems to me that there are lots of things you are enjoying. You have seemed so energized."

"I like the research. I like trying to imagine what life was like here."

"Isn't that the main thing?"

"No. Unfortunately. It's only the material, it's only the wonky stuff. It's such a cliché, a fiction writer liking the research. And hating the work. That's all I can say."

"Well, I'm sorry," he said. Kate, he believed, would try harder to dispute what Eleanor said, or to show her why she was being too harsh on herself, which was often what the kids needed. But for Harry, you had to start by agreeing to the essentials and go from there. If her novel was not giving back to her—whatever that was supposed to mean—the question was, why wasn't it? "Sometimes if you ask for less, you get more. If you're looking for something big, you don't see something little. That's what being in venture capital taught me. What was wonky was usually the difference between finding a gold mine and sinking into a tar pit."

He looked across at her through the pitilessly white western sun; she was staring out at the water, deep in a thought; a few minutes passed, with Harry's expectant gaze upon her. At last she turned to him, invited the conversation to continue.

"Nothing worth doing is easy," said Harry, thinking that she could probably get as good advice from the newspaper horoscope, but still. What's simple is often true. Another key to Harry's soul. "History is hard."

"But you love it, really. That's why you bought this place. If you hadn't, you'd be still living in Menlo Park with your yellow pads and Mom would be in Düsseldorf, or somewhere, not with you. You're the best person you are, here. It gives you peace to be here."

Yes, thought Harry. He knew this, had felt that it filled a void for him on the day they visited so long ago. He had seen it work on him from that first summer, had seen a marriage in trouble grow into a ferocious, spiky bond, a husk protecting what was sweet inside. How did that happen? He didn't know, but what had come to his mind was that for life to be large and full, it must contain the care of the past and of the future in every passing moment of the present. That's what Joseph Conrad said; Harry wasn't much for literature, but he loved *Nostromo*. When living like that, time overflowed, ran over the lip of the cup, and yes again, he knew about the miseries, the crimes, his crimes and his forebears' crimes, and he had to let them all in, let in the multitude of voices in order to be large and full. This is the sort of thing he might feel staring at a brilliant red sunset, and maybe someday, but not this day, he would try to articulate all this to Eleanor.

"Well," said Harry. "I wish I could help." He did wish he had some literary advice to give beyond his little nostrums. Kate would be a better bet, but he had noticed that Eleanor was never more tight-lipped about her writing than she was around Kate—from a fear of influence, or of interference? "But I believe in you to the absolute bottom of my soul. So there."

"Thanks, Dad," she said. And she meant it, because of all the people in her life, he was the one, the *only* one—*fuck you, Vittorio*—she could speak frankly to about her fears. This old guy, her dad, pushing seventy, years with ups and downs, he wasn't going to be in her life forever. And that was okay: neither of them wanted him to live forever. But now was just fine. He was packing up, folding the beach chairs and the umbrella, and Eleanor was helping him transfer it all to his utility cart, but when all was on board and the dogs had jumped up and waited for their master to get on the road, Eleanor hung back. "I'll walk," she said.

"The French should be coming about five. Will you be on hand to help?"

"Sure. Of course."

"And Alice Howe."

"I like Alice. I wouldn't miss her."

Eleanor watched him recede, easing his silly cart in and out of the deep ruts in the tractor path, the dogs' heads bouncing clownishly. Oh, she had been mean about Dad's dogs; over the years it had become a sort of family affectation to disparage them, and really, having a dumb but loyal pooch to kick around was a nice relief. Each time one of them died or had to be put down, her father grieved, mourned the loss for months, as if this were in his darker days and the dog was the only real friend he had. But forget the dogs. Eleanor recalled that in the opening prologue of her novel, scrawled in her journal the night she started on it, she had concluded by addressing the ghostly Mary Foxley. *But no one ever asked you, did they?* When she was deflecting her father's questions, dismissing everything on her mind as wonkiness, what she was thinking about was the idea of person. Of address. In grad school, Monroe Monroe—sometimes they added a third "Monroe" just to be cute—had arrived with a half-finished manuscript written in the second person, and they had all ridiculed him for it. Why, Eleanor wasn't quite sure, except that it felt pretty hokey, like all those "How to . . ." stories high school girls write. (Hers was "How to Change a Tampon.") But as she picked her way through the fields back to the family celebration, she asked herself the one simple question that might open vast vistas of possibilities in the writing life: What if the novel were a conversation between herself and Mary Foxley? And oh yeh, fuck you, Vittorio, you asshole.

5

From across the creek, Alice Howe could hear the sounds of a family gathering, the squall of a young child, a single, surprised laugh, the slamming of a door, and, of course, on this day as on any other day, that goddamned dog barking. Woof, woof, woof—Alice mimed this, eyes crazed—every morning, and clearly not barking *at* something, not doing anything useful to the pack or to its human owners, but simply barking over and over without the slightest change in tone or inflection, just making noise. Even the geese, in winter, seemed to be *conversing*; even the herons with their disagreeable squawks had something on their minds; even the middle-of-the-night snarls of warring small mammals, death snarls as they sometimes seemed to be, were fueled with desperate purpose. But not those dogs.

Alice had spent most of her ninety-six years on a somewhat modest and blameless farm called Weatherly, which shared the creek with the Retreat and seemed always to fall into its orbit for no reason that could be explained. This had nothing to do with the fact that Weatherly had once been part of the Retreat, the kind of distant history that bored Alice to death. But there were more recent events, such as on that early, early morning in August 1939, when Sebastien Mason stole Alice's sailboat and drowned trying to hide from his father somewhere around Kent Island. Apart from the fact that it was her boat—a Comet—and that she had taught him the rudiments of sailing, Alice had had nothing to do with the event, but a tragedy of that magnitude creates its own gravity and sucks everyone in. Her parents' marriage, never great, fell apart, and then her father, a drunk and a fool, died wading ashore in Normandy on D-Day. Thousands of Americans died that day, but Alice always thought her father had gotten killed trying to redeem himself. Her mother had taken her back to Connecticut but within a few years returned to Weatherly because she didn't know what else to do. Alice happily went to Goucher in Baltimore and majored in Latin and Greek, but she found no Hopkins or St. John's boy to marry, returned to the farm, and that was that.

For the last two years a Dutch girl named Milou—well, she was just a girl when she arrived as an au pair in Annapolis, a job that didn't work out—lived with Alice, took care of the farm chores, the horses, did the shopping and most of the cooking, fended off Alice's cousin Margaret, who would have moved in forty years ago if she'd had the chance, and in these years with Milou, Alice had found a happiness that to her astonishment made her glad to be alive. Twice, once in despair about the pointlessness of her life at forty, and once out of a sort of gratitude that she had made it to eighty, she had brought herself to the threshold of suicide, the first time with a noose in her hand, standing in the loft of her barn, and the second staring into a palmful of pills. She knew—she believed—that her love for Milou was utterly selfish, but at ninety-six, this would not go on too much longer, and when Alice died, Milou would have the surprise of her life.

"Margaret called to say she'll pick you up at six thirty," the girl called into the screened porch. Alice was sitting there, as she did for many hours in the summer, staring out at the boats on the river.

"Aren't all those blue flags pretty," she said without turning. She was watching the Fourth of July armada steaming out of Kent Narrows and heading up the river. "I wonder what they mean."

Milou knew what they were, but did not say.

"Why aren't you coming with me to the Masons'?" Alice asked. For weeks she had been campaigning for Milou to join her—with or without Margaret, though preferably without.

"I don't know any of them. And they wouldn't be interested in me anyway."

Alice loved to hear her speak, words so carefully enunciated in an accent midway between English and German, which made every bit of sense.

"Foolish nonsense." Milou did not react, she never reacted, to Alice's rhetorical exaggerations. "They have a son about your age. Maybe a year or two younger than you. A *boy*," Alice added for emphasis, because Milou never mentioned a single thing about romance of any kind. Whether Milou might prefer boys or girls, Alice didn't know or care, but she wanted her to find love of her own.

Milou was not the classic Dutch blonde with rosy cheeks, but rather, thought Alice, something so much more beautiful, classic. Greek, really. Sometimes Alice couldn't keep her eyes off her, the way she moved, the way her expressions always seemed to conceal deeper thoughts. In morning light her face was soft and rounded, but in the late afternoon, in the slanting western sun, she became all angles, sculpted, one would have to say; in this light Alice pictured a clay maquette, still fairly unfinished, forms and planes. Alice did now look over her shoulder and was horrified to see Milou's arms covered in dried blood.

"Milou!" she said.

"It's not mine. It's chickens'. A fox got in last night." She held her arms out. "I'm just on the way to wash up."

"How?" said Alice.

"I don't know. Some board must be loose."

Yes, some board. There were lots of loose boards around this little farm, lots of roofs that needed attention, but what had sustained it was Milou's business providing care and pasturage for horses in their last years, the Osprey Neck for the equine set. The horses, that is. There was little of show or dressage or hunting in Queen Anne's County, but owners brought them over from the western shore. "Will you call Mike Benjamin, *please*, and get him to clean up a few things around here?" Alice said. Mike Benjamin was a carpenter and handyman, not all that much younger than Alice.

"Did you hear what I said about Margaret?" Milou asked.

Alice groaned. "Yes."

"But, of course, it's not that simple," she said.

"With Margaret, it never is."

"Her car—"

"Oh God," interrupted Alice. "Margaret has not had an easy life, but she is one of those people who seem to have brought it upon herself. Everything bad that happens to her occurs in the space of her pretensions. Like her car." Margaret's car was a twenty-five-year-old Mercedes; the local mechanic was now trying to do Margaret a favor by mostly refusing to service it. He had a nice clean Ford he wanted to sell her, but Margaret wouldn't hear of such a thing, and the Mercedes limped along.

Milou smiled, but she would not encourage Alice's mean

streak. Imagine, Alice thought, if she had been living with Margaret for all these years. What an absolute shrew—a Xanthippe, she would have said back at Goucher—she would be by now!

"And she wants to stop at the nursery, where there is some sort of sale going on," added Milou.

"Thank you, dear," said Alice, leaving Margaret to her own petty disasters and freeing Milou to her own business. Maybe she had a plan for the evening when Alice was at the Retreat. She did take days off, and during her disastrous employment in Annapolis she had made some friends; could Alice really argue that Milou would have a better time at the Retreat?

"Are you going to wear your daffodil skirt?" asked Milou. "Do you want me to set it out for you?"

"Yes, if you promise to wear your blue sundress. The one I like." The day Alice fell in love with Milou, she had been wearing that dress.

Milou lowered her head to look down at the chicken blood dried on her arms and on her overalls. "I will wear that sundress because you like it. Someday soon."

"If Margaret doesn't come, you'll have to drive me."

"I won't need to wear that blue dress just to drop you off and pick you up."

Alice stuck her tongue out at Milou and watched her go. Yes, when they read her will, Milou would have the surprise of her life. And so would Margaret, who otherwise would have the place on the market on the same day the deed was in her hand. Every time Margaret walked into the house, there were dollar signs in her eyes. A few years earlier a quite fine silver creamer had gone missing, and though it was not even plausible that poor Margaret had stolen it, the suspicion remained in Alice's mind. No, Margaret had not had an easy life, and she had to watch her pennies, but Weatherly was not coming to her.

Alice remained on her porch, feeling quite satisfied. She went back to talking to herself. No wonder Milou was reluctant to go to this party. What do I think of the Masons anyway? This was Alice's thinking style, responding to her own rhetorical questions, which, of course, were not rhetorical if someone actually responded to them. What did she think about Harry Mason buying the place back; what did she think about Kate Mason living in a house that destroyed its women; what did she think about Simon, who had become such an odd little man—one never knew what he was going to say next. What did she think about this party, which she had attended on and off over the years; she wasn't sure why she had accepted this year, but assumed it was because she doubted she'd be alive next year. Wouldn't she rather just stay home? Of course she would; she hadn't set foot off Weatherly in months. What was out there that she needed? Nothing. So yes, it was partly because she wanted Milou to see the place, wanted to show her off, wanted her to meet the neighbors, because soon enough they would be *her* neighbors. She would like Kate. But also, Alice accepted the invitation because of the boy, the drowned boy, all these years ago, a life that never got to be lived. This party was, had always been, a gathering in remembrance of him, even if not a word would be said about him, first and foremost would not be said about him by the only person besides Alice who was alive at the time, his brother, Simon.

How to poach a whole (fucking) salmon, *selon* Martha Stewart, with additional notes from Kate Mason:

Step 1. Rinse fish under cold running water, washing away any blood around the gills, which would cloud the stock. Certainly would not want cloudy stock! Pat the fish dry inside and out with paper towels; place on a clean work surface. Trim the fins from the back, belly, and near the gills with a pair of kitchen scissors.

Step 2. Cut a double thickness of cheesecloth 17 inches wide and 8 inches longer than salmon. Cheesecloth. Do I have any cheesecloth that mice haven't been living and shitting in? Place the cheesecloth on a clean work surface. Lay the fish lengthwise on the cloth, and wrap the cloth around the fish. Tie the ends of the cheesecloth with kitchen twine.

Step 3. Place the rack in the bottom of the poacher and fill with the cooled court bouillon. Check. Made the court bouillon yesterday, nicely cooled. Using the ends of the cloth as handles, lower salmon into the poacher, adding water if necessary to cover the fish. Cover, and set the poacher over two burners. Cook at a bare simmer for 25 minutes (the water should not be boiling). Of course not. It should be *almost* at the boil, which is like telling someone to turn at the last left before the cliff.

Step 4. Now here's the good part: slide a wooden spoon through each handle of the poaching rack, lift out the rack, and *prop* the spoons on the edges of the poacher so the fish is elevated. "Prop." What a fine word, really; a state of suspension, propped. A bold transitive verb. *Appoggiare* in Italian. *Stützen* in German. *Étayer* in French. That was pretty much how she felt these days, propped up like a poached fish.

Back to Step 4. Raise one of the spoons to lift the side of the rack that supports the head end and expose the widest part of the fish's back. Insert an instant-read thermometer near *where the fin was.* "Where the fin was" is a nice Gothic touch. The fish is fully cooked when the temperature registers 135 degrees. For a larger salmon this may take up to an hour. (For a whale it could take a week.) If the temperature is too low, return the fish to the liquid and continue poaching, checking the temperature every 10 minutes.

Step 5. Using two wooden spoons as described in Step 4—oh yes, as *props*—remove the rack from the liquid, and *prop* it—the fish? the rack?—on top of poacher at an angle to drain, reserving court bouillon. When salmon is cool enough to handle, about 15 minutes, transfer to a clean (!) work surface; let cool completely, about 45 minutes.

Now Martha goes on from there with an aspic glaze: Pour the court bouillon through a fine sieve; in a separate bowl, whisk 6 egg whites until frothy, etc., etc.; whisk the mixture over medium heat until it comes to a simmer, about 10 minutes. The egg whites will "draw all the cloudy particles out of the stock and begin to coagulate on top." No, says Kate, pushing aside her iPad. Out of the question: no more cheeseclothing, no sprinkling of gelatin, no decorating with choice of garnishes. Kumquats? At a Food Lion on the Eastern Shore of Maryland? Are you out of your mind, Martha? This is not the Hamptons.

But the moment approaches. In the background, *ominous music plays*, as the closed caption has it. Kate confronts the fish, which is now lying on a (clean) work surface, which is to say, the section of counter least likely to have recently been used by Harry to prepare the dogs' dinners. Even so, wax paper is always wise. The fish is beautiful, of course. There is no living creature that Kate can imagine more perfectly envisioned for its environment. A horse glides in spite of its knobby knees, its too-big head. An eagle soaring is majestic, but those wings, they have to fold up in just the right way or one of them would snap. Or so Kate thinks. But this fish: it brings its native ocean with it even as it lies on the slab. A dead mammal is a bag of bones; a fish, even dead, could swim like a missile. Well, not counting dolphins and whales, because, of course, they *aren't* fish. Kate lets out a small giggle at this silly meditation; no more rosé for her until they are sitting down to eat! Was that somebody coming in the back door? No. The house is still quiet; the only stirring would be Simon's slight snore, as well as the usual creaks and groans she hears from the less-used parts of the house, the places where in the past the owners would never have had reason to tread. Does a fish have a soul? she wonders. As instructed, she snips off fins here and there. She knows that each one of those spiky appurtenances fills an exquisite purpose, the ability to surface or dive, to turn right or left. Sorry, fish, she thinks. But in all this rhapsodizing about form and environment, in all this carnivorous regret, there is another inconvenient truth for fish: they are a most tidy and trouble-free food. Just empty a small cavity of entrails and the rest is *prêt à manger*. Kate pictures bears in Alaska with salmon in their mouths, and there is nothing ghastly to imagine, very little about a bear eating a salmon that a human wouldn't do.

Poacher strategically placed over two burners, court bouillon ready to do its thing, fish securely wrapped in cheesecloth: in she goes. (She?) Kate dries her hands on a dish towel, considers what she has done, and begins, once again, to count places for the table setting. But she is so bored by this compulsive exercise, so disappointed by the fact that she can no longer, apparently, count from one to fifteen, that she pretty much decides to do the meal, as she says, buffet-style. But no, because, for Harry and Simon, this meal is an act of remembrance and an expression of faith in the future. It requires a certain amount of brio. It marks a moment in time, family time. "What then is time?" asked Saint Augustine. "If no one asks me, I know what it is. If I wish to explain it to him who asks, I do not know." Yes, Kate recalls this fine question and remembers that the bishop finally nailed down the human experience of time by reciting psalms from memory. "In you, my soul, I measure times," he said. Yes, Kate repeats to herself, ritual is remembrance *and* prophecy. So the Mason-Bayly-Lorenz-Gottlieb family will continue, and will be able to mark time with this annual dinner, and in years to come, Kate's survivors will say, *No, it couldn't have been 2019. Mom was still alive for the Fourth in 2019*; or, *Remember that cute girlfriend of Ethan's who lost her glasses? (And what were you doing,* Eeethaan, *when she lost them?) That was 2019.*

Oh, the coziness of these little tales, Mom alive or dead, the girlfriend . . . what was her name? As if these present details were all that mattered, as if history had nothing to do with them. Czesław Miłosz said that about American poets, in critique. Poets have no choice but to face the moral obligations history has assigned to them, he said, or something like that. So it is for aspiring novelist Eleanor Mason: the sweep of American history, the blessed *narrative*, can no longer protect it from its injustices. Kate says all this even while she has her head in the refrigerator, peering into the crisper for the ingredients for a nice tangy *sauce verte*: parsley, chervil, mint, garlic, plus capers and anchovies. What was not to like in any of that?

"Hey, Mom."

Kate was relieved to be brought back to the present by the appearance of Ethan at the door.

"Oh. Hello, Ethan. Are you all back? I didn't hear you come in."

Ethan explained that Dad and Eleanor were still at the beach, Rosalie and Paul and Daniel must be putting the kayak away, Heidi was making one last try to find her glasses. "How are you?" he said. Ethan was the one person on earth, besides Harry, of course, who was allowed to ask that question, to interrogate all its layers: *What's up? How's it going with the salmon? Can I help? Don't do too much here. Any pains, any sensations? Are you thinking about your cancer? Are you afraid of death?*

"I'm fine," she answered. "I was just mulling about the nature of time."

"Uh-oh."

"No. All very abstract. I've been having fun."

"Sounds like a PBS Kids show," he said, sliding past her to take a beer out of the refrigerator. With a jolt, a tightening across her flattened chest, Kate wanted just a sip more of wine, but she fought it back.

"J. and his girlfriend came out to the shore. Dad invited them for dinner."

Buffet-style, thought Kate. Definitely got to do this *boofaay* style. "I'd love to see him."

"When are the French cousins supposed to get here?"

Kate looked at her watch. "Pretty soon," she said. "Dad wants to take them for the tour."

"Huh." He lingered with his Budweiser in hand, and Kate wasn't sure whether she wanted him to stay and chat or to head off; sometimes children just want *air*, their parents' breath, to steal it out of their mouths. "Breathe on me, breath of God," went the hymn from her youth, which she had always found a little disgusting. Maybe she should have gone into her thoughts about history.

"I wanted to ask you a question," he said.

"Of course," she said.

"What's up with Rosalie?"

"You think so?" she said.

He looked at her quizzically—an odd response, but sense could be made of it: *So you think there is something up with Rosalie?* "Well, yeh. I mean, Paul let Daniel fall into the water at the shore, and she lost her shit. And that thing she said to Eleanor at brunch, and from the moment she's gotten here, she's been a real bitch."

"Don't use that word. You know how offensive it is."

"Sorry."

"I mean it." Kate found herself getting very angry. "It's like calling someone a cunt. Would you call your sister a cunt? 'From the moment Rosalie got here she's been a real cunt?'"

"Mom."

"Well, would you? Would you call your sister a cunt?"

"No," said Ethan.

"I get a little damn tired of this."

"Mom," said Ethan, "have you been drinking?" Because that's how Ethan had grown up, with this sense that somewhere off-stage, or in history, there are forces bending the moment; nothing can be understood in the here and now. If Mom wanted to talk about the nature of time, that would have been Ethan's two cents. The sensation of unseen trouble in the wings might be the pentimento of his parents' rockier years, or might be, more recently, Mom's illness, and this summer, it was Mom and her wine. He'd hear the tinny uncoiling of the screw top in midafternoon and he'd know; he'd count the succession of one-finger splashes (the Thelma slices, as Paul's family would say it) and do the math; she was never drunk but occasionally overexuberant, flirtatious sometimes, and sometimes like this, spoiling for a fight.

"That has nothing to do with this," she said, but the moment had passed, the anger in her expression was replaced by the tiniest amount of remorse followed by an appeal for leniency. "You know I hate that word."

"Okay," said Ethan, now regretting that he had let his own impulse take over when really, he thought, for what his mother had gone through, she deserved a break; remembering how, in the first, scariest days after the diagnosis, her solid tumbler of wine as dusk fell lifted all their spirits, paved the way into dinner in the knowledge that she was in a happier place. "Sorry."

"Yes," she said, "Rosalie does appear a little stressed, but that's her business. Having kids is stressful, with a job and everything." Okay, thought Ethan, job and everything; stress. He was learning nothing useful in this conversation, and the truth was, he was feeling a little stressed about Heidi; ever since they'd made love, ever since she lost her glasses, she had seemed bored with him.

"Why don't you go talk to Pop?" his mother offered.

For some reason, he raised his beer in a small toast and left. He found his grandfather where he expected, immobile on the porch, but he realized that the line between wakefulness and sleep in a person Pop's age was a little hard to spot. He tiptoed out the door.

"Ah. The young prince," said Pop, fully awake. "The heir. 'My crown I am, but still my griefs are mine. You may my glories and my state depose but not my griefs; still am I king of those.'"

"Hi, Pop," said Ethan. "Sure."

"And what is on our mind?" he asked expansively.

Ethan never knew exactly how to respond to his grandfather; he was so often a succession of personae, always acting. What an odd way to live, Ethan thought; how much was one supposed to play along? This time he responded with the truth. "My girl-friend lost her glasses."

"Not exactly an affair of state," said Pop, still with the Shake-spearean intonation.

"Well. It's an affair of my state," said Ethan.

He watched as a look of surprise became one of delight. "Oh, Ethie," Simon said, now just nothing but a grandfather. "Good for you. Good answer. Where is she?"

"She's looking for them. We lost them somewhere on the farm."

"Sort of an odd thing to lose, if you need them to see."

"Heidi's vision is kind of in-between there," Ethan lied. "Sometimes she forgets about them because she doesn't always need them."

"Seems to me you ought to be helping her find them. Don't

waste time with me." He resumed his position in the chair, head propped back on the shutter of the French door, gazing down to the water. "An affair of your state," he added, mostly to himself.

Ethan took off, passed Rosalie stowing the kayak in a shed while Paul chased Daniel down a line of boxbush; he stood aside for Dad, and the dogs, returning from the beach in what Ethan thought of as his "electric boat." It was past four o'clock. People would soon begin arriving, and he knew that Eleanor and Rosalie would be pitching in with the preparations, and so should he. But from the way Heidi was behaving, it seemed that unless she found her glasses, she wouldn't show for dinner. She was more than capable of that, simply refusing to budge from the third floor, leaving it to him to make excuses, professing that she didn't care what he said, sneaking down after everyone had gone and helping herself to leftovers. Ethan worried too much about what other people thought; that's what she had said, which bothered him especially because he worried a lot about what Heidi thought.

He passed the stable and rounded the lane skirting the gully that separated the house and the farmyard, and there, in front of the barn where they had, indeed, lost the glasses, he saw Heidi talking to Francis. Who knew what they might have to converse about, but as Ethan got closer, he saw that she was laughing, Francis standing there rail-thin, frail and stiff, and the silky girl almost doubled over, her hand covering her mouth as she guffawed.

"Hey, guys," said Ethan. Heidi had seen him coming, but Francis turned in some surprise, and Ethan could tell that he was disappointed to have this moment interrupted, that he wasn't at all sure he wanted to share with Ethan what he was saying to Heidi.

"Hey," he said.

Heidi glanced at Francis with the gratitude one feels for a funny story; Ethan had never imagined such a moment, as Francis was hardly comic. "I was telling Francis . . ." she said, and hesitated to give Francis the chance to ask her to stop or to pick up the story himself, but he simply nodded. "I was telling him about losing my glasses, and he was telling me about all the places he has lost his teeth."

Francis smiled openly at Ethan, showing off his line of perfect choppers; until then Ethan had not imagined that Francis was toothless. "From time to time," he said, which was as far as he would go with Ethan. "Like I said"—he turned back to Heidi—"things turn up in the funniest places."

"Like the freezer," said Heidi. "Or the mailbox."

"Yeh. Anyway, I'll keep an eye out," he said.

He walked back toward the old help house where he lived with his father, leaving Ethan to wait for further details from Heidi, which she didn't seem inclined to share. "He says being without his teeth feels most natural, which makes sense."

"Not like your glasses."

"I guess."

"I mean—" and it was clear that he was going to say it's not such a big deal or something, that if Francis losing his teeth is funny, then maybe there was some humor here, but she cut him off.

"You don't understand," she said. "You don't understand anything about it."

Yes, Ethan didn't understand, didn't understand what it was that he did or did not understand.

"My parents wouldn't let me have glasses. They thought I was trying to get attention, that the reason I didn't like school, didn't like recess, didn't like other kids was because I was shy. Even when they understood that I couldn't see, even after teachers threatened to bring in social services, they thought I would grow out of it naturally, because both of them had twenty-twenty vision. That's when it started to come out that my dad wasn't really my dad, which was a surprise to my dad, and that my real dad wore Coke bottles. So they split up—they weren't married at that point anyway—and my mom took me to the Vision Center in Hanover, and they were like, 'You mean she's almost ten and she's never had glasses, with her eyes?' And my mom told some kind of story about my vision changing suddenly, and anyway, I didn't care what bullshit she came up with, and the first time I put them on was the greatest day of my life. I mean that. If I live to be a hundred, it will *always* be the best day of my life. For a week I'd go to sleep with them on, and in the morning when I woke up and they weren't on my face, I'd get hysterical. You can't imagine; it was as if I awoke from a beautiful dream. My mom would find them under the covers and put them in my hands or on my face, and it was only because I could touch them, because they were a solid object, that I could believe in them. I have never lost the need to have them with me. That's why I don't wear contacts; because I can't feel them. My face without glasses feels flayed and raw. It feels like riding in a car without a seat belt, as if my face is about to go through a windshield. I was twelve when my sort-of parents got back together and Dad moved back in, and I told him that if he ever said *anything* about my glasses, if he ever *touched* them, I'd mess up his face with a hammer, and I meant it."

They were still standing in front of the mule barn; Ethan looked down at his shoes. He'd known none of this, that her glasses were the key to her past; he had no idea that within her soul was a sore quite like this. This vision of his girlfriend as a child, a child waking up in her bed: it was strangely heartbreaking to him. He wanted to hug her, give an almost parental kind of comfort, to protect her from everyone, starting with those worthless hippies who raised her. But he didn't feel he had the right to intrude upon her story like this, to conclude it with this gesture, and at this point he was probably correct. "Let's try one last time in the barn," he said. "They have to be jammed into a hay bale."

Rosalie stepped into the shower. She felt fat and useless. In the locker rooms at school and college, especially after a win, she luxuriated in standing naked around her teammates even as most of them slouched into the showers, rushed from towel to underwear in front of their lockers. When a body has done such glorious things—a beautiful, feathering pass to an attackman in full stride, a backhand uncoiling like a bear trap—why renounce it? But when a body has betrayed you, it deserves shame. Concentrating on the moment was the secret of Rosalie's considerable academic and business success—focusing on a math test was merely a case of compressing all of time into the point of her pencil—but it left her defenseless against disappointment. Such had been argued by Paul about her miscarriage—oh, I love him, he is my husband—and even now she was beginning to recognize that he was right, which was, of course, a fresh and new source of discontent, as Rosalie hated to be wrong.

On the little table crammed between the bed and the portable crib were the pages of Eleanor's manuscript. Having stowed her kayak hastily and left Paul and Daniel doing something they both loved to do—pawing around in the mud and clay of the marsh near the dock—having showered quickly, and heedlessly clothed her (worthless) body, she figured she could grab a half hour to see what her sister was up to, even if all she was entrusted with was a miserly sample. Rosalie eyed the pages warily, rather like Kate and the fish, and why wouldn't she? What sort of mash-up was Eleanor making of this family material? What right, after all, did she have to do it, even if—as Rosalie had remarked at brunch—she was inventing ninety-nine percent of it? The politics of the project did not concern Rosalie; at best, as a matter of the national discourse, this conjuring of forgotten people in the past provided pleasant footnotes; at worst it was a political cliché; and in between, where were the facts, what was the authority?

She settled in to a description of their ancestor—the Emigrant, as they had always referred to him, which meant he was remembered not as someone who arrived, but as someone who departed, but okay—on an exploratory trip on the Chester in a small boat—a batteau, Eleanor called it—with a boy named Fulke, who Rosalie figured out was an indentured servant. "My husband" was the way Eleanor's Mary Foxley referred to him, which struck Rosalie as a rather clever way to base this fictional character on their Mason forebear without having to name him in the text; Foxley was indeed his wife's real maiden name, but that didn't perturb Rosalie for some reason. An hour and a half ago Rosalie had been paddling in some of these same spots in the Chester River; over the years she had followed every one of the rivers and creeks, inlets and rivulets to the tops of their muddy heads, although Eleanor used what were certainly historically accurate names: "Coursey's Creek" for, Rosalie inferred, the Corsica River; "Lanceford's Cove" for Langford Creek. Someone, along the line, had allowed these names to evolve, and Rosalie wondered why. But it was beautiful, really, the way Nell had reimagined all this as an unknown but lush land, the way she had captured the delight and freedom of sailing through this virgin territory. In fact, Rosalie remembered at that moment the little line drawing of their ancestor, the Emigrant, being rowed in a batteau in one of Eleanor's reference books. Out of this single image, it seemed to Rosalie, her sister had conjured all these scenes, paying calls to the DeCourcys and Goldsboroughs and Lloyds, all of whom—investors in tobacco, Puritans expelled from Virginia, Catholics of immense wealth—were establishing their homes on these shores. As Rosalie correctly recalled, the Emigrant in the drawing was being rowed by people who clearly had no choice in the matter, but Eleanor had cleverly elided that fact by putting her character and the boy under sail the whole time. There was a rhythm, Rosalie divined, between the facts and fiction, between the acceptable and—here was the rub—the unmentionable. Call it a strategy of exclusion. So this is what fiction writers do. Here is where her distrust seeped in.

Mary Foxley had introduced this trip as a guileless effort by her husband to make contact with the native peoples—Rosalie wondered why Eleanor had framed him as a bit of a naïf—and at one point they do encounter some Indians: . . . *rounding a point, they came upon a pair of canoes with about ten men and women angling and spearfishing. They were suspicious, and they pointed their weapons at the batteau, but my husband stood up with his hands empty, offered his chest for a target, if that was what they wished to do, as if foolishness could be mistaken as good intentions. He beckoned that they should beach their vessels and engage in discussion—he mimicked all this, including the hand-to-mouth invitation to share a meal—but they returned no interest in this. They went back to their fishing, and my husband, who had enough sense in this case to push this first encounter no further, sailed on. When they came back down Coursey's Creek a few days later, he hoped that the Indians might have agreed among themselves to welcome him ashore, but they seemed to have disappeared.*

It was as this silent presence that Eleanor had chosen to portray the Indians—mute faces, eyes twinkling in the surrounding forest. "Wicomesse," Mary Foxley/Eleanor called them, and as far as Rosalie could tell, flipping ahead in the pages, there was never to be an Indian character, someone named, which again was probably a wise choice, since there was no way Eleanor could try that without being wrong. In fact, there was only a little more on the Indians, and when Rosalie got to the end of this final piece, she understood why.

My need to engage in social relations was in no way equal to my husband's, but considering how often I had fearfully anticipated hostilities with these peoples, I too was interested in encountering them now that I had learned that hostilities were unlikely. Some of the rivershore lands we occupied had been recently tilled by the Indians but were now growing in again with grasses and shrubs; this was the Indian way. The women would plant their crops for three or four years and then move on when the soil became less fertile. Sometime in the mid-spring of my first year I heard that the women were coming back to these lands to pick greens and blackberries and silk grass, and apparently they paid no mind to us or we to them, though soon enough we would be expanding our plantings of tobacco onto these fields. I went out to greet them one day; when I returned, my husband and even Fulke scolded me for going alone, and I suppose they were right, but that seemed to be the best way to present myself. I was able to walk quite easily through the oak and hickory forests around us, even with a large basket at my side, and by the time I broke into the open, they had heard me and were staring my way. I don't know if the women I saw that day were the last of the Wicomesse or were Susquehannocks, their enemies who were taking their place. They were a tall people, broad-faced and black-eyed, but they appeared undernourished and not in good health. I knew nothing about them, but I did feel that what I was seeing were women who looked much older than their years by our standards. The young children, boys and girls, ran around naked; the women had no infants with them, which meant there must have been some enclave nearby where they left the very young.

When I drew up, they greeted me with the barest of nods. I said hello, and indicated that my name was Mary; I think I heard one of them repeat my name, and they might have understood and of-

fered their own names in return, but I'm not sure. For all that, it was a pleasant scene, a warm early-spring day, a fragrant breeze from the water. What was most noticeable to me was that, as I started to pick plants alongside them, no one objected that this was their patch of greens, that they had discovered the blackberries and were unwilling to share them. What they did not know was that these spaces were within my husband's patent, that Cecilius Calvert had bestowed them upon my husband forever. And for the first time since this whole adventure had been presented to me by my husband five years earlier in Maidstone, I asked myself by what authority the king had ceded this land to the Calverts, and the Calverts had given it to us. The answer was that the king made his own authority. But that king had some years ago been beheaded, and even if, as we understood, his son had been restored to the throne subsequent to our departure, these events across the seas seemed to obtain not at all to what we, the Indian women and I, were doing that day: gathering the fruits of the earth. Would that it could have remained so.

Sometime before the departure of the first colonists for Mary-Land, our lord proprietor composed a letter of instruction for these persons. There were numerous expressions of his desires, some of which I have already mentioned in my account, but the first order of business, after securing sufficient food and shelter for their survival, was to endeavor the conversion of the savages to Christianity. I do not know whether our neighbors made any attempt to do this—certainly my husband did not think he was equipped to effect this spiritual transition among peoples so foreign to us. I knew that Jesuits had been in Virginia in the years before the arrival of Captain Smith, and there had been priests in St. Mary's City almost from the day that settlement was founded. But we did not have the benefit of clergy on our shore.

And so it was a cruel irony for me to learn, many years later, of events now mostly lost to recent history, which included the forcible removal of the remaining Wicomesse people from our region. It was thus that they were converted to our way of life. How, I wondered, in this vast territory could there not be room for us all? Why wasn't God's plan that the planters and Indians simply agree on how to live together? Even now, at the end of my life, my mind is afire with that question, one of the questions about our life in the New World that I hope someday, someone will be able to answer.

So the Masonizing was now beginning in earnest! From where Paul and Daniel were playing, Paul saw a car drive in. Maybe it was the French cousins, or maybe Kate's grotesque *Cousin* Lotte and her impalpable husband, Hector; if Kate seated him beside them again, he was suing for divorce. Which wasn't very funny, considering how the day was going with Rosalie. Yes, he'd complained, a little, coming over, but he did it in good cheer and, in fact, had even hoped that the holiday and the weekend would be a break for them, a change of scene. And he had tried and was now tired of being wrong.

Now that we have that out of the way, he thought, let's look forward. But it wasn't so easy, here, to look forward; this place was all about looking backward. Which Paul did, mulled in that terrible self-pitying way even as he followed along after Daniel, knelt down to inspect the relatively clean skull of a small animal nestled in the grass, raced after the child when he took off for the seawall and the murderous corners of the riprap stones piled in front. He still didn't know exactly what mistake he had made with Ethan's girlfriend; for that matter, he didn't know what was the original sin he seemed to have committed with Ethan. And having gotten all Christian about it, he acknowledged that he had stepped into this WASPiest of all WASPy families with at least some enthusiasm; at times he had enjoyed being the only Jew at family gatherings, as if he knew about a whole world around them that they did not. The same could be said for this heteronormative enclave, all these boys and girls cozily attracted to the "right sort," though Paul knew some things that no one else in the family knew, which was that in college Eleanor had enjoyed a brief but passionate affair with a young female assistant professor and that her sometime boyfriend, Vittorio—still a jerk, as far as Paul was concerned—had never had sex with a woman before Eleanor. The things Paul knew about his sister-in-law, the things she had confided in him! He had to admit that Eleanor telling him such things about her sex life was a turn-on—talk about heteronormative—but mostly he was just flattered that she considered him someone so trustworthy, especially when she introduced the topic by saying, "Don't tell Rosalie this." She had told him about her affair, and about all the low points with Vittorio that made her consider that loving women might actually be the safest course. And so it was, this afternoon, with her bitterly complaining about Vittorio with nonetheless a certain amount of dark humor, that, yes, he had taken his eyes off Daniel for a *second or two*, not in the pounding surf of Atlantic beaches, but the tepid splatter of the Chester River. Still, one could drown in a bathtub, and Paul was horrified and embarrassed by the whole episode even as Harry tried to reassure him, from the edge of the fray, that almost no milestone in a child's life was more routine than getting dunked for the first time. Paul loved Daniel with every part of his being, and he loved Rosalie, and at this point all he wanted to do was pack his family back in their car and go home.

"Time to go, Bear," he said to Daniel, who was covered with streaks of yellow clay; he and the dogs had inspected this shoreline at about the same level of inquiry and discovery. "Time for a bath," he said.

"There you are," said Rosalie, a voice from the other side of the phragmites. She came up to them. "I'm sorry I ditched you. I wanted to glance at Eleanor's novel. At least get a peek."

"Did you?"

"Yes. It's, well . . . interesting. We'll talk about it." She was busily trying to keep Daniel from crawling up her leg and leaving her in need of a new shower. "Sweetheart?" she said to Paul.

"Yeh?"

"Look. I'm sorry. I didn't mean to get so mad. I was scared." She reached down and picked up Daniel, held him as far from her body as she could; the dogs thought this was fun and came over to rub their sodden, gritty coats against her legs. "Mommy didn't mean to yell," she said to Daniel. She looked back at Paul over the top of his hair. "I'm just not quite ready for any close calls these days. You can understand."

"Of course I can," said Paul, trying not to sound either angry or hurt, trying not to sound as if he were Sick to Death of Understanding. Paul kept his gaze out of the mouth of the creek toward the river.

She waited a moment and then asked, "What were you and Eleanor so deep into anyway?"

What? Paul wanted to shout. *This was all about* Eleanor? But he didn't. "Nothing. I can't even remember."

"It wasn't about me, was it? That's all I wanted to know. If she was mad at me."

"No. Nothing to do with you."

For a moment they remained in this tableau, Rosalie and Daniel on the edge of the weeds, Paul still in the flats, gazing outward into the river basin. "Well, I guess it's beginning to happen," Rosalie said. "Cousin Lotte will be driving up any second. I've got to help Mom."

"Sure," he said, looking at his watch. Almost five; these days at the Retreat were always crammed with events—traditions to be observed!—but still could seem endless.

"So? I'm sorry? Can you give Daniel his bath?"

6

Julien Bayly and his daughter, Céleste, had spent the hours between noon and two o'clock waiting for a lost suitcase in the Newark airport and standing in an endless line for their rental car, and when they reached the New Jersey Turnpike, it was jammed, a tangle of construction and decay: even the machinery that was supposed to be fixing this mess seemed rusted and broken.

"*Quel dépotoir*," said Céleste. Then added in English, in order to sharpen the insult by making it in its native language, "What a dump. Explain to me why we ever admired America. Home of the hamburger and the billionaire, and look!"

"New Jersey?" asked Julien. "*C'est ce qu'on appelle le* Garden State."

Céleste fumbled around for another disparaging word, but gave up.

They had been visiting wineries in California and Oregon, but also in Ohio and Michigan, and on this leg of the trip would be making stops in Pennsylvania and Virginia. In the 1890s their family had found opportunity in the humble vineyards of Languedoc, and today they still sought out terrains and climates and cultivars that the press overlooked. Not that they had found anything all that splendid in Ohio or Michigan. But for two weeks they had drunk at the American cup; without knowing or noticing it, their own conversations were half in French and half in English. Céleste, making this trip with her father for the first time, had had enough of America, was eager to get back to her home in Montpellier with her partner, Armand, and their two daughters. And now this stop at a farm in Maryland to visit the family that had enslaved some of her forebears. Why were they doing this? Everything she had been raised to understand about this place was that it was hell on earth.

Julien shushed his daughter, reminded her to be respectful and polite, even if he too regarded the United States with increasing dismay, with a sense that this nation was simply unwinding, peeling itself like an orange, ready to be broken into slices. Idiotic. *Liberté, égalité, fraternité*: well, it was nothing but common sense, which America, from the beginning, had had very little of. He'd said much the same to his wife, Amélie, on the phone earlier today, but Céleste's harping was getting tedious. "It is their holiday, after all," he said, trying at least to make some sense of the traffic.

"Please." Céleste needed no reminders, with all the flags waving. The red, white, and blue of the Stars and Stripes and the almost teal blue of the Trump banners—"Trump: 2020"; "Trump: A New Order"; "Trump: Setting Us Free"—which, in the gritty neighborhoods along the New Jersey Turnpike in the north and in the farmlands beginning to open up in the south, seemed the more numerous. "Do we really think they'll make it to next July? That Trump won't bring the whole thing down, whether he gets reelected or not?"

There was more to this than Gallic disdain; Céleste had been begging this question ever since they landed, and for her it was about business. They already owned vineyards in Sonoma and Santa Barbara, and Céleste had been arguing fiercely against investing more in the United States until it was clear what direction the country would be going in. She thought Romania and Moldova were far safer bets for business. And for climate. Julien found her expression a little melodramatic, but he couldn't fault her impulse to move cautiously, the result being that they had made no deals this time around. Indeed, he would have loved to sell their properties in Sonoma, which, as now seemed plain one way or another, this year or the next would be consumed by drought, heat, and flames. The California vineyards were simply going to burn up, that was the view from Europe.

"*On verra, ma chérie,*" he said, meaning: *Can we just drop this for now?* The truth was, he had long been curious about the birthplace of Thomas and Beal, his great-grandparents who had fled from America and founded their family's fortune in the hills of Languedoc, exiles who'd left America, never to return. Even growing up in France, Julien had understood that the best thing about America was that it was a place for immigrants to be welcomed and to prosper; his family's story was the reverse of this, and the reason for it was race, America's special sin; but Julien had no interest in legacies of shame. The French, he believed, had survived as a country even though there had been injustice and failures and calamities, yet all of it could have been so much worse. This was, thought Julien, a peculiar form of optimism, French optimism. And so it had seemed for Beal. She had been a lifelong diarist—a number of her journals, volumes she had written in French, had been published by a small press in Montpellier—and these writings were never more beautiful and poignant than in her descriptions of home, of the little enclave she called Tuckertown. Apparently Thomas, Julien's great-grandfather, who died the year before he was born, never looked back, never talked about his youth as the scion of a large southern farm, a plantation, as Julien thought it was called, never wrote, never said a word about his American past. And so over the years Julien had asked himself this question: Why did the man who had everything want nothing to do with it, and why did the woman who left little behind in America grieve to her death for what she'd lost? If a business trip could take them within a hundred miles of answering that question, would it not, as the Michelin guides have it, *mérite un détour?*

"They have invited us to their house for dinner. Harry Mason has offered to show us around. Aren't you curious?"

"*Non,*" said Céleste. "*Je resterai dans la voiture.*" If she said she would wait in the car, there was a decent chance that she would do just that; she'd done it more than once as a child, a small ball of rage sitting in thirty-degree heat in furious protest against some unplanned stop that displeased her.

"*Comme tu veux,*" he said.

"Who is Molly Pitcher?" she said after a long stretch of silence. She was already trying to find the answer on her phone.

"*Ça me dépasse,*" said Julien, but he had *some* idea, had noticed this peculiar naming of rest areas on the New Jersey Turnpike on previous trips, though he had never put it together that all the namesakes were famous New Jerseyans. All except Molly Pitcher, who was a myth.

"No service," said Céleste. "Can you believe it?"

They both went back to their thoughts. They were rolling down the turnpike through farmland, with the occasional warehouse complex or corporate headquarters alongside, and then they were fighting their way across the Delaware Memorial

Bridge into a maw of chemical plants and mostly abandoned strip malls. "Thank God for Google Maps," said Julien as they were guided south, and soon enough, once again, they were in farmland, cutting across Delaware and Maryland as instructed. Flat land, a featureless expanse; if you loved such a place, what would you say about it? Julien's native landscape was the *garrigue* of southwestern France, wild land, scraggly trees, ravines and gullies five hundred meters deep, the air fragrant with rosemary and lavender, the occasional clap of the church bell in the valley, the dull clang of cowbells, the braying of sheep. Always something going on; his land, he thought, teemed, abounded, with collective forces, human, natural, sacred. And here? Well, not lifeless, not barren, certainly—even now he could feel the fecundity of this thick air—but solitary. He could appreciate the vast horizontal line of this landscape, its humility, its openness, but it seemed to amplify his sense of emptiness, as if whatever life was there could be seen from a kilometer away. Earlier he had looked across one of the broad fields and seen, in the distance, a single deer grazing in a field; it could have been the only deer in existence.

And such a waste, all this corn, he thought: sandy soil, he assumed. Perhaps a tolerable amount of clay to introduce a little muscularity, as in Pomerol? Not that he had any interest in merlot or cabernet. But vidal blanc, barbera, maybe? Chambourcin was the obvious option, and so far it was proving not to be a bad grape. And if chambourcin, why not tannat? Okay, a bit of a stretch, but it might be worth a try, despite the warm climate. He was musing in this way when suddenly, far off the roadway, across a field planted with soybeans, shimmering slightly, he caught sight of a vineyard. For a moment he thought it was a mirage, a hallucination after two weeks of seeing almost nothing but vineyards, but Céleste saw it too. "*Attends une minute,*" she said.

They were too far away to discern the *cépage*—almost certainly chambourcin, thought Julien, and if so, might there be some chardonel on this estate?—but the pruning and trellising were visible to their eyes and presented all sorts of intriguing possibilities. "Looks like someone who knows what they're doing," he answered, now driving dangerously while looking back over his shoulder. "Imagine. Here."

"We've got to stop," she said.

He looked at his watch; it was—even for as good an English speaker as he was, numbers remained difficult—*seize heures moins le quart.* "We don't have time," he said.

Céleste was still turned around, looking back longingly like a schoolgirl being driven away from a crush, and through his side mirror Julien likewise could see that something quite unusual, quite professional, was going on here, a slight irony to find the work of a true vigneron in this wasteland of fast food and corn. Even Céleste was intrigued. "We can come back tomorrow," he said.

Harry came into the kitchen somewhat soaked, not from swimming in the river but from giving baths to the dogs. He could do little about the skunk smell, but Rowdy looked so pathetic, so clearly understanding that he had been stupid again—*I know! I know!*—that Harry wanted to console him; a nice hosing always cheered Rowdy up, part Labrador that he was. The "worst part," according to Kate. "What about the other parts?" he asked. "Worster and worsterest," she said.

"Any word from the French?" he said, grabbing for a clean dish towel.

Kate was standing at the stove. The salmon was out, cooling, looking nicely, well, salmon-colored. She had squash and zucchini sliced on an enormous sheet pan, ready for roasting. Ethan and Heidi were sitting at the table cutting up strawberries. Or, Ethan was cutting up strawberries and Heidi was drawing on her pad, darting her head up and down, peering at Kate through her dark glasses. For a moment, Harry watched, not entirely with pleasure, as this girl charted the effects of age and illness on his wife's face. Could Heidi imagine how pretty Kate had been, with her lovely, thick brown hair, her pointy nose and tiny cleft in her sharp chin, the same person who was now leaning on the counter, fuzzy scalp and overalls, mopping her face with her bandanna, looking not especially beautiful to anyone but Harry, but not discontent, pricelessly herself, the spouse of the long marriage, the solace for every ill, the succor of every small victory.

"No," said Kate.

"Alice Howe?"

"Still on, as far as I know. She's hoping she can get the girl to come."

Harry had seen Milou at the Food Lion now and again, knew who she was, that tall, kind of Eurasian-looking young woman, but he had never introduced himself; she was always so intent on her shopping. She had no idea, it seemed, that the young manager of the store—a very competent guy named Jason—was clearly smitten. A handsome couple they would be. "You know Alice is going to give the place to her."

"Of course I know it. Everyone in the county knows it, except Margaret."

"Seems a little mean," said Ethan.

"Margaret is one of those people everyone is mean to," said Kate meanly. "She nurtures it."

"Still. It sucks."

"Yes," said Harry. "It does. But it's Alice's choice, after all." He went to the refrigerator and took out a seltzer; even as long as he had been sober, he was still grateful and relieved that he was free from the desire to take out anything else. "So how many is that?" he asked Kate.

"You tell me." She straightened up from her relaxed pose; the moment of her repletion, now riddled with loose ends and question marks, was over. "Ethan says you invited J. and his girlfriend."

"Of course I did. I hope they come, but I doubt they will."

"So how many is *that*," she said, throwing Harry's question back to him.

"You invited Francis."

"In what possible world would Francis actually show?"

Harry did some math. "Even with Lotte and Hector, that would be what, fifteen? If *les français*"—this was meant to jolly her; Harry speaking French, or any language other than Southern California English, was a family joke—"don't show, it'll just be us."

"Did you set a place for Daniel?" mimicked Kate, ignoring the invitation to lighten up, still being mean, this time about her own daughter. Why am I acting this way? she asked herself. Well, okay, Rosalie *is* being disagreeable, but before Harry came in, she'd been feeling that she had mastered the salmon, feeling that things were coming together. She riffled back over a few of the events of the day to see if she could discern the cause of this bad karma, but all she came up with was a line from Sylvia Plath: "The tulips are too excitable, it is winter here."

"Look," said Harry. "Here's what we are going to do. We're going to set fifteen places, and if more come, we will cram in, and if less, we'll spread out. We've got enough food to serve all of Queen Anne's County." Besides the salmon, the peas, the roasted veg, Kate as usual had also prepared a huge pan of chicken Divan for the fish-averse. "I'll be responsible for the count. It really isn't all that complicated, unless you want to *make* it so," he added. There was a stirring behind from the kids; perhaps he had spoken this more harshly than he intended, the sort of thing he used to do when he was drinking. And yes, he saw that old look of hurt, and anger, in Kate's eyes as she put down the dish towel and walked out of the room.

An uncomfortable silence. He turned to Ethan. "Was it that bad?"

"Just bad enough," said Ethan. "Just barely over the line of badness. You'd have been all right except for the 'want to *make* it so.'"

⁂

"Sweetheart?" He was standing outside their room, announcing himself, asking to come in. The door was closed, and at the moment, that made their bedroom her space. She didn't answer, but his gesture was enough for him. He cracked open the door and found her lying on her back, her bandanna balled into one palm, her other hand on her forehead, staring at the ceiling.

"What?" she said.

"Look. I'm sorry. The Ethan-meter is with you on this one."

"Oh," she said.

He advanced a little into the room. Through the open window he heard, of all things never to be imagined, the sounds of Rosalie and Eleanor playing catch with the lacrosse sticks. Unimaginable, Rosalie offering, Eleanor accepting. He went to the window just as Eleanor actually caught one. Behind them, one terrace closer to the water, Pop and Paul were chasing after Daniel. "Family Happiness," the scene could have been called, an instant of perfection that would be gone in a second or two if Francis or Heidi didn't put it in a bottle. "Will you look at this?" he said.

"What?"

He described the scene, though clearly she was not interested. "Maybe it will loosen Rosalie up a little. Have you noticed that she's been a little grumpy?"

Kate did not stir. "Why don't we just bag this. Okay? You show the French around if they ever get here, take them for their *to-ur* of *Tuckertown*"—she said this in a sarcastic little chirp, for some reason pronouncing "tour" in two syllables; Harry couldn't tell if it was he himself or Julien who was taking the heat here— "we send Lotte and Hector and Alice Howe back with some kind of apology. Blame me. Blame my illness. Eleanor can drive Pop home, maybe even take him for a hamburger at Ruby Tuesday; he'd love that more than anything, and it might cheer Eleanor up. The salmon is cooked, and the kids can just forage for dinner and go out on the boat to watch the fireworks. No one wants to do this. I bet every single one of us woke up saying, *Ugh, the goddamn Fourth of July at the Retreat.* I know I did. Everyone's in a shitty mood. This kind of enforced event is just the sort of thing that I am *not* going spend a *single second* of my time on. I mean, what's it for? It's not tradition; it's just habit. The only people who really want this to happen are you and Margaret Howe."

She had not taken her eyes off the ceiling, and when he sat down beside her on the bed, she shifted over a bit, either to give him room or to keep her distance, it was not clear which.

"Well. We wouldn't want to disappoint Margaret, would we? It would kill her to miss a free meal."

She let out something between a grunt and a snort. Harry chose to read it as conciliatory.

"And Pop."

"Pop doesn't want to do it just as much as he wants to."

Harry paused to figure out, amid the negatives, what she had just said. Unfortunately, it turned out she was right; his father in this place was like a helpless bit of scrap held suspended between the poles of a magnet. "Okay. But it's a little late in the day to be canceling, don't you think?"

"That was what the oncologist said."

Harry tried to ignore that. "We won't do it next year, okay?"

"Next year," she said. "What a thought." She said this as if Harry had no idea what he had just said.

"Yes. Next year, dammit. Next year for the Fourth of July, instead of being here, we'll be in Paris, and we'll stagger off the plane and screw like teenagers as soon as we can get into our room at the Hotel Cler. The same room. The same bed. Then we'll have a little walk to the river and come back to Le Petit Cler and have *une bavette goûteuse* knee to elbow with a crush of beautiful young Parisians, all of them smoking and drinking Campari and soda, and we'll look at each other across that tiny table, gray hair and blotched skin, and agree that it is a miracle, a blessing, that we came so far together just to be back where we started."

"We started in Berkeley."

"Yeh, well, fine. You plan the trip." *If you are going to act like this, then the hell with you* was the tone.

He'd landed a clean, legal, and not unkind blow; she was silent for a few seconds. "You think?"

"I think what?"

"You think I'll live that long?"

"Yes. I do. That's what I think, because this time they had it in their sights, fired the torpedo, and killed it all. Okay? They killed it all."

"That's what they said last time."

"Then our odds just doubled. Even more certain that they're right this time."

They lay beside each other and after a second her hand found his; her hand felt bony and crabby and needy, but he was grateful that it was offered.

"I'm sorry," she said. "I was feeling good, happy, and then all of a sudden this anger took over. I can feel so put-upon, put-upon, as if garbage—I mean literally, garbage—is being poured on my head."

"I know."

"And sometimes the way my mind works, or doesn't work, scares me. It's changed, you know. I'm never going to be the same person inside my head."

"I know it has. I know you won't."

"But really."

"But really what?" He heard the screen door crash downstairs.

"This Fourth of July thing. Can't we find some other more innocent weekend to all get together, sort of spontaneously? All that matters is us, our family, now. Making it into a tradition invites trouble. I don't want people to come here just to be troubled."

"What's wrong with tradition? It helps us focus on who we are, on who we'd like to be—"

"Tradition is just narrative with all the bad stuff taken out. It's history with a mulligan. That's what tradition is."

Harry did not think this was the time to debate these matters, but if it were, he'd say that history is not fate; if Harry believed anything about the human species, it was that from one century to another, from one Reformation to another Enlightenment, from one Norman Conquest to another fall of Afghanistan, people were slowly inching closer to what it might take to be called humane. And if the species were moving forward like that, then he could at least claim a seat on the train. That's what Harry thought. "Then maybe what we can do to make it better is confront what we'd rather forget, because we're better now. That's the ethics of it. While giving thanks for what we have, for our mercies"—he risked inflaming their spat by pounding on this word, but she let it pass—"we become aware of the injustices of the past."

"Really, Harry. On any kind of scale of ethics, 'being aware' is right down there with waterboarding. It's like those people who start meetings giving thanks to the indigenous peoples for allowing us onto their land."

"They don't say 'allow us.'" Harry tried to remember the last time he had encountered this newly popular custom.

"Well, it's the same thing, in the end. *We stole your land, and we're not giving it back, but we acknowledge . . .* They're just waterboarding the Indians all over again."

"Gee," said Harry. "And I'd have thought you'd approve. No mulligans allowed, as you were saying."

"No. That's just a different way *not* to talk about it. A different tradition, no better than the last."

He let it go. It was a few minutes past five, and he was beginning to fear he had been stood up by the French cousins, at least for the tour part of it, and just when he realized how relieved he was, how this might even allow time for them to go out for the tiniest little cocktail cruise on their decrepit Mako 20, it sounded as if a tour bus had just arrived downstairs . . . or the fire department. All hands were on deck. They heard Pop's surprisingly shrill laugh—the sort of staccato pip, pip, pip that is made by people who never laugh without fear that they will be misunderstood. The dogs were barking.

"Okay. So, your *français sont arrivés,*" said Kate.

"So what'll it be? Bag it, or get the show on the road?"

"You go down. Just give me a moment to retie my bandanna."

Kate remained on the bed for a few minutes after Harry left. It was sweet of her husband to talk about Paris, to recall all those details, to promise that trip again, to force himself to believe every word he said about her treatment and prospects, even if nothing was that certain. Yes, that trip was not where they started out, but it was just when Kate was beginning her blog and she was trying to make connections with the French publishers, and they stayed on rue Cler because it was close to the American Library, which had given her a tiny grant, and she hadn't felt that excited about herself since Berkeley. Every day they had breakfast at the Café du Monde and then she'd be off, chirping like a bird. So Harry wasn't wrong to speak of this as a beginning. But that trip hadn't been quite as Harry remembered it. Because this had been their first venturing forth *sans enfants* after he'd quit drinking for good—"quit drinking," they said, rather than "getting sober"— and she hadn't been at all sure that he'd make it, that he wouldn't relapse, and he had. She allowed him to make a sort of game of this, telling each other that what happens on rue Cler stays on rue Cler, and yes, the part about screwing like teenagers was true, every night, doing things they had never done before and never did since. But yes, he would have been at the cafés by the time she returned from the library, and she remembered those dinners as an exercise in holding her breath. Which is hard to do when eating. Slightly terrified that when he stood up from their tiny table, he would stumble and send diners and tables and chairs and ashtrays and glasses of Campari and soda flying.

Maybe she had been too quick to condemn the idea of a narrative with all the bad stuff left out. Maybe she wished she could do that now, because for all the disappointment of the relapse, Harry hadn't behaved that badly, didn't ever stumble, didn't do anything a million other vacationers would do with no harm done, could not have been faulted in the least if it weren't for all the baggage she'd dragged over to Paris from the years before. Harry had proved himself again and again since then, yet this small malignancy of memory, this enumeration of crimes done, still inserted itself into her consciousness, saying, *Yes, but*. How was that fair? Shouldn't values hold some edge on deeds, as long as the deeds aren't so terrible?

There was a knock on the door, and Eleanor came in. "Hi," she said.

"I was just feeling that I don't deserve the life I've lived," said Kate, "that it should have been lived by someone more worthy. Someone who appreciated it more."

"Okay," said Eleanor cautiously.

"Next time around, more positive."

"Well. Never too late."

"That's what the oncologist said," she said, thinking it was obscurely clever to be repeating the line.

Eleanor wasn't in the mood to coddle her, and at that moment Kate had a revelation, something came through her thick scalp, which was that everyone, even Ethan, was trying to make sure today was not about her illness, that they were doing this consciously because they thought she'd want it that way. And of course, she did want it that way. Except. Kate directed her tartness of tongue, her slightly notorious candor, inward as much as outward, and in this moment she remarked to herself that she was not ready to move on from her illness and not ready to lose the privileges accorded to the unwell. Maybe they were jumping the gun a little, but they were all in the same race and were tired of false starts. They were already down the track, and she had no choice but to follow. They were looking ahead because they loved her. Yes, this all, this remission, could prove in the future to have been an illusion of hope and longing, but in the meantime she was simply going to have to do what the healthy do. At that, she took a deep breath, *cleansing*, as they say. "What's happening? Where is everyone?"

"Rosalie and Heidi are setting the table. For fifteen," she stated with some conviction: clearly she had been warned not to get Mom started on that again. "We'll set out the food on the kitchen table and people can serve themselves. Okay? Dad and Pop are going to take Julien and Céleste for a driving tour of Tuckertown. That won't take long."

"No, it won't. I think Julien asked him."

"Yeh. He's great. Smooth as they come. I can imagine him having a twenty-five-year-old girlfriend, along with a beautiful wife. Named Amélie, by the way. And her! Well, I'm completely intimidated."

"Her?"

"Céleste. I just said so. Julien's daughter. About my age, and so, so French. Her hands and gestures, it's as if she practiced in front of a mirror. But all so disinterested, slightly disdainful. Good old-fashioned haughtiness. If she could teach that style to women in New York, she'd make a fortune."

"All right. We've established that the ambience at the Retreat has taken a big step up with our French guests. I'll be down soon."

As was *their* style, in the midst of Kate and Harry's quarrel about the meaning of tradition and the arrival of Julien and Céleste, Kate's cousin Lotte and her husband, Hector, had slithered in through the summer kitchen and assumed their posts. Everyone felt the chill. The house, its spaces and its spirits, didn't like Hector; it resisted him, and he heartily returned the favor. The Retreat, as far as he was concerned, was an impertinence. His post was a chair in a far corner of the wraparound porch, where he could sit and chain-smoke—and I'm the one who gets cancer, Kate had reflected. What was he *thinking* about, all those hours, smoking all those cigarettes and staring lifelessly at the view? Hector had never uttered a word that could be taken as frankly political, an aggrieved man wandering aimlessly on the edges of the American scene; it was assumed that before Trump came along, he'd never even bothered to vote, but after that blessed event he'd gone all in. That was the family theory, as in recent visits he had seemed, unfortunately, to have found his voice. But whatever it was that snaked through the nooks and crannies of his brain, it seemed to hold his attention, or at least divert him from staring at the clock. Clearly, he loathed this event in a house filthy with the years, grounds full of chiggers, people who nattered endlessly about art and climate change, and those goddamned dogs. The more he shooed them, the more he kicked at them, the more irresistible he became.

Lotte's post was the kitchen; this was where she felt she could compete with Kate on even ground, even if it was, after all, Kate's kitchen. What a delight to come in just as Rosalie and this young girl were setting the table! "No, no," she said, casting off her handbag. Lotte was one of those tall, skinny women on whom age does not wear well; more witchlike, thought Rosalie, by the year.

"No what?" said Rosalie. Lotte's arrival, finally, had cast her deep into the pit of her discontents; when Paul woke up that morning with an ugh and a "Shit!" about driving to the Retreat, it was confronting Lotte that Rosalie was dreading.

"We're having the salmon, I assume."

Rosalie pointed to the fish on the counter, which, peacefully lying on its side, seemed happily unimplicated in the fray around it.

"Not those forks." Lotte was clattering through the silverware drawer. "This is impossible," she said, pointing into the drawer. For decades Kate had dutifully separated the silverware into trays until one day a while ago she said "Fuck it," ripped out the trays, and dumped the dishwasher basket into the drawer in a heap. They'd all gotten used to it, pawing through for the utensils they needed; Ethan liked to keep rattling until everyone screamed at him to stop.

Are we really going to get through this? Rosalie asked herself. Mom apparently wanted to call the whole thing off. The French had arrived with the dazed and confused look of shipwreck survivors. If they were, indeed, cousins, the generations in France had removed any trace of the Retreat. The daughter could not even pretend to be interested in the tour; one look at her, and Rosalie knew they had their work cut out for them. She and Paul, these days, were not ready for prime time, which this most certainly was. A family day like this one has its ebbs and flows; there are fair winds and following swells, but also shoals to be avoided, ports of call to be bypassed; and now, with Lotte's arrival, it felt to Rosalie as if the tide had just turned in the Bay of Fundy and the whole lot of them were being washed out to sea.

"That's how Mom likes to do it," said Rosalie.

"She always was so messy," Lotte said, continuing to hunt through the drawer. "Mutti thought she was feebleminded."

Mutti, thought Rosalie. She still refers to her mother as *Mutti*!

"These," Lotte said finally, holding up a specimen. "Fish forks."

"Aren't those dessert forks?" said Heidi. "I mean, if we're saying."

Lotte wheeled around in what looked like horror and rage, corrected by this child in an area in which she clearly would have no expertise. Lotte and Hector had never had children; Lotte said it was because of the demands of her teaching career, but Kate believed it was because Lotte and Hector had never had sex. "We haven't been introduced," she said. "You are?"

Heidi didn't answer, barely even acknowledged the question, soundlessly threw these bad manners back into Lotte's face, and all of a sudden Rosalie found something to live for again. "This is Heidi," she said, providing no more details. In solidarity and pride, she patted Heidi's shoulder, the way she might with her partner in a doubles tennis match. Teammates.

"Why is she wearing those sunglasses?" Neither Rosalie nor Heidi bit on that one either, which left Lotte to continue with the forks. "I know they are dessert forks, dear, but they're better with the fish."

"We aren't just having fish," said Heidi. "Like, what about the peas and the chicken?"

"We have to make some compromises."

"Besides, if we use them for the main course, what are we going to do for dessert?"

Lotte had no answer for this, and when Ethan walked in, she looked as if she might cry. "Hey, Cousin Lotte," said Ethan. "What's up?" He went to the refrigerator for a beer.

"Nothing is 'up,' dear. We are setting the table." She pointed at his beer. "Are you sure you need that?"

"Huh?" he said. He appealed to Rosalie and then took a long sip. "You heard about our cocktail cruise?" he said to Heidi. "You're coming, right?" he said to Rosalie. "I'm headed down to the dock."

Heidi was not completely enamored of the idea, this cocktail cruise, as they called it; she'd seen the boat with its streaked sides and torn cushions, and like almost everything else on the Retreat, it might have been high-quality once, but decades ago.

The only boats Heidi had ever seen were on the Connecticut River, dweeby, middle-aged people drinking on pontoons, fat kids floating alongside in inner tubes. Cocktail cruise? But okay, she thought, anything to get away from this freak.

"A most impolite and irritating girl," Lotte said to Rosalie after they left. On the way out of the kitchen Ethan had snagged a six-pack and a bottle of pinot grigio from the refrigerator. "Your brother is drinking too much. This runs in your father's family." As usual, none of this required a response. Lotte was now clanging through the dish cupboards. "Where are the platters? Have they been moved? Are they being used as dog dishes?" This was supposed to be taken as delightfully nasty.

"Mom said we're just going to do buffet."

"What does that mean? 'Do buffet'?" Fully Frenchified on "buf-*fet*."

"Serve ourselves at the stove, I guess."

"Oh no. With this lovely salmon?"

And here, as much as she wished she didn't, Rosalie agreed with her. Because what was the point of gathering like this, schlepping from far and wide, straining her marriage during a difficult time, enduring unsupportable people like Lotte and Hector, if they were all simply to stand at the trough and feed like animals? On the matter of decorum and etiquette, Rosalie was an oldest child all the way. The dining room, with its massive fireplace, crystal sconces, and elegant sideboard, was almost never asked to live up to its promise. Why not give it a chance to shine? All of this, this day, this reunion, was really just leading up to the meal, and why not give it the ceremony it deserved? Why not take time when time is given to us? The salmon on a platter at one end in front of Mom; the chicken Divan—the old backup—in front of Dad; the peas and roasted squash and tomato platter and pots of *sauce verte* in the middle. Plates being passed, a sort of hand to hand, giving and receiving, a communion; *just a little of that chicken, please, Harry.* The magnificent gentleman in the robe and ruff collar who presided over the dining room from his perch above the fireplace—Oswald, the prosperous Kentish grocer, the father of the Emigrant—would approve of all of it. And no seating plan? Let people just gravitate toward their own little corners? Why not just call in from curbside and eat in our cars?

Her mother was tired of all this, and Rosalie did not blame her, but by God, people had come here for a family meal and that was what was going to happen. She had already begun to sketch a chart, complete with contingencies if Ethan's friend J. or Francis showed up, or if the French stood them up; the main problem was Lotte's husband, with his suffocating cigarette stench. When it came to being assigned a seat for dinner, people like Margaret Howe, who couldn't complain if she was used as filler, were particularly useful. And actually, Margaret seemed to be sympatico with Lotte and Hector, which figured. The problem was Hector's other side: in years past, it was true, it had seemed that Paul was best suited to endure him, but days ago he had said he would eat in the kitchen if she did that to him again. So even though she believed she would live to regret it, she had surrendered, sent Ethan and Heidi out the door for the boat ride, turned, faced Lotte, and reported for duty.

As Harry had warned Julien when attempting to arrange earlier visits, there was very little left of the village where Beal had grown up; Harry came here rarely, feeling as if he were trespassing, driving down this dead-end street only to gawk. He explained that this little strip of houses, straddling the boundary line of two large farms, was typical for the region, that before the Civil War they had been communities of Free Blacks, and after emancipation had provided the labor in an economy that had changed very little. He offered that there were others like it in the county that might be in better repair. Today there were only five or six dwellings, and except for one house at the head of the lane that was original, the rest were trailers and ranches, with brown lawns and pickups out front. The houses and shacks that had lined the lane had burned, or been demolished, or simply allowed to fall in upon themselves, Harry didn't know when or why, but Pop had told him that into the 1950s this was a bustling community, with people coming and going, children lined up for school in the morning, and in the evening families sitting on porches watching the day end. But still, for Harry to imagine what it must have been like, there was enough here: the obvious house sites, a rosebush, a tree that had once provided shade for a front yard, a rubble of bricks that was all that remained of a chimney, a well and a tumbled-in water tank, the shapes and imprints of human life. If you listened, Harry thought, you could hear the voices in the breeze.

And for Julien too, even with so little to go on, there seemed, oddly, enough for him to feel that this was the place his great-grandmother had described in her journals—the angle and color of the sun in the late-summer afternoon, perhaps; the narrow slash of the road and the houses pressed between the woods of larger holdings; the sense that even today people without wealth or advantage were making the very best of what they had. He recalled how she had described her own family's house: two stories and an attic, with a tiny round window looking out onto the lane; a swing bench on the porch where she and her brother and sisters loved to rock in summer; the hard-packed clay of the lane where people, in Beal's description, always seemed to be out and about. He could imagine the gardens in back where the old people spent their days even under the hottest sun, and he believed he could see the rubble of the barn, where two or three of the more prosperous families, like hers, kept a mule and a wagon.

"What happened to them?" asked Julien. Harry had said that except for the young white family that had bought and restored the house at the corner, this was a Latino community now, and on their way down to the dead end of the lane they had passed a handsome but very short young man—Peruvian, it seemed to Julien—walking a tiny white dog on a leash. "What happened to the Black families?"

"I don't know," Harry said. "I wasn't living here then. Pop knew it way back when," he said, tipping his head toward his father. Pop said nothing. This was all getting silly. Harry had expected, was counting on, Pop to explode with tales and historical factoids from the moment Julien and Céleste walked in, but he had been strangely silent. Something had been said to him, perhaps; Harry had to manhandle him into the car. The *to-ur*: Kate's churlish little parody echoed in his head. A tour to see where something had once been: Who would sign up for that? "The houses would have been pretty marginal," Harry said after it was clear that he'd get no help from Pop. "Not necessarily worse than other houses built for farm labor, but freezing cold in the winter. The families who were here must have moved into town as soon as they had the wherewithal to do it. Maybe they were able to get something for their land, a few thousand dollars, maybe."

"I suppose you're right," said Julien.

"But after all, these little strips of houses were an invention of slaveholding times." Harry offered this as a way of introducing the topic that hung over this jolly little outing; he wasn't sure how much of this American story these French cousins would know.

"But then all these plantations," said Céleste, "are inventions of slavery also. *Non?*"

This woman's lack of enthusiasm for this visit was clear

enough; when they'd driven up to the Retreat, it seemed for a moment that she wasn't going to leave their car. But of course she was right. "Yes," said Harry. "They are. And the mansion houses, as we say in Maryland, endure. Like ours."

Harry let that inequality settle in as he drove back up to the top of the street, took a right, and about a quarter mile down the county road pulled into a lane where the AME church had once been. There was now a tidy double-wide on the site. He left the others in the car and explained to a woman through the screen door of the house that he was there to visit what was left of the church burying ground. "I have some people with me from overseas"—he beckoned at his car —"who have ancestors buried here. Could we take a look?" Harry had never known quite what the arrangement might be for an orphaned burying ground like this; even if deconsecrated, if that was the right word, he assumed it was legally protected in some way, some sort of right-of-way to the graves, some sort of assurance that the site couldn't be dug up for a swimming pool. He felt the same must have been true for the graveyard on the Retreat during the years it was owned by strangers. The reaction he got seemed to confirm that.

"It's over there." The woman waved toward the long grasses. She wasn't being hostile, just a little defensive in the face of someone who might know that they had driven their mobile home onto the ashes of a Black church. "Getting a little overgrown," she said apologetically. "It was for colored," she added, as if, having glanced at the people in the car, she wasn't sure who could be a descendant. "My husband thinks he ought to go back there and weed whack, but it don't really seem our place," she said finally.

Harry said he understood that, he'd feel the same way. He pulled the car forward, and they got out. The airless site was surrounded by a dense copse of scraggly trees, raspberry bushes, and honeysuckle vines; it was silent except for the low murmur of country music coming from the trailer. There were about ten graves, with markers of some sort, most of them a pour of concrete with a name scratched in, though undoubtedly there were many, many others buried here—the most recent was from 1960, a low stone tablet, the name and dates, a World War I veteran. In the middle of all these, rising above in ways that were both impressive and forlorn, were three white marble stones with the names carved in.

Harry said nothing, stood back as Julien and Céleste and Pop wandered from grave to grave, kicking aside the overgrowing grass to read the inscriptions, information that could mean nothing to them. But it was as if they were paying respects to the lives commemorated by these more modest memorials before standing before the three that meant, or might mean, a great deal to them. Eventually they all ended up in front of the white stones: Abel and Una Terrell, who lost their youngest daughter, Beal, when she fled to France; and the brother, Randall, who had been murdered before she left. Their descendant, the great-great-grandson, this slightly stooped but stylish Frenchman—the blazer, the pocket square adding a dash of color, the expensive shoes—reached forward to brush the leaves off the tops of the stones.

Julien and his daughter said a few words in French to each other, and then Julien turned to Harry, saying, "We pass by their daughter's grave"—*daughter*, he called her, because if she was a great-grandmother in France, she was forever a child in this place—"almost every day." He didn't need to complete the thought; with this visit from three thousand miles away he was reuniting these people, carrying some sort of *all's well* from daughter to parents, some sort of greeting from sister to brother, and when Julien returned home, he would stop at Beal's grave and deliver their responses. The uniformity of the stones suggested to Julien that they had been erected at the same time, after the last of the three burials, the burial of the patriarch, Abel Terrell, and he was right; they had been ordered and paid for by Simon's father, Edward Mason, a surprisingly reverent gesture for a man so focused on himself. But in the end these marble monuments and the splashes of concrete seemed to have suffered the same fate, the same fate as the village that had once provided the congregation for this church and the souls for this burying ground. In France, Beal—like her husband, Thomas, of course—had been surrounded by people, living and dead, who loved her and admired her; her grave had never seemed lonely to Julien, she had been interred in the soil of her own world. But now, viewing these graves, he realized he had known only half the story, as if the narrative had been torn in two, and this new information told him just how far the girl had gone after she left this place.

"She never came back?" Céleste asked after a long silence, and when her father, lost in the moment, seemed unwilling or unable to answer, Simon at last broke in.

"No," he said. "Her mother"—Simon pointed to her grave— "died before the war, but Beal could have easily come back to see her father in the twenties. I have always wondered why."

"She couldn't bear it," said Julien, rejoining the conversation. "That's what she said in her journals. Her brother's death, their escape to France. It was an unhealed wound. She had to live as if it had all happened in a very different way. More ordinary, I suppose I mean."

"Yes," said Pop. "Sometimes that is the way to go forward. To pretend. To the grave." Céleste heard this and turned to Simon with the zeal of a dentist itching to go at his mouth with her instruments, to work down his throat to the weak seams of his soul, but she did not interrupt. "I met her, you know. Beal," said Pop. "I met them both, and your grandfather Randall too." Harry knew this story, that in the thirties his family had visited Thomas and Beal at St. Adelelmus, their winery in Languedoc. "I was six, I think. My brother, Sebastien, must have been thirteen. We were in an enormous car, and my mother kept telling me how beautiful your farm was. That's about all I remember."

"And about Beal?" asked Céleste. She had softened a little; the walk was doing her good.

"I had no idea who or what any of these people were. I do remember that she was quite dark. I think I was afraid of her."

"And then you came here and your brother drowned. That is the right story?"

"Yes," he said. "Two years later. My father went back to England, and I went to Chicago with my mother."

"I'm sorry. That must have been very hard for a child."

This slight expression of sympathy had the effect, as Harry knew it would, of putting an end to this moment of reflection and truth. Simon had spent his life avoiding sympathy, as if accepting it required him to accept some responsibility for what had happened. It had always seemed to Harry that his father could not distinguish between being a victim and a perpetrator. Pop had a storehouse of personae, stage figures that he fled into at times like this, and this time it was the old reliable carnival barker. "Well, young lady, stay over, and tomorrow we can go visit the grave of Sebastien Mason and his lovely mother, Edith." Julien could not imagine what could have brought this on and what it meant, and he looked at Simon—now standing with arms wide, drawing in the crowd—with considerable puzzlement, as if language were the problem.

"Pop," said Harry.

"It's in the lovely and historic churchyard—see here the portrait of a rector painted by Charles Willson Peale—where one can also find the remains of such revolutionary heroes as—"

He stopped when Céleste put her elegant hand on his sleeve. He looked down at it as if it had just slapped him, but when she gave his arm a squeeze, his whole body, coiled into the strands of this stage moment, relaxed.

"Why don't we go?" said Céleste. "Is it far?"

"No," said Harry, thinking that his father would never permit this. But Simon shrugged—*sure*—as if this would be of little interest. So after wandering around for a few more moments, they went back to the car, and just ten minutes later they were standing in a very different type of burying ground: stones of various tasteful sorts—conspicuous monuments were discouraged, it would seem—a healthy green lawn, trimmed privets and boxbushes; somebody had been out here weed whacking and a good deal more. There was an immaculate brick sanctuary and a fine rectory on a circular gravel drive. "Historic" said the plaque, mentioning the once-proud Lloyd family and other planter families, and Julien remarked that he had never seen the word "historic" used as often, and as proudly, as he had on road signs on this trip. Driving across the country, they had come to feel pistol-whipped with peculiar boasts about the past, about wagon trains, battlefields, ghost towns, buildings built with corncobs. "The word must mean something different in English," he said.

"Perhaps it means something more, or something less," answered Harry.

They were chatting while standing back and letting the unlikely pairing of Simon and Céleste wander down the gentle hillside toward the graves. Harry knew well where they were, had visited them over the years, read the names and the inscriptions. In this place of decorous Episcopalian rest, some literary license was allowed, some flowering in the attestations to piety, industriousness, community service. But over the years, in the occasional travel piece or tourist brochure about this "historic" churchyard, the inscriptions that often got mentioned were those on Sebastien's and Edith's graves: "Lost Son" on Sebastien's; "Lost Mother" on Edith's. What the guidebooks did not know was that despite the similarities, these inscriptions had two different meanings, two different speakers. The epitaph on Sebastien's was his father's: Lost Son because Sebastien had died tragically at age sixteen; Lost Son because whatever Edward Mason thought he was doing to raise a child, he had failed with this one; Lost Son because Sebastien had drowned in hopes that if he disappeared for a few days, his father would have to go back to England without him. And Lost Mother—Harry remembered hearing his father direct the monument company in Maryland to visit the churchyard and copy exactly the design of Sebastien's stone—was Simon's response. Lost Mother because she had failed Sebastien, the person who loved her the most. Lost Mother because on the day Sebastien died, a good part of Edith, the mother part, died with him. Lost Mother because even though Edith lived, Simon was mostly raised by his aunt Rosalie. And it might well have said "Lost Grandmother"; if Harry had a grandmother, it was Aunt Rosalie as well.

"I don't know how long it's been since Pop was here," he said to Julien. He was not reluctant to show that he was leery of this, but he knew, he had already seen, that letting his father do this with Céleste was the right way to do it. The story behind these twin graves and twin epitaphs could be Simon's to tell, or not to tell, without Harry standing by; the hurt and sorrow Simon had experienced in his life could be his to reveal, to seek comfort from, or not. Whichever way he wanted to go, Harry believed that Céleste could help him do it.

"Why wasn't the boy buried in the family graveyard, at"—Julien hesitated on the name as if he might get the usage wrong—"the Retreat?"

"For one thing, the whole place, the whole idea of the place, was falling apart. Who knew who would own what in the years to come? And another, I think, because Edith couldn't bear to think of him in the place he loved but would not live to enjoy. So much 'lostness,'" he added, "in this whole story."

"Is that why you bought it back?"

"It seemed a duty. I can't tell you why. It seemed to me I had no choice." Harry gave out a small, unconvincing laugh. "My wife thought it was crazy."

"It's a lovely place to live. It seems to have worked out for you."

"What I didn't realize was that the family sorrows and sins, or at least the responsibility to reckon with them, came along with it. Kate understood that, but I did not."

"I must tell you," said Julien, "that I am very grateful to you for showing all this to us. Without seeing this . . ." He trailed off, and Harry wanted to probe this dropped thought, but he held back, and Julien started up again. "You may apologize that so little of the village remains, but I am surprised how much endures."

"For better or worse," said Harry. "It's hard for us to know whether we make too much of it, or too little."

"*Pour le meilleur et pour le pire,*" Julien repeated. "But thank you."

They stood for a few more moments, enjoying the little breeze that came up from the creek at the far end of the cemetery. Pop and Céleste were working up the hillside toward them, and though Simon had taken her arm in the courtly manner to assist her in her heels, it was clear to Harry that her tight grip was steadying Simon, not the other way around.

7

Back when Eleanor conceived of her novel on Mary Foxley, she called her graduate school friend Monroe Monroe— a Virginian, it hardly needs to be said—who told her in no uncertain terms not to write it. "A novel about the South? Slaveholders? You'll get killed," he said. "Eaten alive. No matter what you say about anybody, someone will come looking for your"—here he paused with self-acknowledged chagrin—"hide. You may think you'll get a pass because you are a woman, but you won't. Believe me, I know what I am talking about. You can't believe the crap I hear from customers." Eleanor's call had caught him doing his early-evening shift at a bookstore in Washington, DC. "And I am not talking about writers of color. I'm talking about the people who are looking to atone for the sins of their forefathers. Writers of color are just trying to get the facts out; they speak for themselves. White writers, white readers are looking for absolution. That's all history is now, a way to get clean of the crimes of the past. That's why the novel I am working on is about a mother and daughter making a pilgrimage to Lake George with the grand-mother's ashes"—they both laughed ruefully—"or something else, I am not sure. Actually, I am writing a novel about a recent Excelsior University MFA called Madison Madison working as a clerk at a DC bookstore called Policy and Words while he tries to write a novel about . . . Wait. Hold on a minute, Eleanor . . . Yes, of course. Twenty-four ninety-nine. Would you like it in a bag? Here's the schedule for our readings in August . . . Eleanor, are you still there? Write an ethical novel about an ethical person who owned slaves? Are you fucking out of your mind? You think you could pull that off? You think calling it *fiction* protects you? No, it makes it worse, because no matter how much research you do, people will just read your facts as *attitude*. In case you haven't heard, that's what history is: attitude. That sound you hear is your body sizzling on top of the third rail of contemporary literature. You were born in California, for Chrissakes. You were born free. Me, the second I open my mouth, people see me with a whip in my hand, but you, you're invisible. Why do this? Jesus, Mason, what are you thinking?"

Monroe called her the next day to apologize. "I mean," he said, "with your family and all, why not? What have you got to lose? Don't ask me how or why, but I just found out that one of your ancestors was a groomsman at Robert E. Lee's wedding. Maybe writing about it will get you off the hook."

"'The third rail of contemporary literature,'" scare-quoted Vittorio with deep scorn after Eleanor told him about this con-versation. Vittorio had only barely tolerated Monroe in their group because Eleanor liked him, or at least she felt she owed him a certain mid-Atlantic loyalty while others were savaging the chapters of the novel he had naïvely and foolishly volun-teered for the first workshop of the year. The novel *was* pretty bad, thought Eleanor at the time, though not because it was in the second person. Or not *just* because. "What an asshole," Vittorio said.

"That's what he said about you," said Eleanor, or said the brassy, truth-telling, blunt Eleanor who existed only in this cohort and especially when it gave her cover to score a point against Vittorio. She could also speak this way to Rosalie when she had to, but that won her nothing in the world outside the family. "He said, 'I bet that asshole Vittorio told you to *go for the heat.*'"

"Such a coward. You know he's a coward. That's why he's working in a bookstore."

Eleanor might have said that people who worked in bookstores were already two pegs above unpublished writers in the literary pecking order—the peg in between was someone who worked in office supplies—but she did not say that, because Vittorio was not entirely wrong. Monroe, with his patrician manners and his fear of alienating his parents, had already eliminated about half of his personal material worth probing, and for the rest? Well, the reception he received arriving at Columbia too fresh from Sewanee—Phi Beta Kappa, *summa*—had spooked the rest out of him. He would never, ever write a piece of autofiction, as he had joked he might *Yes, Monroe,* she might have said, *Vittorio did advise me to go for the heat. Quote, unquote.*

Eleanor was sitting in her little study over the kitchen. She checked her messages for the umpteenth time since sending him that kiss-off, but the most recent text in the string still began with *You can fuck* . . . Was he in her apartment at this moment, packing up his things, or was he, as Eleanor had invited him to do, fucking the first man or woman his eyes fell upon in the street? Maybe fucking someone in her bed, so *two birds,* as one of her fellow MFAs liked to say.

But as mostly always, as too-damn-often always, he had landed a blow with his crack about cowardice, which was not really an attack on Monroe, but a challenge launched at her. *Show me you're tough enough to create art. Show me that people saying don't do it is all the justification you need for doing it; that's how you know it is worth doing. Are you in the academy or in the streets with the artists?* So, in the face of all that, she dove in.

In graduate school Eleanor had created her own niche as the class structuralist—under the influence of her adviser, who was, for a brief time, her lover at William & Mary—and in the hidey-holes of theory she had often found a safe place during workshop discussions; but here it seemed to have led her into a dead end. What was becoming clear was that the more she tried to make Mary Foxley an ethical person of her time, the more of an apologist she made herself in the present day. Or vice versa. She could join in the attack and indict Mary Foxley for her sins—*Dear Ethicist, I have just found out that I own a portrait of a slave owner. Is burning it enough or should I also burn down the house where it hung?*—but what would such a book get her, what insight would that offer when, presented this way, there was almost no choice for the reader to make, and fiction is about choices, for writer and reader. No? As Henry James would say, whom would it profit? And besides, she *liked* Mary Foxley, the person she imagined she must have been, liked her humility but also her boldness, a side Eleanor had endowed her with; after all, she grew up on the docks, or at least that was what Eleanor imagined. Eleanor could easily picture this Mary Foxley snickering a bit—hmm, *chortling* better here? *tittering?*—when she'd scored a win in business, and she must have scored a lot of them. That was one fact for which the evidence could not be denied: during the years after Mary's husband's death and when she was his executor, a period when the tobacco market was a bust and patents like her husband's were being abandoned or sold for pennies, the Retreat thrived.

With almost everyone out for Dad's tour or the boat ride, the house was quiet, except for Lotte rearranging her mother's kitchen cupboards and Hector's constant, chronic throat clearing. Eleanor glanced at the ten or so volumes in her traveling Chesapeake history collection with the feeling that a way out of this dilemma lay somewhere in the totality of those pages, but just as Monroe had predicted, they didn't help all that much; Monroe knew all about the particular burdens of fact. Maybe, if American history was her topic, she should write a novel about *Monroe*—her Monroe, not the other one—his conundrums after all being the same as hers. Hmmm, scribble, scribble. Pop had told her long ago that it was his mother, Edith, who had taken over this little space as a private writing room during the brutally cold winters they spent there in the thirties. Maybe it was just one winter; she couldn't remember, but the unquenched misery of that sojourn had come down to her from Pop and from her father, who described his grandmother, when he visited her in Chicago, as "catatonic with grief." This was *twenty-five* years after her son had drowned. What is it that keeps a wound so raw for so long, what phantom pain continues to reside in that spot after the skin has healed? Electroconvulsive shock therapy would probably have been advised back then if she had sought help, as it might be again today, but instead her insides were allowed to be feasted upon by the worms of her past. Why, Eleanor wondered, couldn't she have written a novel based on *Edith*—hmmm, her grandmother's ashes sprinkled on the waters of the Chester River in the spot where her son had drowned—but the answer came right along without a moment's delay: not as long as Pop was alive. For that matter, not as long as her father was alive. Not as long as Alice Howe was alive and almost anyone else coming to this party—and yes, there was perhaps now a thump of car doors and screen-door slammings and general social murmur; that point was now upon her. She should, at the very least, be helping her mother, but she was still mad at her, mad at her drinking and then staging that little hissy fit. On the other hand, Eleanor had to admit to herself that she was anxious about confronting these French descendants of American slaves, men and women who may have indeed been enslaved by her own forbears on the Retreat, though that was a little hard to pin down. What in God's name do you say to such people? *So sorry that my people—who were, of course, your people—enslaved your people, who were never my people?* And really, the reason she had been willing to forgo her seat in the boat was—God, what a fool's errand—to have time to glance at the chapter she had been working on about Mary Foxley and slaves, just to refresh her own recollection in case the whole question of her novel came up. At the moment, this first rough pass—yes, "rough pass" was what they said in workshop in order to pretend that they didn't care what people thought—was on her screen.

After about six months of attempts to plump up the novella she had written in a fury—the fury was what she had dreamed about upon embarking on a life as an artist; the doldrum that followed was never in the plan—the old familiar ache was back; the anxiety dreams returned. Beware the watchers at the gates; this, said her mentor/lover at William & Mary late one night, was what Friedrich Schiller had once advised a young artist in despair; beware of the voices in your head that stifle your creativity. No problem, thought brash, sexually emboldened Eleanor. Oh, everything about this had once seemed so easy! Well, a whole battalion of watchers had taken up their posts since then, but oddly, the one person Eleanor could think of who might be able to make some sense of this was one of the people who had put the sentries there to begin with, her old pal Monroe Monroe.

"Why didn't you show it to Letitia?" was the first thing he

said. It was a frigid mid-Atlantic day in January; they were sitting in the coffee shop in the moldy basement of the bookstore, her manuscript on the table between them. She'd sent it to him a month earlier. "She'd give you a good reading." Letitia Mower was a Black woman who was tangentially part of their group at Columbia, but she was a very sweet and kind person and ended up on her own island, her own neutral Switzerland, between their group and Miss Decorum's.

"I know," said Eleanor, "but I wouldn't want to hurt her feelings. You know, say something that put her in a bind. Besides. You were the one who told me not to do this."

"Well," said Monroe; enough of the sweet and kind, gloves off. "You stink in first person. That story of yours in our first year about the woman who fed the wild boars in her backyard? That was first person, right? In each line I see you trying to pretend to be someone else. It's so fakey. This sounds like a romance novel." Eleanor was stung, but this was the way they talked about each other's work, analogizing without apology; his infamous second-person manuscript had been described by ann smith as "Lorrie Moore after botched gender reassignment surgery."

"Listen," he said, reading aloud barely above a whisper, which made the whole exercise even more painful. "*Fulke Todd has been with me since the day I landed, and indeed that is also a miracle, because none of this would have happened without him. My husband favored no young man as much as Fulke, and he became overseer to all my enterprises; such was my husband's suggestion in his will, though he did not feel the need to appoint Fulke before the court. It would not have mattered if he had. Fulke was already acting in that role, and when I die, I plan to leave to him one of our farms, just as I will do with Richard and would have done to any son who survived me. When the price of leaf was unfavorable*"—Monroe gave "the price of leaf" an extra ironic flourish—"*it was Fulke who brought in the grain, and it was Fulke who helped me buy the failed farms around us and put them on the road to sufficiency. When I bought out the last of John Coursey's holdings beyond Reade's Creek, Fulke moved himself and his family to the house Coursey had begun to build, but he has remained the manager of all I put into place."*

"So?" said Eleanor.

"It's not just the voice. You're trying to hang too much material on her testimony. Too much fruit on the branch."

Yes, she thought: everything *plumping up* the novella, *hanging* on this prose, had come from her research. Talk about fruit! This was like watermelons on a cherry tree.

"But there's some interesting stuff," said Monroe. "Your point about the lack of labor." He ruffled through the manuscript and pointed to a spot and they both read along: *And so we struggled year after year, not against the climate and not against the Indians and not against the vagaries of the market, but against the lack of labor. Against the dwindling number of persons wanting to depart from England; the lesser sort of persons who might be willing to indenture themselves, could they be found; the departure of newly freed indentures to the west, to Pennsylvania and down the River Ohio; in brief, the shortage of labor. It began to seem that labor was the fatal flaw in this whole plan along the Tobacco Coast. That it had been created for commerce and no other reason, and commerce was dying. From John Smith's first flag in James City, bonded labor was the foundation of our survival, but for a time, we could believe this was a temporary matter; I think we all thought that our system of headrights—*"Headrights?" asked Monroe; "You got fifty acres for every indentured servant you brought in," answered Eleanor—*could create a sufficient English population. We were seventy years into this great enterprise before that was proven false. So many of our servants would die in their first few years here, and if they survived and married, either the husband or the wife would almost certainly die in the first few years of marriage, and their children stood a good chance of being orphaned and raised by persons who as stepparents would be two or three marriages removed from their parents at birth. Most of these children, even the children of the planters, would never reach their majority, would never live long enough to inherit the property that was, at the beginning, the reason for all this suffering. Such was the life here.*

I had learned over the years from Captain Nickerson—

"Oh yeh," said Monroe, pointing to the name on the page. "The love interest. The Yankee trader."

"He gets lost at sea. I know that will disappoint all my faithful readers who are waiting to have her undergarments ripped off her on the rivershore during a storm. I mean . . ." said Eleanor, still rankled.

"Anyway," said Monroe.

—that this was not the way of it in New England. The sons and daughters did not need to seek new lands to find a living and were happy to find employment in and around the villages of their birth. I had been so long gone from that life that I could barely imagine it, a village, a parish, a community where people—so Captain Nickerson claimed to my disbelieving ears—often lived well past sixty, even beyond seventy, years of age, and the generations lined up to continue the work their forefathers had begun. I cannot say I grieved over the loss of this life; it seemed, I might even say, to lack challenge. And, based on Captain Nickerson's initial astonishment about my role in our commerce, it could not be so in New England, as it was not in our home country, that a woman would be allowed to exercise her talents as I had done ever since my husband's death. The Tobacco Coast was founded in the minds of men but put into being by their widows.

"Hmmm," said Monroe; he had marked that last sentence with a check. "I like the power thing, the matriarchy thing. I like that line"—he ruffled back in the manuscript—"about the women dying young or dying old and the men dying in between."

Eleanor tried not to take this as a compliment, as a crumb of praise; that such patronizing morsels would never be tossed into the pen was the upside of their group's brutish customs. But still, she did think it was a pretty good line.

The café was filling up, people getting coffee before a reading, perhaps. Eleanor spotted the writer sitting with one of Monroe's colleagues, a pleasant-looking woman in her fifties, dressed in a seriously neutral outfit with a silk scarf. The scarf was Givenchy, but still she was looking nervously and imploringly around the room, and when customers were invited on the PA to gather upstairs for the event, no one but staff left the room with her. Eleanor thought of all those readings she had skipped at Columbia, until she was invited to dinner with a visiting writer who spoke of his upcoming reading as "another exercise in public humiliation." Oh God, she thought, this was a mistake, sending the manuscript to Monroe, meeting here in this temple of her dying dreams.

"Eleanor?"

"Oh yes. Sorry."

"And here too—" He was pointing at the final pages of the section, and he was still speaking in a tone of praise; the scene was where Mary Foxley finally assents to Fulke's pleadings and the first of her slaves is brought to her. "What you have done with this moment of contact, this willingness to put her there. It's the original sin, buying the first slave, the Big Bang. Yikes. No one can say you didn't try to take it on. This moment, well, Eleanor, I'm glad it's you trying to do it and not me. But notice what you did."

The two men, brothers, it was said, were brought by Fulke to the entrance hall of the house, where all business was done. This was the custom with new indentures, still groggy and pale from the long trip at sea, wordless but animated, peering about, taking stock of this new world that had opened its breast to them. Whatever had brought them this far, this was a beginning for them. She always told them that she too had landed in this place in circumstances that were not all that different, a young woman with her son William in her arms; she wanted them to feel the responsibilities but also the opportunities of labor and duty in this place built out of nothing but honest toil and steadfast determination. And on the day that their service was done, for those who had survived, the ceremony was reversed; they were welcomed into the community of free men and women.

But on this day there was no babe in arms in her mind; there was no promise, at the end of service, of a life among the free.

Fulke brought the two men, brothers, it was said, because such family ties purportedly kept them docile, amendable, more likely to accept servitude. They had been born in Cape Verde but had grown up in Saint-Domingue, it was said. That meant they would have acquired some knowledge of European laws, some French or Spanish. They had been accepted as barter by the Yankee trader who had replaced Nickerson; they were just what was needed at the Retreat, the trader said. He was still at the dock, waiting for his agreed-upon pounds of tobacco, or if the Retreat had currency on hand, approximately £60, either was fine.

"Madame?" said Fulke.

Mary had wondered, for years, what she might feel at this moment. She looked at one and then the other; they resembled each other like no brothers she had ever seen, one tall and stocky, the other a much slighter man. They were dressed like everyone else on this farm, the same rough hopsack, trousers tied at the waist. The captain had promised that they would come clothed, but that did not include hats or footwear. She looked at these two men and asked herself not if she should buy them—the purchase was already out of her hands—but what would it do to this place, what would it do to her? Because surely it would do something. To listen to Fulke, it would save the Retreat and all the other land she had acquired, save it for her only surviving son, Richard, now seventeen. But Mary knew that buying these two men would end for good the illusion—an article of deepest faith for her—that for the souls that had worked for her, the Haven was simply a brief pause, a rung or two on the ladder on the way to a fuller life.

What was the nature of this thing she was doing? Mary had never been a person who let unanswered questions rattle her brain; either/ or was not a solution. She looked at the two men standing just in the doorframe, with Fulke behind them. She said nothing, and they made no attempt to vocalize; the moment was soundless. She wondered, What was she buying? Not their souls, not their bodies, not even their labor; labor was easily paid for with food, housing. Why would you have to enslave a man in order to feed and clothe him? So what was she buying? Their futures, maybe. Was she buying the time that God had given to them? Yes, she supposed she was. Their freedom too, she supposed; somehow that Yankee trader had gotten hold of their free- dom and was in a position to sell it to her. It was as if he owned their shadows. She didn't want to own their freedom, had no use for it, and yes, Fulke still waited behind them, looking over their shoulders for the last assent, her last nod, but it was happening whether she wanted it or not. What was she buying? Was it, in the end, their silence? Did twenty thousand pounds of tobacco win her the privilege of never having to face what she had done? Was the whole world changing, and yet she would not have to hear a whimper?

She looked at the two men, who did not return a gaze, had not, even when their eyes met, given any sign that she was standing before them. She was no more human to them than they were to her. The taller one was perhaps twenty years old, his skin still quite flaw- less; the shorter one seemed the older, pocked and scarred. They had names; she had been told what they were but at this moment could not recall them. Names would be used in the years ahead, but not today. She had resisted this moment, she had combed her thoughts for a dif- ferent path. But nothing could survive the lack of labor.

"Madame," Fulke repeated.

She gave commands; the men were led off.

"See?" said Monroe.

"See what?"

"You switched to third person. You couldn't do it. You couldn't be that person."

Eleanor looked at her manuscript, and it was true, she had. No wonder, as she recalled, these lines had come more easily to her. "Okay," she said. "But what about the scene? What about her decision?"

"Oh," said Monroe. "Nice try, but you're still screwed. The soul that got sold that day was hers, and hers alone. No way out of it."

Kate had promised Eleanor that she would rejoin the party, but from her corner room she had heard the house emptying; from the land side the Tuckertown tour had assembled and departed, and from the water side she heard the thumps and splashes of a boat party trying to get under way. Miraculously, the outboard sputtered to life, and she heard happy voices shouting above the hum and then a frothy departure for the open river. In the rest of the house she heard the little mouse tracks of the few who were left. A few minutes laid themselves out to her, and she leaned back into her pillow, feeling a kind of warm buzz in her veins that reminded her of the all-too-pleasant blur of oxycodone after her surgery. It had all the advantages of death without the permanence, and with that in mind, Kate pictured herself laid out in this very bed, on her back, arms crossed over her abdomen. Comfort closed in on all sides; she spoke for it, this comfort, telling herself how kind were its intentions, not to resist, not to quarrel, and she fell asleep. As soon as she was out, she was closed into that Dada dreamworld reserved for deep sleep too late in the day, a fever of images, her father's scolding voice, being lost in a market square in Europe somewhere, a grotesquely leering man leaning against her in a crowded bus, herself sitting naked on a barstool.

She awoke, frantic that she had either died, in fact, or slept through the dinner, but no, still just twenty minutes to six; she'd slept just enough to empty her mind of this demonic cavalcade of anxieties. Once aware that neither of these events had occurred, she regretted not being released; but really, what was the problem here? Her husband, her children, her grandchild: she was blessed with them and it was *damn sure time* for her to acknowledge that, to "shape up" and "fall in line." These were expressions her father had used. Was he saying something like that in her dream? *Shape up*? Stop *lollygagging* or *skylarking*? The navy veteran. He would have been happier if he had stayed in the navy, would have done better with sons, would have known how to talk to them— a thoughtful, decent man, but in the end, the only time he was ever truly happy was alone, fishing, lost in a meadow, throwing a line into a creek.

She sat up, tried to blink away the crusts of sleep still clouding her vision. Now, with her ears free of the pillow, she heard voices, the sounds of a party, long planned, finally coming together. She went to the mirror, selected a nice fresh bandanna from the drawer, and bound her head snugly. She liked this feeling; if a moment became too confusing, something would keep her skull in one piece. Wrapping her head this way reminded her of what she had been taught to do with the three children when they were newborns: bind them tightly in the hospital blanket, which did seem to calm them. Freshened up, she came down the back stairs into the kitchen, relieved to find everything staged for the dinner and no one there. The truth was, she'd depended on

Lotte; even hiding in her bedroom, she knew Lotte would never allow dinner to be served buffet-style. So, no problem. She continued through the kitchen, glanced out the side door onto one end of the porch, and was satisfied as well that the drinks and glasses, the ice bucket, the wine, the seltzer, the iced tea and beer were all on the table, attractively arranged and ready to serve. Nothing to fret about there either, although instantly her resolve to drink nothing this evening began to waver; she did rather too much want a little sip of that delicious rosé, and why the hell not?

On her way into the hall she peeked into the dining room, and yes, a dining room this size, a table of these dimensions, lies waiting and hoping for events like this. "Tonight, grave sir, both my poor house, and I / Do equally desire your company." Hmmm, thought Kate, haven't read that old chestnut in years. "No simple word / That shall be uttered at our mirthful board, / Shall make us sad next morning or affright / The liberty that we'll enjoy tonight." Nice! Would that it be so here at the Retreat. From his perch above the mantel, Oswald seemed content. To top it off, Kate noticed that place cards had been set, a few of them with scribbles of crayon; she pictured Rosalie and Daniel doing this and decided not to peek in advance to see what Rosalie had devised. The concerns that had been weighing on her—as she had put it rather pungently, the garbage on her head—were lifting, and she felt a little light-headed, probably because she had overdone it with the bandanna. She kept going into the hall, hearing, from the porch, the best sound she could imagine from that vast space: voices, young and old. Yes, Ben Jonson had it right: "My poor house, and I do *equally* desire your company." If any "house" can be said to desire something, this house could: the trees that had been felled for its timbers had never died; the footsteps on its floors and stairs still reverberated; the thump, drone, and fizz of earlier days were still in the air. But Kate loved this sound from the porch, the way, growing up in Connecticut, she had loved the sound of football games on the TV on Sundays; she wasn't interested in the games, but the sound meant that men, or boys, were in the house. Her family was just her sister, her mother, and her father, who traveled for work a good deal, which meant that quite often men were *not* in the house and the distaff side coursed unchecked through the modest ranch; innocent words became barbs, inculpable objects became weapons. From time to time, mousy, gawky, miserable Lotte would come to stay while Mutti was "off" and spend all her time crying in the (one) full bathroom. In the company of nothing but women? Thank God they had Ethan.

She was just about to head out to the porch when the knocker crashed behind her, and when she opened the door, to her delight, there was Alice's girl. Such an unusual-looking person; any description of her would make her sound homely, but she was in fact a combination of strength and grace, of firm features—heavy nose, full lips, broad forehead—handsomely arranged. Kate had seen her around town, waved at her in the pickup Alice had given her, bumped into her at CVS, and each time she was aware that this girl looked like no one she had seen before. No photograph could capture all this, Kate thought, even while loyally wondering if Francis could manage it. "Milou!" she said. "What a pleasure to see you."

Milou seemed a bit taken aback by this fulsome greeting and didn't return the cordiality, but Kate could see that she had other things on her mind, mainly that she needed help conveying Alice up the five concrete steps to the landing. Alice was at the bottom, leaning on her walker; imagine still being able to stand on one's feet at age ninety-six, imagine still being alive at that age. By this time Harry and Ethan had come from the porch, and each took an arm and guided Alice safely up the stairs. She rested there for a second and then said gaily, "Margaret was detained!"

The girl made certain sounds indicating that she was just dropping Alice off and she would return when called, but Kate took one look at her and knew exactly what she was seeing: she was in jeans, pant legs that went on for miles, but she was wearing a stylish crepe shirt and had even, so Kate observed, made a pass at makeup. This was not a person who was going back to the farm to muck out a stall. "Oh, don't be silly," said Kate. From behind Milou, Alice cheered Kate on. "We were hoping you would come," Kate said. "Rosalie has set a place for you." And off Milou and Alice went, on Harry's arm, to the porch, to a round of greetings and introductions accompanied by a tremendous screeching of chair feet over the tile—okay, Harry hated the screen door slamming, but Kate hated this fingernail-on-blackboard squawking, and Harry was the worst offender. "Ah, the Arrival of the Queen of Sheba," exclaimed Simon; with surprisingly good pitch, he hummed a few bars of what Milou alone recognized as Handel. Alice responded with a warm*ish* "Simon, how nice to see you"; there was a multilingual meeting of the two European women, with Lotte trying to butt in in German— Kate was still in the hall and had not yet laid eyes upon the notorious Céleste—and a general round of gracious welcome to all from her three children. Good job, kids. Drinks were spoken of, with Harry and Julien—Kate's first peek of him; she knew he was a winemaker, but she had not expected him to look like Yves Saint Laurent—passing by the door on the way to the bar. And still Kate did not move from her spot in the hall, under the lamp, directly in the center between the highboy and the portrait of the colonel—who is he, again?—pointing to the battlefield where he'd died. She thought, Everything is perfection in this one spot, this certain kind of place and time, this *chronotope*, as Bakhtin called it (Berkeley, Doe Library, 1982, *The Dialogic Imagination*, just dumped by what-was-his-name); if I move so much as a toe, it will be broken, changed. Is this what it is like to be a ghost, to be frozen in a place for all eternity?

"So where is Mom?" she heard Ethan say. Ethan said this, but he, and maybe his father, were the two people in the gathering who knew exactly where she was, still in the hall, lurking, observing, eavesdropping, thinking, thinking, thinking.

"I'll go," said Harry, but he had seen her in her spot, and she had met his eyes with a nice smile, and beyond that, he wasn't going to intrude. Julien, of course, had brought wine for the evening, and he brushed past Harry with two glasses of something cool and refreshing. Someone, Ethan probably, had told Julien that Harry didn't drink. Julien sat down between Eleanor and Rosalie, who both swooned. Unfortunately—no one had planned this—but like a cat who unerringly jumps onto the lap of the person who loathes their kind, the loathsome Hector had wound up beside Paul, and Paul was nevertheless being a dutiful son-in-law and doing his best to engage him, until he was saved by Daniel, who had wandered off and needed to be retrieved. Down the lawn, between the trees, past the terraces, through the cattails and sea grasses, the creek was calm, still greenish in this western sun. The party was on.

Alice turned to Simon. They were sitting in the middle of the large circle of chairs, wicker and teak and iron; like the farm implements in some of the barns, the confused ensemble told the brief history of a hundred years of porch furniture. "And how are you, Simon?" she asked. "How are things at Osprey Neck?"

"All is well," he said. "There is a coffin next to mine that has just become available, if you're interested. Only used once. Very plush. Satin-lined."

"Kind of you, but I think I'll stay at Weatherly."

"Weatherly," he said, pointing through the screens and across the creek, as if picking out a landmark on a distant shore. "There was always Weatherly."

"As there was always the Retreat," answered Alice, although she was not quite sure what Simon was saying.

"I meant that when we were here, your parents and you and your house were some kind of ideal for us. You had electricity. We could see the white light through the trees. It looked warm and ordinary while we were living like moles in the darkness. Your mother was someone we could count on."

"Little did you know."

"Yes. It's how little we know that most surprises us. But I mean it about your mother. She was the only one of the four adults in that ménage who cared a bit for the children, for you and for us. She did her best."

Alice did not disagree. "Thank you for saying that."

In answer, he dropped his hand onto Alice's forearm; so rarely now did anyone touch her body out of affection. What was so baffling, to her, about Simon, was that he had an extraordinarily kind heart. In many ways and perhaps uniquely for Alice, the sweet, industrious little boy he had been was still there; he was a person who, for all his nonsense and bluster, could see in an instant where mercy was, where grace was, when a touch of human kindness, like a hand on a forearm, might be welcomed. That game where you ask which of your friends you might go to in times of trouble? Well, ridiculously enough, thought Alice, if it were just advice one needed, Simon was a man whose good intentions, whose good heart, you could count on; and as far as trouble went, he'd had plenty of experience.

"We visited the graves this afternoon," he said. He described the excursion to her, the drive through what was left of Tuckertown and the stop at the site of the Black church.

"I went to a funeral there in the sixties," she said absently. She tried to recall whose. "I haven't been back there in years. Every time I drive by, I think it odd that someone would put a house there."

"There's no rest to be had in an untended grave. You'd think otherwise, that the dead are better off not being meddled with. Let the dead bury their dead? But it didn't feel like that. One of the saddest things I've ever seen. It felt as if these people wanted to be remembered and weren't, and then there was Julien, seeking them out from thousands of miles and a hundred years away."

"Yes. How nice that you paid them a visit," she commented, still mostly absent from this conversation, still expecting Simon to veer off into absurdities, even to the point of calling her a sucker for taking him seriously—oh, thought Alice, those old words, like "sucker"; did children still use them?

"Good people buried in lost graves. They were calling to me. I made a fool of myself."

Yes, this was the sort of thing Alice was thinking about. The Shakespearian fool was a role she'd seen him play many times, but he did seem to be sincere, and she wanted to respond sympathetically. "You're always trying to lighten the load, Simon. The heavier the load, the more you try. That's what you were like as a child. You're afraid of darkness because you know how dark it can be."

"Thank you, honey."

"And?"

Simon knew what that "and" meant: *And what about the other graves?* In fact, when he said "graves" to her, she did not have Beal's family's neglected final resting place in mind; she was thinking of the lost son and lost mother. Her last memory of Edith in 1939 was as a perfect profile, annealed by her grief; when Alice saw the photographs of Jackie Kennedy under a veil at JFK's funeral, she thought of Edith. When Simon brought her casket back from Chicago to bury alongside Sebastien, Alice had been one of three in the funeral party; the other two were sixteen-year-old Harry and an elderly Black woman named Valerie Turner, who had cooked and cleaned for Edith during her stay at the Retreat in the thirties.

"Still there," he said, answering her question. "No one is going to be running pigs over their headstones."

"I know you don't like to go there, but I would think your thoughts might have changed over the years."

"No. I still beg Sebastien to forgive me. I still tell Edith she was unworthy of his sacrifice."

Anyone else in the world—even Harry—would have to ask Simon what he meant by that, but not Alice. She understood. These events from eighty years ago, and the roles they had each played in them, were as fresh in her mind as they were in his.

While Alice was reflecting on this, Simon went off in a new direction, one Alice much preferred. "Isn't your girl lovely," he said. "What a joy for you. You act like a guy with a new car: you can't keep your eyes off her."

Alice basked in the sentiment. She had half an ear out for Milou the whole time and was interested that Céleste and she were talking about music; Milou had a violin with her at Weatherly, and once in a very long while Alice would hear her playing it in the barn; the sound was so mournful, the behavior so furtive and secret, that Alice had never said a single word to her about it. But here this French girl had Milou chattering away; Berlioz was the name she recognized.

"Yes, look at her. I am so glad she came tonight. I hope she will come here many more times in the future."

"So I understand," said Simon slyly. "You're sure she will stay with you to the end? Not go back to Holland and marry?"

"Often I worry that I am stealing her youth, but yes. I am sure. It won't be that much longer. A few months?"

"Are you ill? At our age all it takes is a sniffle."

"No. Alas. No sniffles. But it can't be much longer, can it?" Alice looked around as if Margaret might have sneaked in. "Do you think that it is cruel? To Margaret? I'm going to help her out as much as I can."

"'For what can we bequeath, save our deposed bodies to the ground,'" Simon answered, deepening his tone into a proper stage utterance.

Alice did not know what exactly he was quoting, but he had said it more to himself than to her, and since being obscure always seemed one of the purposes of Simon's tics, she was surprised that he actually went on to explain it to her.

"Richard the Second," he said. "He's saying that wills and legacies are all bunk. He's saying when we die, the world goes along and does whatever the hell it wants to."

"Oh," said Alice. "I guess that's right."

"I played him in a production at the University of Chicago in 1951, and I have never forgotten a line. Probably because this was the happiest event of my life. Martyr or monster, King Richard has never failed me."

"Not Harry's birth?"

"Harry's birth?" From the corner of her eye, Alice saw Harry take a start at hearing his name. Yes, thought Alice, Harry has had one ear cocked toward his father ever since he was old enough to understand words. If they were both in a room, you were talking to the two of them, whether you liked it or not.

"Your happiest moment?"

"Oh, it always surprises me when people say the births of their children were their happiest moments. I don't believe it for a second. I found it terrifying, like going onstage and forgetting all your lines. I'm still terrified by being a parent, though now that Harry is almost seventy, I guess I've gotten over my initial panic."

"Oh, Simon. We both have so much to be thankful for." She nodded toward his two granddaughters, deep in conversation with Julien.

Harry was talking to Ethan and Heidi while monitoring his father's behavior and utterances, always ready to bust it up, but he, like Alice, was surprised where it was going. He hadn't thought his father made a fool of himself at the graves; it was just that, as so often, his reaction was hard to read. No harm done, certainly not with Céleste, who seemed to perk right up when she heard it; she had a fine eye for broken things, that was clear. Harry would have loved to know what she said to him, whispered really, but he could already hear Simon's response if he asked: *Oh, just some French nonsense.*

"Shouldn't we check on Mom?" Ethan asked Harry.

Yes, this time he probably should, and he was relieved, glancing back over his shoulder into the hall, that at least she wasn't still lurking by the highboy. Most likely she was in the kitchen making the last preparations with Lotte, who had torn herself away from Céleste and Milou. In fact, Harry would have very much liked to take the seat Lotte had just vacated, and he was both surprised and intrigued that Heidi, only slightly involved in the desultory father-son chatter, picked herself up and crossed the tiled floor to this prized spot. Rather a gutsy move, especially as Harry had noticed Paul eyeing the place for himself, but in its own way perhaps not a little hostile? Seeking out a nook the farthest from the family core? Of course he did feel bad for her having to navigate what would soon be diminishing light with those dark glasses.

Ethan watched her go. Didn't the fact that they were lovers

give them both some power to influence the other? he wondered. If so, it went only one way with them. Is love impossible? "I mean . . ." he continued after this pause, meaning, *Mom's not getting drunk, is she?*

"Don't worry," said Harry. "She's happy. Being happy these days is almost as difficult for her as being unhappy. But no, she's not getting drunk."

"I wasn't—" Ethan started to protest, but Harry was suddenly overcome with love for his gawky, sensitive boy, who, it seemed, had just been ditched; Ethan, born so much later than the girls, had been raised as an only child, as clued and tuned in to his parents' dramas as his parents were to his. Harry reached over, pulled him into his side, and gave him a kiss on the temple. This was going to be fine no matter what—the day, the dinner, their places, thought Harry in a threadbare image, at the table of life. Ethan squirmed a little, but Harry didn't let him go, and for a second that seemed to freeze in time he enjoyed the varying expressions that this public gesture elicited around the room: from Julien, a fatherly nod; from Hector, scorn; from Alice, an instantaneous and uncontrollable glance over at Milou; from Rosalie, irritation that he was willing to make this public show of affection for his son but practically *recoiled* from his grandson; and from Heidi—the person this was all meant for anyway— complete indifference.

Heidi's heart was pumping as she headed over to the chair between—between!—the two women, but once she saw this place open up, she almost helplessly lunged for it, even as she had already gotten the impression that Céleste was a rather chilly piece of work; it was Milou that Heidi really wanted to talk to. To her relief and joy, when she was halfway over, she saw Céleste turn to engage Eleanor, and Milou looked up at her with a welcoming half smile. But as these things can sometimes happen, while she was crossing this divide from the place beside Ethan to this new land, the realization came to Heidi that she was ready to move on from Ethan in every other way, that later tonight she would ask him to take her to the train station the next morning, before the "bridge traffic" about which she had been hearing since she arrived, and that by the time they returned to college in the fall, the memory of this strange weekend in the South and of their fuckship, as she tended to think of relationships that were now done, would have been reduced to a few unlucky snapshots. So when his father gave him a kiss, it was from that future perspective that she saw it, and the gesture seemed strangely tragic but, even so, not her concern.

"I'm Heidi," she said after she had settled into the decaying, unsteady wicker chair—perhaps the oldest item in the collection—that had been brought up from the far end of the porch. She rocked her body a bit to make sure the legs weren't going to collapse under her.

"I'm Milou," Milou answered, eyeing her cautiously, though she could see no eyes in return through the unusually opaque lenses, not mirrored, but worse, a black pit where the eyes should be. Milou could not imagine why she was wearing them at this gathering; something degenerative? Nearly blind?

"Everyone has been talking about you. Hoping you would come tonight."

Milou reddened. "That is kind. You and Ethan?" she asked, nodding toward him. Ethan was sitting alone; his father had left, and he didn't seem in any hurry to join another conversation.

"Well, yes," said Heidi. "We're in college together."

"How nice."

There was a pause, and that anodyne phrase threatened to set the tone. Heidi glanced at Milou and saw that nothing else was coming. She searched for something to say, thinking that maybe this great interest in Milou was all overhyped, that she had come to the U.S. as an au pair and now was working as a companion for an old person and as a keeper of horses, and none of those things made much of an impression on Heidi. It was true that she was wonderful-looking, those sharp, high cheekbones—Heidi's fingers itched for her pencil—but maybe that was all there was to it. She had overheard her and Céleste talking about classical music, which suggested something, but Heidi knew nothing about classical music. Still, she thought that might be a place to start.

"I don't know anything about music," she volunteered. "I grew up in Vermont."

At first Milou couldn't figure out what Heidi was talking about; in fact, she had been warned by Alice that Simon Mason was liable to blurt out almost anything at all and she shouldn't be thrown off. Perhaps that was the way all these people talked. But then she figured it out. "Oh, because we were talking about Aix?"

Heidi had no idea what X was and what this could have to do with music. She looked back blankly, all the more unreadable because of her dark glasses.

"The music festival," said Milou. "In Aix. In France."

"Oh," said Heidi. "Yes. That was it."

Again, a deathly pause; Heidi glanced across the room at Ethan, and he seemed to be enjoying the fact that she was getting nowhere, which she would have deserved even if she weren't planning on dumping him. Which Ethan had realized at the same time she did; all day he had been thinking about what was really happening with this weekend, even—maybe especially—when they were having sex in the barn.

"Do you like music?" Heidi asked.

How to respond to a question like that, which for all its magnitude is so hollow that it echoes?

"Classical music," Heidi added.

Milou was now completely nonplussed, especially since some of the attention of the group seemed to have switched to her now; she had no idea what this American college girl wanted of her, why she had let herself be persuaded to come into this house when her intention had been simply to drop Alice off, help her get settled, and then split for Annapolis. There seemed nothing left to do but give the full story. "I played violin all during my childhood. I was in a local youth orchestra at home. Bernard Haitink conducted us once and gave me a pat on the top of my head. If you know who that is. Then I went to the annual music festival at Aix-en-Provence"—she enunciated each syllable as if that would put the matter of this small French city behind them—"as a student in a master class, and from the first moment, I knew I was in over my head. All my practicing and dreams had come to nothing. The teacher was mean to me, and then I overheard two other students, a Russian girl and an Israeli boy, making fun of my playing. When I got back home, I cried in my bedroom for two weeks, and then my mother showed me an ad for an agency that placed au pairs in the U.S. I am the oldest of four children, and I never minded taking care of my sisters and brother. I miss them, but my brother—he's twelve—is coming over to spend August with me. Alice bought him his ticket," she added. At this point, Milou noticed that all the conversation on the porch had stilled, that except for the two men in the corner, they were all listening to her. She looked over at Alice and saw that she was in heaven, so she kept talking. "Going to America seemed as good a thing to do as cry in my bedroom. With my music I had never planned to go to college. So I applied and got accepted by a family in Maryland. I signed an agreement to stay with them for two years in return for my plane fare, but from the moment I walked into that house, I knew it was . . . I mean . . ." she said, but faltered a bit.

"It was not a good situation," said Alice.

"Yes, not a good situation. With the father."

Eleanor thought she might interject at this point that what Milou was describing fit a good many of the stories of indentures that she had read, masters who abused the servants bound to them, especially the girls, and she hoped that she was on firm*ish* ground in her novel in characterizing Mary Foxley as protective of the women. The wives of the planters *must* have been protective of the girls, right? Unless it was their own husbands abusing them. But of course, this would all be too much of a mouthful to throw into the conversation.

"I used to take the children to a playground," Milou said, "and I was sitting on a bench talking to my mother on the phone and telling her what was happening, and she was freaking out, which freaked me out even more. I was sort of defending the guy because, well, I thought I was at fault. And the guy hadn't taken advantage of me yet, really, but . . . And so there was an older woman sitting there—"

"'Older woman,' says Milou kindly," interjected Alice, "but really, she was just as ancient as I am. An old friend from Goucher. She was at the park with her home health caregiver. She died quite soon after this."

"At Osprey Neck," said Simon, "we all know when one of the staff asks you if you want to take a walk out to the end of the point, the answer is *no*. This is the Walk of No Return. They're taking you out to say goodbye to all that."

"Really?" asked Rosalie.

"No, dear," said Harry. "Shhh."

Milou continued. "And why would there be at that time, in that place, sitting beside me, a woman who spoke Dutch? What are the odds? Isn't that the expression you use? What are the odds? I mean, the reason we Dutch are so good at other languages is because no one knows our language, which is impossible anyway."

"Rather a coincidence," said Harry. A stupid remark—he was just trying to be encouraging—which she turned into something profound.

"When you look back at events that have changed your life, it all makes sense. It had to have happened this way for it to happen at all. Nothing is a coincidence. But when you're moving forward . . . well, who knew it would lead to this?"

Yes, reflected Eleanor. This is just what that asshole Braithwaite had said about plot, about reading with the "anticipation of retrospection." Which Braithwaite stole unattributed from Peter Brooks in *Reading for the Plot*. As if no one else had read it. And his cute little habit of drawing tiny icons—he called them "intaglios"—in the margins of student manuscripts: the small lump with smell lines rising above it, a shovel, a violin, a pair of angel wings; "Did you see my intaglio?" he would ask, eyebrows dancing.

And Rosalie also reflected on what Milou had said, wishing that she was now well beyond this current point in her life, with all seeming to have become uncertain overnight, with everything being held together merely by their wits; she wished she were looking back on it with wonder and surprise.

"Her father was Dutch," said Alice. "In the navy. He taught something or did something at the Academy."

"When I hung up with my mother," Milou said, "this person apologized in English for eavesdropping. She said it sounded awful what was happening, that my mother was right to be concerned. No, she said, that man should not enter your bedroom without knocking, no matter what he says about who owns the house. No, he shouldn't tell me he likes my nose." She reached up and ran her thumb and forefinger down the length of it—a fine, solid nose, thought Harry; all the sculpture of her face depended on that nose. "No, an older man in America does not tell a young woman she must model her new bathing suit for him. I was embarrassed."

"Why embarrassed?" asked Rosalie. "Were you being—well, indiscreet on the phone because you assumed no one would know what you were saying?"

"No. I was embarrassed because of what I had already let that man get away with. Because I had been defending him to my mother. And then this woman said she had a friend on the Eastern Shore—I didn't know the 'eastern shore' of what—who lived alone on a farm and needed some help, and what did I think? I met Alice, and she got a lawyer to get me out of my agreement. She saved my life."

"Oh," said Alice. "I wouldn't go that far."

"It seemed so to me at the time. Anyway, that's how I got from Aix to Weatherly," Milou concluded, turning back to Heidi as if this had all been between them alone.

"I once had great ambitions for myself in the arts," announced Simon. "An unkind remark—from my own father, yet—was all it took to make me abandon them. But I don't think I was wrong to abandon them. I still got great pleasure as an amateur."

Eleanor gulped. Her career like Pop's? Pleasure as an amateur: keeping a journal, general agreement that she wrote excellent letters and emails, a surprisingly compelling memoir in manuscript found by her grandchildren? What if this was in store for her? As they all joked at Columbia after a rough workshop, time to take the LSAT. It was sort of funny then, sitting above the fray at the hearth of the Chosen. On the Amtrak coming down to visit her family that first Thanksgiving, she felt as if the eyes of the other passengers were on her, that they *all knew* she was in the Columbia MFA program.

"And the horses?" Heidi asked. "You keep horses at Alice's place?"

"I grew up in the city, but my grandparents had a little farm they worked with horses. We spent our summers there."

"Hippies," said Heidi. "Hippies and draft horses. This is something I did learn about in Vermont."

Milou did give her a smile at that, but no, she said, not hippies, just old-fashioned.

"Well," said Harry. "We're all glad you're here. And with Alice."

In the kitchen, Kate had settled in beside Lotte as she caviled about the peas. Frozen. On the Fourth of July. "You always were so lazy," she said.

"So you have said," answered Kate without a shred of animus. *Have been saying for sixty years*, she didn't need to add. "I think we'll make all six packages," she said, pointing to the bags Lotte had taken out of the freezer.

"Five would be plenty."

"Okay. You're probably right." She cracked the oven to check on the chicken. Lotte, she thought. Harry may be tied to his family's past by tradition; Kate was tied to the past through Lotte, the one person in her life who had forgotten nothing. The vehemence of those memories could drag Kate back to the source at any time, but family forgives. That's all there is to say. What is one to do but to keep on, in this case, to keep on with the person who, in some respects, knows you the best in the world, better than your own sister, who never took all that much interest in you. Lotte had no choice but to study her two cousins, to become expert in their ways and their faults. She lived with Kate's family for months at a time, and Kate's mother tried to bring her in. At Christmas she made outfits for the three girls, and in photographs of these occasions Kate and her sister looked cute enough, but there was poor Lotte at age twelve, towering over them on her pasty white thighs. Kate was mean about Lotte, naughty to make fun of her in front of the kids, because hers had not been an easy life. For anyone who had a mother who was as much of a b . . . —the point is, Ethan, that you save words like "bitch" for people who really are that bad—bitch as Mutti, just surviving is a triumph. Kate remembered all those times when Mutti reappeared after one of her absences—either drying out or off to Europe with some man she hardly knew—and she would make a point of lavishing attention and gifts on Kate and her sister, Martha, but gave almost nothing to her own daughter. There was nothing to be gained for this woman in being kind to her daughter; even as a child Kate had understood that equation. Lotte had survived into adulthood by becoming as unpleasant as her mother, without the evil, sociopathic intent, which made a certain amount of sense when you thought about it. Lotte had refashioned her mother's behavior into something merely disagreeable, something that could pass as brisk and decisive, which was a way to salvage something of her childhood. But no wonder she and Hector never had children.

"That girl simply has no manners," Lotte said. "I don't understand why parents raise children without manners."

Kate knew she was talking about Heidi, and not about any of the other "girls" in the room. "She's very sure of herself. Ethan has got his hands full."

"And those sunglasses. I don't know why you don't tell her to take them off."

Kate had no interest in this topic. Heidi, yes; her glasses, no. What Heidi could have been making of all this, this day, was a mystery to Kate, but it was a pleasant mystery, a welcome obscure note interjected into these all-too-familiar activities, a bit of added intrigue. Yes, for all her little-girl cuteness, Heidi was way too much woman for Ethan at this age, when boys were still just trying to catch up. Kate hoped she would let him down easy.

"There you are," Harry said, entering with an unmissable rankled twang. "Why are you hiding here? Why haven't you come out to greet the guests?"

"Lotte and I are cooking. You know, *dinner for fifteen*? I thought you had everything under control." She meant that earlier, when she was standing in the hall and their eyes met, he was saying that he'd cover for her, that she could take her time.

"Well, Julien is eager to meet you." Behind him he heard the commotion of someone arriving; more guests to be entertained.

"I am not hiding," she said, but she didn't have any idea why she was acting in this peculiar manner; maybe it was because she had peeked at the table setting and found that Rosalie had seated Julien beside her; they would have plenty of time to talk, and she didn't want to run the risk of exhausting their inventory of topics before they sat down. Or maybe it was because at this point in her life—and what point was that?—meeting new people was much more trouble than it was worth. Without a future, the present is pointless, she thought. "Anyway, I think we're just about ready."

Okay, he thought, drop it. "The salmon looks magnificent," he said, a token of appeasement. "Your best." They always said things were the best yet, our best Christmas tree, our best Thanksgiving turkey, our best car; it was a joke between them that had lasted forty years.

"Saving my best for last."

Harry had been about to offer more notes of gratitude and admiration about the meal to come, but *the best for last*? He felt his mouth hanging open, waiting for the right words. What came to him? First, of all things, anger. Why say this now? He stood there dumb in front of the two women. How many years of this! he thought. He was tired of being the one whose job it was to fix things, to be the one of hope and cheer, to have faith, to *believe*. He'd been irritated about it all day, her resistance to this event, the energy he kept having to pump into it. But this anger, so misplaced, receded no sooner than it had been registered. He understood. He understood that these comments were her way of relieving the pressure, like miserable teenage girls cutting themselves. And yes, as Kate stood there beside the notorious Lotte, he could see the relief in her eyes, the relief of death foretold, and at that moment he finally accepted that the only way to go forward, now, was to admit that she was dying. Oh, he'd done the vigils, awakened at three in the morning with the nightmares, felt the convulsive horror of bad news, imagined and imagined and imagined cancer taking her away. But this was different. This was not about her illness, but about mortality, not just hers but his. The end of life, coming sooner than we want, but when is that? What is soon? We're all dying, of course, and it could take years; but as the scorecard seemed to mark it, at this time she was doing it faster than he was, and someday soon her hand would slip from his.

"Your best," he repeated. Lotte had gone back to her busy-work; Harry's and Kate's eyes remained riveted, and hers were saying, *See? See?* Somebody was coming in the door behind him. "I'm sorry," he said, and turned for the door onto the porch.

"Dad?" It was Ethan who had come in, but Harry was moving fast now, sprinting for the outside, and he did not delay. From the side door of the kitchen he took the side door of the porch, hurrying for the pecan tree, and when he reached the safety of the far side of that massive trunk, tears burst out of him as he sputtered and gulped in an effort to muffle the sounds. He rocked back and forth and then, when he had regained some control, put a hand to his forehead and rested it against the rough surface of this ancient being; the bark expressed a faint herbal scent, sage perhaps. The sounds of the party on the porch continued, oblivious, heedless, of the truths that Harry was just now staring into so deeply. And so he took his time, because time, every second of it, was the issue now. He turned and sat with his back against the tree like a barefoot boy in a straw hat; he pulled up a long shoot of grass and put it in his mouth, chewed on the tender white meat. Rowdy was delighted by this, coming up and resting his dumb Labrador head in Harry's lap, which helped. Harry figured that Kate could see him from the kitchen, but she would not follow. There were guests to greet; she would not interrupt, because she knew he must do this. It would be better now, between them—the last act would be, could be, the best one.

8

Throughout the cocktails on the porch, Rosalie had been darting out from time to time to check on Daniel—against all principles and better intentions, they had plugged him into Blippi in the study—and to adjust the seating chart. She had initially placed Daniel between Paul and herself, but Paul had been more than a good sport with Hector at cocktails, so she decided to reward him with Eleanor to his left and Heidi to his right; she was unaware of their earlier contretemps. That put Daniel between herself and Heidi, which Heidi would probably not like, but he wouldn't last very long anyway. She couldn't resist putting Pop and Alice on either side of her father at the end, creating a sort of grown-ups table, but why resist it, especially since Pop was doing pretty well on the porch; the three of them together were the kernel, the reason, the soul even, of this event. Rosalie liked the feeling of parochial gravitas at that end of the room, anchoring them all under Oswald's glowering visage over the mantelpiece.

Hector was the problem, as much as anything for the cigarette stench, but then—what luck!—she perceived the unmistakable perfume of tobacco smoke on Céleste, and thus her fate was sealed. She'd give her mother Julien and Ethan, even though in every respect *what Grammy should want* was her grandson at her side. *You just enjoy your supper, and I'll take care of him*, she should say. But no, none of that from Mom; Rosalie had never imagined that she'd made certain assumptions about her mother as a grandmother, but it turned out she had, and Mom had failed her every time and in every way. She had no idea, thought Rosalie, how much her daughter would appreciate a little help *just now*. On her last trip through the dining room she moved Milou next to Ethan, because everybody saw how Heidi had treated him at cocktails, and she was removing Margaret's place setting and chair—which would mean Lotte would end up beside her husband, but okay, they deserved it—when the door knocker boomed through the house, the screen door crashed, Daniel started to wail, both dogs barked furiously, and Margaret, disheveled but full of the triumph and majesty of the moment, came in shouting, "It's okay, all. Everything's fine. I made it!"

The roar from the crowd might have been somewhat less than poor Margaret wished for. For one thing, the only person in the hall when she entered was Rosalie, who was rushing into the study to comfort Daniel in his fright. It was Ethan who came forward, and he was only there because he knew something was up between his parents—he always knew something was up between them before either of them did—and was going to the kitchen to check it out.

"Oh. Hey, Margaret. Awesome," he said. Margaret was always in tweeds, winter and summer, grays and browns, a shabby, harried look; she smelled like a closet, ancient wool and moist shoes. The skirts were below the knee, which made her look even stumpier than she was. The only reason Ethan knew the word "tweed"—this was not a term that had much usage on the Eastern Shore or at college—was because he had once asked his mother why Margaret looked so dingy and she answered that it was because she always wore tweeds. "Why?" he asked.

"She thinks it makes her look grand. Old money. English, I guess. She thinks it makes her look like Queen Elizabeth."

"Does it?" he asked.

"Yes. Unfortunately."

Still, Ethan did not like being unkind, hadn't liked it earlier when everyone was trashing her; Margaret had always treated him okay, like a person. Ethan understood that Margaret was someone who did not have the luxury of looking down on anyone, even the smallest tot. Some people who don't have children feel that in order to acknowledge children, they have to instruct them, scold them for something. That was not Margaret's way.

"Ethan," Margaret said. "Where is everybody? I hope I'm not too late."

"No. We were waiting for you," he said, knowing this wasn't true but recognizing it could appear so and would make her feel good to hear it.

The pleasure duly registered on her face, but the dogs were still huffing and circling them stupidly. "Could you put the dogs out?" she asked. "They're so smelly."

He opened the door, gave Rowdy a solid kick in the butt, and then counted the seconds it would take for them to run around to the blasted-in screen door on the side of the porch. At this point, people began to migrate from the porch to the hall: Eleanor, thinking, I knew it wasn't that asshole; Milou, wondering if this meant she could split; and an elegant olive-skinned man whom Margaret deduced easily was the French cousin she had heard so much about.

"Excuse me, madame," he said to her. "I am a little lost," meaning, *I was just trying to find the WC.* But having come upon her, he introduced himself and said that he gathered Alice's cousin might come and thus, she must be this cousin.

Once again, upon hearing that she was spoken of, that apparently people were anticipating her arrival, she beamed. "Have you been having a nice visit?"

"Yes. Very nice. Harry took us for a tour of the place where my great-grandmother grew up."

"Beal, yes. Tuckertown. I expected he would, but it's almost gone."

"Yes, it seems so. But now I have a place to imagine her in."

"So much history!" exclaimed Margaret. Julien responded to this only with a courteous smile, so she pursued the point. "So much history all around us here."

"I must say I have sensed that. To my surprise, if I may say so. It's been a very interesting visit."

"Of course we only go back a few hundred years. Not like the French," she added admiringly. "*La gloire.*"

"Oh, all our kings, Louis XIV and all that, and revolutions and republics, all those rises and falls. In the provinces, those were all tempests in the distance. For the French, that kind of history is just a warning that nothing is permanent and that we should pay more attention to our own lives."

Margaret was left pondering the distinction Julien was making between this sort of history and that, permanence and impermanence. "We Americans think of everything in Europe as getting passed down from generation to generation."

"Not at all. *Pas du tout.* That's the English. The English bequeath and inherit; that's what matters to them. The French just pick up the pieces," he said, and because he laughed so fully and in such a friendly manner, she did too. By this time everyone on the porch was wandering into the hall and Julien was freed to "find his way."

Milou came to Margaret's side. "We were worried. How did you get here?"

"Billy drove me."

Billy McCready was the mechanic who had refused, or tried to refuse, to have anything to do with Margaret's Mercedes, but it seemed that this time, once again, on a holiday yet, he'd been ensnared.

Milou groaned. "Oh, Margaret," she said. "I would have come and picked you up and you know it."

And then Lotte came out of the kitchen and pulled plump Margaret aside a bit, saying, "Thank God you're here. At last someone we can talk to," and Margaret Howe had never in her life felt, and would never again feel, so welcome, so needed, so beloved—as if this party was for her and she was about to be shown to the head of the table. Ethan was free to continue toward the kitchen just as his father went out the side door. He found his mother pretending there were yet more details to take care of, and he all but dragged her into the hall. "This is Mom," he said to Céleste, as if, thought Kate, he were introducing a reluctant first grader to a new teacher, and he went off to find his father. He found him on the lawn, no longer hiding behind the tree, thank goodness, but Ethan knew he was upset.

"What's up," he said.

Tears filled his father's eyes.

"Something with Mom?"

"Oh, Ethan. Until the day you die, remember what you did for us, for your parents, being with us, being for us."

Ethan was not taken aback; he never for a moment was unaware of his duties. "I know," he said.

"I think we're going to lose her earlier than we thought."

"What happened? In the kitchen?"

"No. Nothing bad. No revelations. Nothing that should worry us today."

"Really?"

"Just . . . we have to be ready."

Ethan shrugged. His father, like his grandfather, had an operatic side. Ethan had heard more than a few arias over the years, and he always took them as sincere, if overdramatized. But what could that mean, be ready for Mom's death? The prospect had loomed up in their lives, and if Ethan had ever believed that anything he did or said could diminish it, those hopes had died after the first round of chemo. "Yeh," he said.

"You go back," said his father. "I'll just take a moment more. Thank you." He put his hand on Ethan's shoulder. "I'm sorry I kissed you in front of everybody."

"At least it wasn't sloppy."

Okay, okay, thought Kate, watching Ethan approach Harry on the lawn, time to grow up. She greeted Julien and Céleste, at last, in pretty good French, she thought, and they responded in French, and this being done meant that for the rest of the evening everyone, even Lotte, could speak in English without demur. The notorious Céleste struck her as not so bad, not so witheringly stylish as all that, an attractive brown-haired young person, even if slow to smile. They met, in fact, conjoined as two women who were not entirely into this event but were there to support the men in their lives.

"Then let's sit down," Kate announced, and at that moment, Lotte, darting invisibly around like subterranean Disneyland staff, threw aside the pocket doors to reveal the full magnificence of the once-proud, once-influential, once-esteemed Mason table. Oh, so worth it, thought Rosalie as Daniel squirmed in her arms. The candles and sconces were lit, but lambent late-afternoon sun was drifting through the French doors; the room itself seemed to have captured a magical hour. Oswald had rarely seemed more satisfied with the arrangements. Jeez, thought Heidi, this is some shit; maybe she was being too hasty about Ethan. The salmon looked quite magnificent—thank you, fish, thought Kate—and the peas, roasted veg, and sautéed leeks . . . even the chicken Divan in front of Harry's place looked elegant, which is hard for such a homey dish to do. Kate invited everyone to find their places, and standing at the end, she watched the guests come to roost, and she could only be impressed and grateful for the job Rosalie had done. "Oh, how nice," said Lotte, louder than she intended, discovering Margaret between herself and Hector. "At least they didn't put us at a card table in the hall," said Simon to Alice. Harry, at last coming in from the porch, took his place at the head of the table and tried to signal cheer to Kate; *I know*, she signaled back.

"Sit. Everybody," he said.

"Aren't you going to make your speech about all of us being here together again?" asked Rosalie, disappointed with this breach of tradition. "About the privilege of being a family in this unique place? Your joke about the clown car and the circus?"

"Well, thank you, Rose. I couldn't have done it better myself." He said this through an almost closed mouth, and Ethan did a double take, thinking, *This frail old man at the end of the table. Is this really my father?*

"Could I say something," asked Margaret, boldly rising to her feet. "If Harry isn't going to speak and we don't have grace?"

"Of course," said Harry.

"I would like to say that we all gratefully acknowledge the native peoples on whose ancestral grounds we gather, as well as the diverse and vibrant Native American communities who make their home here today. Thank you." She sat down and was mostly pleased that Hector leaned over to congratulate her, but he whispered, "Let's see what they do with that," which had not been Margaret's purpose. The rest of the table was silent; Céleste and Julien, as they had earlier in the graveyard, exchanged mystified glances: *Et puis quoi encore?* Harry put his hand on his father's arm to restrain him from making a crack.

"Thank you, Margaret," said Harry.

"Well—" said Kate.

"I know there are no Indians to speak of here today," said Margaret. "But if there were, it would be nice."

Eleanor tried not to sound confrontational. "Do you know why there are no Indians here today? Do you know what happened to the people who lived on this land when the English landed?"

"They left. Didn't they?"

Eleanor felt an obscure rage rising, compressing, in her chest; what Margaret had done was an innocent gesture, Eleanor thought, on a topic in which there was no innocence to be found. "Do you even know what they were called?" she asked. "As long as we're acknowledging them?"

Margaret froze under the blinding glare of these questions. She appealed to the rest of the table.

"Nellie," said Rosalie.

"Yes. I know," said Eleanor to Rosalie.

"As I think everyone knows, Eleanor is our expert on colonial history," said Harry, turning to Eleanor. "I'm sure Margaret isn't the only person here who doesn't know the answer to your questions."

"The Wicomiss," said Eleanor. "Wi-*co*-miss," she repeated, pedantically emphasizing the accent on the middle syllable. "John Smith called them the Ozinies, but no one else did." Even just saying this much, taking this small amount of refuge in the embrace of her research, being the one who had seen the truth, calmed her a little. She continued in a slightly less haughty tone because, of course, she had nothing to be haughty about. "They were a small community that was being squeezed out by the Iroquoian-speaking Susquehannocks in the north and the Nanticokes and Choptanks and the other Algonquian tribes in the south. They never engaged in a treaty with the English; they just tried to play the middle. They were pretty much gone as a unit by the time the Masons got here, but in 1668 a Wicomiss was accused of murdering a planter, and the English and the Choptanks hunted down those who remained. Those who resisted were killed like dogs, and the survivors were sold into slavery in Barbados." All this landed with an enormous dispiriting thud. "I don't know whether Richard the Emigrant had anything to do with it. Probably he did. He might have led the charge. He was sheriff of the county by then."

"Could we go back and just say grace instead?" asked Ethan. "You know, 'For these gifts which we are about—'"

Eleanor ignored Ethan's joke. "I'm sorry, Margaret," she said. "I don't mean to attack you. I think what you did shows a good heart."

Margaret looked unconvinced.

"It's just that it doesn't get us anywhere. Just saying it. It doesn't get us off the hook."

"I don't think Margaret thinks it does," said Lotte. "That was neither her hope nor her intention. Was it, Margaret dear?"

"At the Historical Society we always begin our meetings like that."

"Well," said Eleanor, trying hard not to lecture or scold, "the history here needs to be reckoned with. We can't do that if we don't know what happened."

"But this story about the tribe," said Rosalie, not remembering the name Eleanor had just offered. "Those details aren't in your book. At least not in the pages I read."

"Not yet, actually," said Eleanor, trying to sound as if there were a deep thematic or structural strategy in play. In fact, she didn't know what to do with this story, so damning to the Masons so early in the book. In this draft she had portrayed Mary Foxley as only learning about it, without details, years later, but what difference would that make? "But they will be. Obviously."

"Obviously," said Hector, sourer by the minute. "Wouldn't want to miss something as juicy as *that*."

Harry knew he'd better dive in fast, but he was waiting for Kate to comment; just two hours earlier she'd said that these acknowledgments were like waterboarding the Indians. He waited for her but then realized that this was a fray that was beyond both of them, a new way of grappling with the past, to be sure, not something to mock even if it lacked marrow. "I think the point of all this, as Eleanor says, is to reckon with it," he said finally. "Thank you, Margaret. We're all the better for the discussion you've inspired. El has learned some pretty arcane stuff."

Kate took up her serving fork. "Now, everybody. The food is getting cold. Send up your plates."

Eleanor had been feeling okay with most of this—so few people knew the story of the Wicomiss—but now she was beginning to feel ganged up on and, worse, that her father was patronizing her. Our expert in colonial history. Thank you, Eleanor. Arcane stuff! Tell that to the oncologist, thought Eleanor. Growing up, she was always being patronized because Rosalie had been the much better student; we're helpless when we hear the sounds and whistles from the cradle. So she was back to feeling that Margaret's little piece of politesse was insipid and self-serving—I mean "ancestral grounds"! what Disney writer came up with that?—and she couldn't help thinking of all her fellow liberals all over America intoning this kind of crap. The next thing Eleanor knew, she was saying something so much bigger, so much more present, really, present not just in the land but in the very structures that sat on it. She was saying the thing that did not get invoked at the beginning of the County Historical Society meetings, because it was simply too hot to handle. "Why stop with the native peoples? Shouldn't we acknowledge that we are on land and in a house sustained and maintained, created, in fact, by enslaved labor? Should we thank their descendants for their service, or give them the keys?"

"Oh dear," said Alice.

"You mean reparations?" said Hector. Clearly this man hated all the Masons, hated their guts, wanted them and their highboy and portraits put out into the street. Talk about being patronized; Hector had watched his wife being demeaned, belittled, barely tolerated, scorned by these people *all her life*, and still she came back for it every time. Well, time to get even, beat them with *their own stick*. "It would not be difficult, I would suppose, for you to locate descendants of the people this family 'enslaved.'" He evoked the scare quotes with a clownish smirk.

Whoa, thought Ethan. This party is DOA. He was just glad J. hadn't shown up, because from the day they became friends, from the day they'd been identified as talentless and relegated together to the percussion section of the school band, the unspoken question Ethan could never entirely evade was whether his ancestors had "owned" J.'s. Then Heidi piped up. "Well, why not? Why not give away a few acres? What difference would that make to the farm?"

Daniel had already begun to squirm, but there was no way Rosalie was going to leave the table now. She had been fine with this irritating girl when they were on the same side, but this comment was simply too naïve to be left unchallenged. "For one thing, as you wouldn't know, the whole estate is under a conservation easement. It can't be subdivided."

"Gosh, Rosalie," said Ethan. "Does that really answer the question?"

"Well, Ethan. Which acres would you have in mind? If we could."

"This is isn't about land. I was using the land as a met-a-phor." Heidi said the word slowly, sounding out each syllable, as Milou had done with "Aix-en-Provence"; as Eleanor had done with "Wicomiss." The girl missed nothing and was ever ready to shovel it back. "You know, forty acres and a mule? I'm just asking, why not do something?"

"Let's unpack this a little more," said Paul, intervening with the questioning, Socratic tone he used in seminars to bring down the temperature, to separate students who were going at it. Rosalie had always loathed the fake diffidence of his professorial voice, and here it was being used on her. To defend this little twit-in-dark-glasses who had—who's patronizing who here?— just treated her like the stupid kid in the class!

"And I am only asking for realism," Rosalie snapped.

Which irritated Paul, who felt that if a calm, relatively neutral take on the family history was needed, he was the one who could provide it; when the subject was the Masons, he was the only true realist in the room. "Isn't the question beyond realism, Ros?" he said.

"And what realm is that?"

"The practical. For example, I would think the least that might be done is to make this family's papers available to anyone trying to research their own family's past. African Americans especially, but indentures also. No, Eleanor?"

Rosalie got in one last riposte—that all the papers *were already available* in the Maryland Historical Society—but by then

the numbered looks around the table had registered on the com-
batants. Kate's serving fork was still hopefully poised above the
salmon; Julien, Céleste, and Milou were trading tentative expressions of solidarity; poor Margaret was terrified that this argument would sooner or later be traced back to her; and Hector
was reclining in his chair with everything but his hands clasped
triumphantly behind his neck. It all came back on Harry, and
for the moment, the only thing he could think to say was that
it was the responsibility of the new owners of this farm to write
a better chapter. To make this very evening the best, most just
and fair, evening of its three-hundred-and-fifty-year history. He
meant, less obscurely, to stand up for justice today because they
couldn't do a whole lot about what happened yesterday. And
when it came to the disposition of the keys, he might try to as-
sert that if he now owned a place built by slave labor, he owned
it not because he had inherited it, but because he had written
a check to the man his father had sold it to; maybe the money
had gone to the wrong person, but that wasn't Harry's fault, was
it? Anyway, in terms of family crimes, he wasn't sure whether
that lacuna in the legacy amounted to anything. And indeed, his
remark earned nothing from anyone, except from Hector mum-
bling about getting all PC about slavery.

Said Harry, "Hector, one thing I am glad of is that my political leanings do not require me to argue that slavery has gotten
a bum rap."

"I am wondering what our French *cousins* feel about this,"
asked Hector, weaponizing the word; when he was growing up,
his cousins picked on him, and Lotte's experience with Kate's
family only fanned his resentment. "As I understand it, by blood,
they're from both sides."

From opposite corners of the table Julien and Céleste took
each other's measure. Do we really have to wade into this swamp?

Après toi, ma chérie. Kate was pleased to see that for a moment Céleste seemed at a loss, and she kept her gaze upon her. Finally, Céleste said, "I have never imagined that I had anything to do with American history except for the fact that some of my ancestors fled from it. My blood is French."

Julien did not mind Hector's question; actually, he was amused by Hector, his churlishness was refreshing. And he didn't entirely disagree that slavery was getting too much attention. That men and women had been enslaved on this very farm was grotesque to him, but he wasn't sure that it made much difference that some of them *on both sides* were his ancestors. What good would it do, he thought, to see them, to see himself, through that lens? They had lived and died; that was what mattered to Julien. Let these Americans figure out the weights and measures of the topic; based on the conversation at the table thus far, *bonne chance* with that. But he welcomed the immanence of the past here; Margaret had not been wrong to effuse over it. This whole detour to the source of the quarter of his blood represented by Thomas and Beal—or, more important, to Julien, the eighth of his blood represented by Beal herself—was driven by a powerful yearning he did not entirely understand: wanting to see, wanting to touch. But he was not going to say any of that.

"It will probably not surprise you to hear me say that this evening is the first time in my life that I have been asked to reflect on the fact that some of my forebears were American slaves," he told the table. "This has been quite a day for Céleste and myself. There's much for us to consider."

Alice might never have directed a seminar, but she had been to a dinner or two, and she knew a thing about raised voices and awkward pauses and when it was time to move on. "Kate, the salmon looks perfect," she said.

"I think the one crime none of us wants to commit today," said Harry, "is to let Kate's wonderful dinner get cold. Except the salmon, of course, which is supposed to be cold and is otherwise blameless. On that can we all agree?" There was, at last, a general relaxation of breath and a murmur about the food. The serving had begun, plates were being passed, the communion rail was as Rosalie had envisioned it. The salmon was now in the final stage of its four-thousand-mile journey from the Alaskan seas to the plates at the Retreat. Most of the table was also in for a scoop of chicken. "Mom's *famous* chicken Divan," announced Ethan. He was right there with Alice and Dad: keep the discussion on the food for as long as possible; he knew well enough that food, like everything else in this modern age, had become an issue on which one had to take sides, but he figured that the present table, with its protein options and vegan roasted root veg, was probably okay.

"Believe me, dear," Kate said. "There is nothing famous about chicken Divan. When I was growing up in Connecticut, the secret ingredient was a can of Campbell's cream of mushroom soup. If my mother wanted to be really decadent, she'd use two cans. Topped with crushed potato chips."

Everyone at last had a chance to ask for the salt and the *sauce verte*, take a scoop of veg as the platter was passed from hand to hand. Rosalie was finally willing to take Daniel back to the study; he'd been fussing and fidgeting this whole time, but his small voice had not been heard. They all dove into the feast like Romans. "Boy, this corn is special," said Paul, perhaps to himself, and most people at the table looked confused, as if they had missed a dish, but Heidi, sitting right next to him, perked up with the eager smile of the student who has the answer. "*Deliverance*," she said. "Ned Beatty at the rooming house at the end of the movie." She'd just taken a course called Hollywood and the American Culture, and on this happy note, it seemed that the table now might be allowed to break into smaller conversations about trivial matters. And eat their dinners in peace.

Harry was feeling better; the conversation had wrung every bit of self-pity out of him, and he thought he might offer the traditional welcome that he had ducked earlier, raise a glass, and propose a toast. But to what, exactly? At her end of the table, Kate was thinking that maybe they would survive this, as a family, intact. That the family would live on, muddle through in its own basically well-meaning way. She glanced down at Harry, and he returned a happier squint; he was being brave now, and it broke her heart. Why did it seem so hard for them to be brave at the same time, to be afraid at the same time, to love at the same time? For the past three and a half years they had been jolted from side to side, smacked and whiplashed; they had survived it despite all possible misalliances of spirit and mood. Cancer was tiresome for everybody, the most tiresome of diseases. That comment about the best for last; it was unfair to him, trying so hard to pull the evening off, but he had gone too far with that Paris thing, and she didn't want to be left there floating on that hopeless dream like a heroine about to be swept over the waterfall. She knew that her control of her moods was infantile now; the higher the high, like that moment standing in the hall, the lower the low. But it all balanced out. Couldn't Harry see that? Couldn't he do the math and recognize that, in sum, she was the slightly volatile but ultimately practical woman she had always been?

"May I pour you some wine?" asked Julien. "This is from South Dakota. We thought it interesting." In the course of cocktails, Julien had been producing a bottle of this and a bottle of that, and the pinot grigios and Provençalish rosés and nondescript reds she'd bought at the local drive-through Liquor Mart had been quietly replaced. If Harry still drank, he would have taken care, pleasure even, in selecting wines; as it was, all Kate ever wanted was *the usual.*

"Thank you," said Kate. She glanced guiltily at Eleanor, and then added, "I missed cocktails so I could have wine at dinner." This had the double virtue of explaining her absence and getting Eleanor off her back, but it wasn't entirely honest; the little half-full juice glass in the kitchen with Lotte—she called such nips cooking wine—simply didn't count. Even if there had in fact been two of them.

"Yes," Julien answered. "Our wines today have too much alcohol. Too hot, too much sugar in the grapes. This is a problem that we need this young man"—he indicated Paul, who was now deep in conversation with Heidi, and when eyes turned toward them, they both looked as if they had been discovered in bed—"to solve."

Paul had not caught the intro, didn't realize the issue was the effect of rising global temperatures on the wine industry, but the word "solve" was enough to inform him he was on. Every time someone learned what he taught, the next word was "solve," or "solution," or "get us out of this." This was especially true of the once and future deniers and the entire coastal real estate profession (not counting his wife), who blamed him for being right. These days he'd begun to think of his academic discipline as a chronicle of death, an organism studying itself as its systems failed one by one, which was the main reason he'd become so bored with it. But after all the history lessons, Paul believed, this party couldn't take another downer. Besides, he was having fun talking about movies with this girl, who seemed much more eager to be ingratiating now than she had earlier in the day. Favorite dinner scenes, beginning with Ned Beatty and his corn: *The*

Dead . . . American Beauty . . . Alien! All this party needed was to have a monster explode out of someone's chest. To Julien's comment he responded only that if he could solve it, he would.

Kate took a sip of wine, and those few drops crashed like surf on the back of her skull. A slight panic—oh God, as much as I vowed not to do it, am I drunk?—but then she swallowed, took another quick assay, and concluded that all was not lost; she believed she was acting coherently. Still, she was staring into the social abyss otherwise known as having absolutely nothing on her mind to say to her dinner partner. Her mother once told her that a woman must always have two topics stored at all times, along with a syntax to present them: a question, an assertion, a speculation. That was, to some degree, Kate in the old days, pre-illness, but these days she couldn't keep that much straight in her mind, even dead sober. Topics scattered like hares when she went for them. Also: Harry *knows* I don't like dinner parties, she thought. Julien saved her, for the moment.

"But why salmon and peas?" he asked. "I gather it is an American tradition for the Fourth of July?"

"A New England tradition," corrected Kate. "In the South the tradition is hot dogs and deep-fried Snickers bars."

"Mom," said Ethan, "could you just . . ."

"Sorry," she said to Julien. "It was because the salmon were migrating up the coast at about the time the peas were ripening. Late June. Early July. By the end of the runs, I'm sure people were sick to death of salmon, and of peas. But somewhere along the way somebody called it traditional for the Fourth of July. Probably as much truth to that as the myth of the first Thanksgiving."

"But not this fish," said Paul, despite his earlier resolution not to introduce any more discord. "This is not Atlantic salmon. This is Alaskan." He was thinking that he had been nasty about the salmon upon arrival this morning, had been dismissive of Julien a moment earlier, and was trying trying to reassert himself as a helpful source of information, the professor willing to linger on an ancillary point for a moment or two. "There's no real wild Atlantic salmon fishery anymore, and farmed Atlantic salmon have escaped from cages and entered the habitat of wild populations, which has genetically altered the native populations and decreased their viability and character. This was a long time coming. By 1850, the fish Kate is talking about, *Salmo salar*, was all but extinct, at least completely gone from American waters. Most of their habitats and breeding streams had been blocked. Basically, they'd been wiped out. Like the passenger pigeons."

Once again the conversation came to a shuddering halt, and once again it was Hector who unsheathed his dagger. "So we have to feel guilty even about the *salmon*?" he said in a voice high with scorn and disbelief. "What about the chickens that lost their lives in this?" he said, pointing at the casserole in front of Harry.

"It's a lucky thing Kate didn't serve pigeon," said Simon.

"I don't think 'guilty' is the right word," said Paul, the realist. "I don't think anyone at this table is guilty of anything. Historically speaking, of course."

"Seems like an easy way out," said Heidi. "Like it just allows the system to keep going."

"The culture is guilty," said Paul. "Yes."

"Oh, right," said Hector. "We hold these truths to be self-evident, that all men are created guilty. *Men*," he added for emphasis, providing an extra seasoning of grievance.

"Saint Paul would strongly agree," said Harry. In certain fissures and cracks in Harry's well-ordered brain there remained the detritus of the few years that his father had insisted he acquaint himself with his Catholic heritage. That was before Simon became concerned that Harry might be gay and tried to interest him in NASCAR.

This, the day, the dinner, the conversation, all were getting out of hand—Saint Paul! Next up, Immanuel Kant?—but Eleanor kept at it because the answer mattered to her; she clung to it now with the urgency of one who has lost all faith. "Then what?" said Eleanor to Paul. "I would really like to know."

"What *what?*"

"What word, what single word, encompasses this family's experience with its past? A word that acknowledges, that does not deny, but at the same time does not condemn. People are already filling in that blank. I mean, our family name is being chiseled off high school facades as we speak." No one volunteered such a third path through the horns of the dilemma, so Eleanor continued. "All I want to do is to boil it down to a single word or two that does it all. Like one of Mom's poets."

"I thought you were trying to make the truth more understandable, not less," said Simon.

"No. One word can do it, and the word is not 'guilty.' That isn't what I thought I was doing with my stupid book, but it turns out it is."

Harry was jumping in to tell his daughter that she shouldn't refer to her project as stupid—good old Harry, thought Kate, the kids will be in good hands when I'm gone—but there was indeed a word on Kate's mind, a word she had often thought described this family's experience with the past, and she let it fly.

"Haunted," said Kate.

"Say what?" interjected Hector. "Clanking chains and the smell of rotting flesh?" He thought he still had the Masons on the run, but he didn't realize that things now were moving on without him, that his barbs were no longer hitting the mark.

In fact, Lotte was giving him a withering and silencing glance; she would have been made dean if not for his performance at a certain disastrous dinner party in Fauquier County, Virginia, in 2003.

"No, Hector," Kate said. "Just haunted. That's the word that describes this family's relationship to the past. For me."

"Could you explain?" This was Julien.

"This house reeks of this family's past, but what haunts it are the stories that haven't been told. If you want to get political about it, stories that have been repressed. That may be all but unrecoverable. This haunting may be as close to any of it as we ever get. I think Harry"—she nodded at the end of the table—"sees it as the reason to preserve this place, giving the people who have been harmed a chance to speak. Maybe he's right."

"Maybe not," said Simon, but he was not making a joke.

Kate gave Simon a warm nod; he knew something about this topic, being haunted by this house. "There are certain rooms in this house—views from a window that feel alive to me—and I wonder what happened there. Sometimes when I am in the kitchen I get the feeling that I can hear voices coming down the stairs from the servants' quarters if I want to. That if I stop and listen, I can hear."

"Why don't you?" asked Eleanor. It was the silence, the silence from the indentures, the Indians, the slaves, from Mary Foxley herself, that had been tormenting her ever since she started her project. "If you could hear their stories, wouldn't you have a responsibility to do it?"

"What they are saying is none of my business. We all know about their misfortunes, but their lives are private."

"It seems that Céleste and I are right in the middle of all of this," said Julien. "Does everyone feel this way?"

None of Kate's family stepped up, so she kept going. "I think that is true for all of us. There is something spectral that ties us to this place. Something out of joint."

"Harry would agree?" asked Julien, glancing down, but Kate did not give Harry a chance to answer.

"*Especially* for Harry. He's come to terms with it. Really, what Harry does is haunt himself. If that makes sense," she added, not at all sure that it did make sense.

"What do they want, your ghosts?"

"Justice."

"How does one confer justice on the dead for what happened in the past?"

"I don't know. I suppose Harry could give everything away, renounce all this privilege and all these possessions. As your great-grandfather Thomas did, in effect. But I don't think the dead can be bought off, and I'm not sure the living have a right to share, to lay claim to, their pain. Maybe the dead just want revenge."

"Since Kate didn't allow me to answer Julien's question"— Harry said this with good cheer—"I'd like to ask Ethan what he thinks. He's the only person at this table who grew up among these mysteries."

Julien looked across the table at Ethan, a fine-looking boy with a pretty girlfriend, a son of wealth, a person of privilege. But he had the feeling that this boy was strangely burdened; it seemed difficult, maybe impossible, to get his full attention. For one thing, he seemed to take it as his responsibility to police his parents and sisters, not so much to arrest them if they erred, but to encourage their best, most lawful behavior. It appeared likely that he had been seated at his mother's right hand in order to keep her in line, just as the elderly Simon had been seated at Harry's left.

"What do *I* think?" Ethan asked.

"Yes," Harry said. "Excuse me." Meaning: *I am sorry I asked you this important question in the third person.*

"About guilt? About Margaret's Indians? Slavery? About Paul's salmon? About Mom's ghosts? Like, sure. All of it. Sure. History's, like, a funnel."

Kate let out a little repressed giggle, parental cover. "A funnel," she said gaily—*isn't the boy being très drôle?* "What could you possibly mean, dear?"

"I mean, *Mom*, that you can't pick and choose. I don't care if you got off the boat in 1660 or last week. The day you set your foot ashore, you take on the injustice done to native peoples, enslaved peoples, because without that injustice, America wouldn't exist. New England would try to deny it, but the South, well, the South is America's inconvenient truth. You live in America, you dream of living in America, and you're no more innocent or guilty of the crimes of the past than anyone else. Every American myth has death and injustice attached to it. All goes into the funnel. The funnel misses nothing, it's the end of the line for history. It's where everything America has done gets shoved down our throats. Open wide, Mr. Goose," he said, head back, eyes wide, mouth gaping, volunteering to turn his liver into foie gras.

Eleanor had been listening to all this, watching a discussion play out that, as far as she was concerned, had become a referendum on her novel. That was the way she saw it: all about her novel, even Ethan's funnel, soon to become a legend in this family. She pictured her keyboard as a concavity, catching everything she knew and was trying to say and ever narrowing it into, finally, a concentrated drop of text, her single word, but she wasn't sure whether this unlikely image was a comfort or further reason for despair. Maybe this concavity was a bottomless well, maybe even a black hole from which light cannot escape, from which, most certainly, no three-hundred-page novel might emanate. But as Ethan was finishing this thought, she heard sounds coming from the kitchen, a thumping, someone out there; the dogs had heard it and had shuffled off to investigate, which meant it couldn't be a ghost. Well, hallelujah, Eleanor thought. It must be Vittorio; yes, odd that he had come up through the kitchen from the old wing of the house, and yes, she had texted him to fuck off, but honestly, thank God! She needed him. Because the thing about Vittorio that no one understood was that however disloyal to her he was in every other way, he was an outspoken and unwavering champion of her work, and right about now, a champion was needed. As an unfaithful lover, he was a joke: no stray personal item on the pillow, no obscure but incriminating text was required to catch him with his pants down. This was the Vittorio everybody knew, but in this disregard for even the most trivial of conventions lay the soul of the artist, the truly psychoneurotic mind that is the prelude to greatness. Eleanor had no doubt that he would be great. And this man, this artist, believed in her, and he could knock her about a good bit and she'd still come back for more if he kept believing in her work when she did not.

"I'm sorry," she said. "I'll go see who that is."

As she was leaving, Rosalie expelled an exasperated breath; Ethan rolled his eyes.

"Vittorio?" asked Harry.

"Don't be an idiot," said Kate. The whole table held its breath while, from the kitchen and the hall, voices mumbled, papers rustled here, and footsteps went there.

"I'll go check on Daniel," said Rosalie after a minute had passed.

In the lull—how many more body blows can a party take?—
Harry had to say, "Eleanor has a boyfriend she hoped would be
able to join us." Everyone munched along on the last of their
dinners until Rosalie reappeared and, of all things, beckoned
Heidi to come with her. Which now left their side of the table
missing Rosalie, Heidi, and Eleanor: Paul remained alone until
Daniel padded in and yanked on his hand. He wanted a parent,
and Paul was suddenly more than willing to attend to his needs.

All these mysterious departures and beckonings were, for
Kate, part of a perfectly logical sequence of events: this was the
kind of thinking, leaps of inference that she could do these days,
a mélange of scattered facts, shards of ideas, half-overheard bits
of talk; being slightly drunk only loosened the flow. The person
who had arrived was Francis—what other "guest" would enter
through the summer kitchen? Why did he ask for Heidi? Because he had found her glasses, which, considering what they
all assumed was the real story of their disappearance, made this
discovery a little dodgy. But okay, Francis had found her glasses.
Which left Eleanor, humiliated and devastated, retreating to her
study and Rosalie trying to comfort her.

"Perhaps we should clear," Kate said, and when she stood up
and took hold of her plate and Julien's, Milou followed her lead,
and then Ethan followed hers, an excuse to go find Heidi. Lotte
went out to supervise the preparation of the strawberry trifle and
coffee. This was the moment when Hector and Céleste slipped
out to have a smoke.

"This is like a Buñuel movie, or an Ionesco play," said Simon.
"Look at all these chairs."

"Why don't you join us," said Harry to Julien, who was now
completely deserted at the other end of the table.

"With you down here, the median age might drop below
ninety," said Simon.

"This thing with Eleanor and her boyfriend," Harry said, as if that were the only cause of all this. "I apologize for subjecting you to our ferment."

Julien had to think for a moment about this expression. "Not at all," he said with a pleasant smile. "Busy lives."

🙣

Rosalie expected to find Eleanor huddled—maybe "cowering" was the better word—in her little writing nook, and then she looked in her bedroom, and when she didn't find her there either, she had a vision of her sister wandering down the lane in the dark, a jilted heroine in a hooded cape heading for the waves, the cliffs, or whatever. Rosalie was wondering whether she was going to reach the extreme of setting out after her, but in the end, coming down the stairs, she saw her at the desk in the study, leaning over a small stack of papers.

"Here you are," she said from the doorway, meaning why are you *here?* Despite the fact that this was where Daniel had been deposited with Blippi for so long that his eyes were crossed, it was not a room anyone lingered in. In this space, finally, too much history, too many ghosts of the wrong sort, too politically uncorrectable. The bookshelves on one side were filled with the literature of the British Empire: the complete Sir Walter Scott, Kipling bound in three-quarter purple morocco, Macaulay's *The History of England*, a copy of Baden-Powell's immortal *Scouting for Boys*, the complete oeuvre of H. Rider Haggard, the early travel writings of Freya Stark. Eleanor had realized that if the Mason family's Confederate past didn't disqualify her from the New York literary scene, this library collection, a cabinet of horrors for her postcolonial friends, would surely decide the matter. As if to underline the point, there was a floor-standing globe on which the African continent was neatly and helpfully depicted as a patchwork of colors: magenta for England, light brown for France and dark brown for Belgium, yellow for Italy. The only country marked as independent, in powder blue, was Ethiopia.

"I thought cowering upstairs would be just a little too pathetic."

Rosalie came into the room and stood above her. She saw that the paper in front of Eleanor was a section of her manuscript. "Nellie," she said. "I'm sorry."

"It's just so embarrassing. To play this all out in front of everybody. It's like everyone is in the room watching me have sex with the guy. Which isn't great, by the way."

"We're all on your side."

"Oh. I don't care. I really don't. What would I be doing now if he came? Listening to a lot of bullshit and lies about the difficulty of renting a car, how he had to go back to his place to get his wallet before he left."

"He could have rented a car without his wallet?"

"See? Bullshit and lies. I'm happier here."

Rosalie drew up behind her, gave her a few firm squeezes on her shoulders—more precisely, on the trapezius—and then lowered her head to rest alongside Eleanor's, cheek to cheek, feeling the unbristly warmth of her sister's skin, breathing in the fragrance of her beautiful black hair. Rosalie would have liked to stay there for a long time, in this perfect place, and not return to the labors of her job, her mortgage, her child, her marriage. Eleanor responded by raising her shoulder and tipping her head, as if closing a trap.

"That's nice," said Eleanor. "I need nice."

"You're nice," said Rosalie.

"You know . . ." said Eleanor. "I mean, I'm sorry if Paul and I weren't watching Daniel closely enough at the beach."

Yes. How complicated everything seemed these days to Rosalie, a person who, like her father, had a mind for reducing the most twisted conundrums into manageable strands; it wasn't working so well these days. Was Paul and Eleanor a strand? "Oh," she said, "don't worry about it."

"Can we talk?" Eleanor asked, knowing that this would come up again, this Paul and Eleanor thing. Unfaithfulness was not the issue—there is no way to describe how repulsed Eleanor was by the thought of having sex with Paul—but disloyalty? Well, yes. Paul and Eleanor's entire relationship was founded upon disloyalty to Rosalie. And how, if they both loved her, could this be?

"We should get back to dinner," Rosalie said, but made no motion to leave.

"I just had a thought I wanted to jot down. It was something you said about replacing the American myths with honest fictions."

"Really? I said that?"

"Rosalie, you were always smarter than me. It's a lucky thing fiction writers don't have to be smart. Better if they're stupid, actually."

"If you say so. But that's sweet. If I thought you were stupid, I wouldn't feel flattered."

"Okay," said Eleanor. She deflected the moment by picking up the small disorganized sheaf in front of her. She thumped it into a neat pile.

Rosalie had straightened up a little, but she was still looking over Eleanor's shoulder, and in this posture they were both staring at the pages on the desk. The words "Madam Lloyd" appeared in boldface. "Who was Madam Lloyd?" she asked.

"The richest woman, the richest person in Maryland in the seventeenth century. A Catholic married to a Puritan. A piece of work, as far as I can tell. There's quite a lot known about her. She and Mary Foxley sealed the deal."

"The deal?"

"Married their kids to each other. Our Richard the Second and her oldest daughter, Anna Maria, two children who survived long enough to marry. It's the end of Mary Foxley's story. The native-born elite were off and running. God help us. It's a big theme in colonial Maryland history." Eleanor read aloud, "*Was there any other society in the world where this could be so remarkable, a cause for wonder and celebration? We women of the Chesapeake, we were the handmaidens of death, we wiped the brows, offered the last sip of water, we were the last voices heard, we closed the eyes, and then we got to work, washing for the last time the most emaciated of bodies or the most ghastly of bodily mutilations, we dressed them in such burial suit or gown as they might possess, we folded the hands as if in prayer and sent them to a better life. But at the last, my last born had survived; my work was done. And I could now look forward to my own ends, the peace of privacy, a final moment alone.*"

"Did the young couple have a say in the matter?"

"I think they probably didn't, but it's not as if they had a lot of suitors to choose from. They seem to have been happy, eight kids, seven who survived—quite a lineup, actually. Go out tomorrow and read the epitaph on Anna Maria's slab. Even by the standards of the day, it's over-the-top. That's her behind us, by the way," Eleanor added.

For a moment Rosalie had the image of a third woman standing with them, a ghostly cheek on the other side, papery and cold, but still a solidarity of women going way back. But then she realized that Eleanor was referring to the portrait over the fireplace. They both turned to look at it. It was an oval, like the picture of Mary Foxley in the hall, but in this one the young woman, the *girl*, had been painted wearing a simple dress, her red hair allowed to flow almost voluptuously; there was a small spaniel curled in her lap. Rosalie's eyes had passed over it hundreds, maybe thousands of times, but she had long taken to thinking that this was a much more recent ancestor, even from the 1920s. Someone who loved her had painted this portrait, had so exaggerated her youth and freshness that she appeared to have been born two hundred and fifty years later than she was. How cheerful this girl looked in spite of God knew what kind of harsh realities, how uncomplicated this painting made her life seem. Both sisters were thinking roughly the same thought.

"You didn't give me those pages," said Rosalie.

"I know. I'm thinking of junking the whole thing."

Rosalie was shocked to hear her say this, but in fact, the threat didn't seem entirely genuine, perhaps was meant to be squelched. She told Eleanor that. "You seemed so energized writing this. You were having fun with it, I thought."

"Oh. I had some fun imagining the wedding." She pointed down at her manuscript. "The two were married in January of 1699, and Mary Foxley died a few months later, but I moved it all to September so I could describe something golden, glorious, and festive. I was picturing something between Handel's *Water Music* and Katherine Mansfield's 'The Garden Party.' The boats begin to appear in the creek at midmorning, little girls take their places on the pier to watch as the boats draw nearer, and they come scampering—yeh, 'scampering'"; she pointed to the word in her text—"up to report each new sighting. Even these kids can spot each family by the boat that brought them: the red sails of the Ringgolds' batteau, the sleek lines of the Goldsboroughs' small sloop, the crisp strokes of the oarsmen carrying Mary DeCourcy around from My Lord's Gift. Et cetera, et cetera. Can you feel the *authority* of those period nouns?" Eleanor paused and looked up at Rosalie, a self-deprecating sneer on her face. "More work-shop bullshit," she added.

"Oh, Nellie, just stop being that way."

"Okay. Sorry. Some boats fly pennants, family coats of arms, a gay armada shimmering in this pleasant early-fall light; the colonial governor arrives in a ship that draws too much water to moor at the pier, so he comes into the creek in a boat rowed by eight sailors resplendent in naval livery. I know; laying it on a little thick, but see, I'm contrasting this with the opening scene, when Mary Foxley arrives forty years earlier, rowed ashore in order to live in a hut with a dirt floor."

"Yes," said Rosalie. "I see."

"Yeh, anyway, through the trees, and perhaps through squinted eyes, it looks to Mary Foxley like the busy harbor of Rochester, where she had grown up, and for the first time in many years she feels the sharpest pang of sorrow at the vision of her father waving to her as she left all those years ago. She feels that she will now see him, that she is dying, which she is. Finally, Anna Maria arrives with her brother, Edward Lloyd, they come through the bushes at the bottom of the lawn—I mean, how different, really, might it have looked back then? No lawn, like something mowed, but the slope up from the water to the house. That's permanent. She watches them approach from her bedroom. Beautiful. Rich-ard and Anna Maria get married in a pavilion constructed for the event, and that is that. I had fun with that, but okay, maybe it all sounds fakey in first person."

"Fakey? Who says fakey?"

"Oh. My friend Monroe Monroe. Don't ask."

"What's that typeface, anyway? The pages you gave me didn't look like that."

Eleanor peered at her pages. "I was trying it out. You don't like it?"

"Sort of dorky, I think. I like Garamond. Seems more fitting for a historical piece."

"Fakey and dorky. You guys are great to me."

"Oh, come on. You know I love you." She gave Eleanor's shoulder one more squeeze. "You're going to come back soon, right? I can't imagine what the French are making of all this."

Eleanor promised, and Rosalie left, and as soon as she was gone, Eleanor grabbed her notepad and scribbled *Garamond!* And *Fiction replaces myth!*

9

When Rosalie returned to the dining room, she discovered that the party had taken it upon itself to rearrange her seating chart, which was to say that except for Ethan, still in his assigned spot beside Kate, and Alice, still in her spot beside Harry, the men in the party were at one end of the table and the women at the other. Rosalie could sense, as she walked in to the comfortable chatter, that everyone was quite happy with this, that after all the exertions on the Indians and the slaves and the all-but-extinct salmon, it was a relief to gather with one's own kind. The only other irregularity in this new order was Francis, who had been persuaded to take up a chair on the corner at Kate's right hand, but Francis would have been happy only there, under the protection of the women. When Eleanor came back, if she came back, she and Rosalie and Ethan would all be sitting together, which wouldn't have been ideal either, except that Rosalie was struck, at that moment, with the idea that they had been neglecting Ethan, that, glasses or no, this irritating little Heidi—typical!

straddling the line between the men and the women—was not to be trusted with her brother's heart and it was time to close ranks behind him.

She sent a salvo across the table. "So Francis found your glasses," she said loudly, to all. She was pleased that Heidi reddened slightly, and Francis squirmed a bit. He was holding, clutching, a grimy manila envelope; he looked like a schoolchild who understood that his precious show-and-tell was not going to be admired.

"Yes. He did," Heidi answered, glancing across the table through her thick lenses.

"How weird. I mean—"

"They had fallen off when we were climbing up to see the carriages in the hayloft," interrupted Ethan. This was the first time he had offered an explanation. Francis volunteered no additional details.

As long as Ethan was going to defend her, and not wanting to put Francis on the spot, Rosalie let it drop. Actually, she didn't want to make this girl uncomfortable—there was too much discomfort in her world as it was—and Francis, now in the room, had already transformed the spirit of the gathering. It was as if, after all this faculty-lounge discussion of history, History itself had decided to pay a call to straighten them out. Francis's father, Bo, had heard all the Retreat's voices over the years loud and clear, knew all the stories of Black and white, knew who'd loved whom, who'd hated whom, where they lived and how they died, and he had passed all of it on to Francis. No one would dream of querying Francis directly about any of these topics; one simply had to behave more maturely when discussing them in his presence. Francis was not flippant; he did not understand humor, Hector's sarcasm or Simon's quips; Francis could not tell the difference between argument and debate, and he hated conflict. He wanted only the purity of the most ordinary and honest truths. Rosalie knew that carping about Heidi's behavior didn't cut it; time for the Mason family to up its game.

Eleanor had slipped into her seat during this final go on Heidi's glasses. She felt better; her latest crisis of doubt had passed. As Virginia Woolf said of Orlando's struggles as a writer—Eleanor had this quote posted on her bulletin board—"he had his good nights and bad mornings . . . and could not decide whether he was the divinest genius or the greatest fool in the world." I'm neither genius nor fool, Eleanor thought; but her pages on Madam Lloyd and the wedding, as she had shuffled through them in the study and summarized them to dear Rosalie—under the table, she reached next to her and gave Rosalie's hand a pat and a squeeze—weren't as bad as she'd feared. None of these pages, she would say, were really anything but *notes*, the *way I might tell it*. Of course, if someone wanted to publish those notes as is—you never know—that would be fine too. An anecdote for marketing the work: *and then my editor said, Why not just publish the notes, and I said* . . . Short bits, lots of white space. Accidental genius. *Yes*, she had earlier scribbled in the margin of her draft, *all we get is glimpses, there is only juxtaposition, no narrative, the past is not a movie.* Except that such was precisely what she was trying to do—*and then my agent said, Let's show this to Reese*—despite all her efforts to dodge the demands of narrative.

"Eleanor?" said Kate.

"Oh, yes. Sorry."

"Everything okay? I'm sorry about Vittorio." She had just finished serving the strawberry trifle; Francis sat with a plate resting on the envelope in his lap, looking miserable.

"You see, what could well happen is that he will show up now," Eleanor said. "This is how he raises his relationships to the level of melodrama. It's instinct for him."

"Then I hope he doesn't come—and if," Kate added fiercely, rising in volume, "he does, I'll go to the front door and send the asshole on his way."

That last phrase rang out, and there was a nice pause from one end of the table to the other. Into the silence, with surprise and gratitude, Eleanor said, "Mom, you've used my favorite word."

"Meaning the boyfriend I mentioned," said Harry to Julien as the separate conversations resumed.

"So hard to stand back from our children's choices," Julien said.

"Not me," said Simon. "From the first time I met Kate, I knew she was a jewel. I told Harry I couldn't believe she was interested in him. I told him he'd better marry her quickly before she realized her mistake."

"You may think he's telling a joke, but he isn't. That is exactly what he said to me." Harry did not think this was funny, then or now, but he knew even at the time where it came from in his father's wounded soul: his second wife, Trinket, had just left him; all love was a hopeless game, a series of feints and deceptions. Harry had also loved Trinket, everybody had; he might have leapt at Käthe Lorenz with such fervor in part because he was trying to assuage the same sense of loss. Trinket. A good and gracious heart, loved to have fun; from others it might be an insult, but as far as Harry was concerned, it was high praise to say that no dog had a cleaner soul than she did. She just wasn't all that reliable.

"This is what I wonder about Thomas and Beal," said Alice to Julien. "Such dangerous choices they made, an interracial marriage in 1893. How their families must have tried to dissuade them, then sending them off to France, never seeing them again. The lives people lived."

"I think there was a great pain in it, for her," answered Julien. "In her journals she wrote about being homesick. For all the admiration people felt for her, they always spoke of her as reserved, as if a piece were missing. A typical exile, I suppose."

"And have you found that piece here? Or some idea of what it was?" asked Alice.

"I have found where some of it had once been. I am very grateful to Harry for showing it to us. I have to say, to Kate's point, I do not feel Thomas Bayly's presence in this house—there's too much going on here, I suppose—but I did feel Beal's presence, as a child, in that quiet place. Céleste thinks I am too *sensible*, but it gives me great joy to feel it."

While Julien was saying this, Francis leaned forward and tapped on Kate's shoulder. He nodded down into his lap as if, Kate thought, he wished she would relieve him of this dessert he did not want; she then realized that he was asking her to do something with the envelope, but she was busy making a point, a scab she had been itching all day.

"With our history, it's hard to get all misty-eyed about the passing of ol' Tuckertown," she said.

"And why is that, *madame?*" said Julien. "I wish there were more of it left."

Ethan figured that if his mother couldn't grasp how much her comment had pissed Julien off, she was truly shit-faced. "Mom," he said.

Yes, thought Kate, I have had too much to drink, and if I hadn't, I wouldn't be saying it like this. *Ol' Tuckertown* was perhaps too much. But once down this road, she felt she needed to complete the thought. "That place was essentially a labor camp. Those buildings were inhumane. It was shameful. Not something we should regret losing."

"*Bien sûr*. But perhaps something you should regret forgetting?"

"Certainly," said Kate, now a bit confused about her own point. No, of course not *forget*, but wasn't this tour of Harry's a little pretentious, more than a little tacky, given the history? That was the part she objected to. "But it's hard for me to imagine joy there." As she was saying this, Francis once again was trying to get her attention, this time more insistently, sticking the sharp corner of his envelope into the flesh of her forearm. "For the man," he mumbled, nodding his head down the table, but Kate was now realizing that she had stepped even further into offense and was desperately trying to find her way out of it. She tapped Francis's hand, meaning, *Wait a sec.*

Julien was not giving her any help. "You haven't read Beal's journals," he snapped. How dare she, from this privileged seat at the table, attempt to eradicate that family's life? Those people lying in those neglected graves were forgotten enough. What did these Americans *want* from history? Half of them couldn't live with it; half of them couldn't live without it. Hardly the way to create a national identity, much less a national purpose. He glanced around the table. This pretty daughter tied up in knots, apparently, about the book she was writing. The other daughter and her conservation easements. And Kate Mason. Lives were lived; what was the difficulty, what was their *offense* against the present that their humanity should be denied? But then again, on the other side, buoyant, guilt-free Margaret and her enthusi-asms. And Harry Mason. Well, Julien liked Harry, was grateful to him, but wasn't it a bit extreme to buy an estate because it had been his family's seat in America? Why not just *visit*, as Julien himself was doing, drop in some Sunday afternoon, when, Julien assumed wrongly, calls of that sort were not discouraged? But he didn't want to get lost in this American conundrum. This formi-dable woman, Alice, had asked him whether he had found miss-ing pieces, whether he had found what Beal so yearned for during her forty years in France, and it was time he offered a more com-plete answer before his pauses got embarrassing. "I think for Beal it was just family. Nothing more complicated than that," he said finally. "In spite of all that was happening in America. As I understand it, they left just as the James Crow laws were being enacted. But her parents sounded like accomplished people."

"*Jim* Crow," Harry corrected. "A racist song and dance popular at that time. In blackface."

"But yes," said Alice. "Abel and Una Terrell were very accomplished. People still speak of them, and of all that they lost."

"Still, I do find this a most unusual region," Julien said, hoping to cap this whole thing off without delay, because rising in him was a fierce, unexpected sense that Beal's people were now *his* people and not anyone else's at the table, that if Kate Mason were to be the author of their story they would be in very bad hands indeed. For a second a question flashed in front of his eyes, whether he was going to have to choose between his white heritage and his Black blood. One thing was clear to him: Beal's parents were no longer fodder for conversation at a white man's dinner party. Especially this one.

"How so?" asked Margaret.

"A landscape unlike anything we have in France," he continued pleasantly. "I find it quite marvelous. But I am not the only European here. I am wondering how Milou finds it."

Céleste and Milou had been in a rather intense if muffled conversation in French, chairs pulled back a little from the table, a perfectly harmless withdrawal from the main chitchat, the sort of relaxed rules that come with dessert and coffee. As hard as Alice tried to figure out what they were saying, her last French lesson had been in 1939; she had not thought they were speaking softly and in French in order to be private, but then she wondered, as they both reacted as if found out when Julien turned the light on them. On the other hand, Kate had heard enough to realize that in all this talk of homesickness a hundred years ago, about origins and the past, Milou was speaking from the heart about similar things to Céleste, who seemed to have this effect on people. Céleste was asking what she was really accomplishing here. Yes, helping to care for this lovely *vieille femme austère*—but for herself, what was she achieving? Was she really part of this life? Wasn't this woman—head tipped Margaret's way, Céleste was avoiding using people's names, evidence to Kate that they were consciously speaking in code—really not the true heiress to all this, her dowdy clothes and her Historical Society? What, after all, is a "Historical Society"? She was encouraging Milou to get on with a university degree. At home. For the moment, though, it was all between Milou and Céleste—and Kate. At Julien's intrusion, they rejoined the table

"Oh, we wouldn't want to put anyone on the spot, would we?" said Kate with a forced, coquettish gaiety that Ethan hated because she only sounded like this when she was drunk.

But Milou answered without much difficulty. "I come from flat land and water. At Alice's farm"—Alice wished she had said *our* farm—"the water feels everywhere. It's what I am used to." She stopped speaking, but it was clear she had more to say and didn't want to say it.

Kate jumped back in. In some way that she had not figured out, relations had turned sour between her and Julien; he was avoiding her glance, there had been a frisson of, well, animus. Julien could not have avoided meeting her eyes more obviously if he had held up a hand as a blinder. Okay, she thought, take this. "And what have you observed, Céleste? This is your first trip here?"

"My father and I have driven at least two thousand kilometers in the past two weeks," said Céleste. "Small *villages*, mostly, *régions viticoles*. Coast to coast, as you say. Such an American expression. Would I be wrong to think that few of you have made this journey recently?"

"And?" said Margaret, once again delighted to be on the receiving end of impressions of America from a foreign visitor, a new Tocqueville or Dickens; she was prepared to be entertained. "From sea to shining sea?" she added proudly.

"I think it's falling apart, *franchement.*"

"*Ma chérie?*"

Lotte roared to life. "And how, exactly, in your view, are we 'falling apart'?"

Céleste was not the slightest bit deterred. "Each town we passed through seemed more confused and nasty than the last. When Americans talk about being proud, it's because they think they are winning; when they start losing, there is nothing there but spite and distrust. Nothing but *méchanceté*, especially from the women; the nastiness we endured, the mistrust! Americans think France is a has-been—that's the expression, 'has-been'?—but we're still proud to be French. We're proud of our *patrimoine*; Americans don't even have a word for it. We believe in *communauté, convivialité.* We believe in *dignité.* From the Pacific to the Atlantic, I saw very little dignity in America."

This comment left Lotte with her mouth open. As Julien had expected, in the shocked pause that followed this, all eyes turned not on Céleste—everyone was avoiding looking at her—but on him, the father, who would now be expected to mop this up a bit, repackage the message as a proposition that might be debated and not necessarily a true statement of her beliefs; show kindness to Margaret—Julien had grasped her tenuous place in all this from the moment he'd met her in the hallway—and perhaps send the whole package along to Simon, who would dismiss it with one of his witticisms. The eyes, including Céleste's, turned to Julien for all this, but in fact, he agreed for the most part with what she'd said, knew she was going to say it all when Kate asked her. It was time, as far as Julien was concerned, for Harry to perform his final duty as host, announce the end of dinner and let them all go home. Nothing had yet been said when a small voice, Heidi's, came from the ladies' end of the table.

"It's all corrupt anyway," she said. "That's why we're falling apart. It's not worth saving. My parents have seen this coming for years. They've been buying guns ever since Trump was elected."

"Cool. What kind of guns?" asked Ethan.

"We're leaving," said Hector, jumping to his feet and throwing down his napkin. "Margaret," he said, "you will come with us."

This was the cue everyone had been waiting for, even if more abrupt than expected. The seat backs had started to poke into the spines; the cushions had lost their give. Alice and Simon remained seated, but everyone else milled around while Hector gathered Margaret and marched to the doorway. "Any more July Fourths like this," he said, "and we *will* fall apart. Then we'll see what the *French* can do when the Chinese take over the world. We'll let them *reckon* with that." Clearly, if he had been slightly snowed by Céleste earlier in the evening, even if they had partaken of a convivial smoke between courses, the glow had been extinguished.

Harry had followed them but offered no response. Hector bellowed for Lotte, who was in the kitchen taking her leave from Kate. "I'd stay to help you with the dishes," said Lotte, "but I'm sure you'll just ignore them tonight. I can't imagine waking up to all this, but that was always your way."

"Thank Hector for taking Margaret, will you?" answered Kate.

"But before I go," Lotte added, walking over to the dishwasher and dropping the door, "you have always loaded the dishwasher wrong. See?" She pointed as if the mistake, the offense, would be obvious to anyone who took a second to look for it, but Kate did not make such an attempt. She allowed Lotte to depart in a final puff of hauteur and then turned to see that Francis was now sitting at the table behind her. In front of him was the manila envelope labeled by a few faded words written in a childish hand; there was a streak of what looked like blood on one side. He had both hands resting on top of it, as they had been all night. She'd seen him like this before, bringing her photographs—the first person, as far as she knew, to whom he'd shown the pictures that most mattered to him. It was a sort of ceremony, something that couldn't be rushed. She sat down, took off her bandanna, and mopped her brow and skull. "I'm sorry we didn't get to your pictures," she said.

"It's all right," said Francis.

"It got a little heated in there," she said, and in fact, the unusual crisp and cool air of the morning had been falling back all day before remorseless haze and humidity, and it was now one of those breathless Chesapeake nights in July when dishes do get left on the table, when there is only a low murmur from the porches, when the prospect of nightclothes and bed is unbearable. Kate let out a sigh but then a slight laugh. As she remembered it, Hector had stormed out last year too, though she couldn't recall why. Nothing as good as Heidi and her parents' guns. And Ethan. Really? "A funnel"? "What kind of guns"? She laughed again. But goodness, she never imagined that she had raised a *Southerner*. She'd have to reflect on that.

"Did you and Bo have a nice Fourth?" she asked.

"Dad gets pretty tired," he said.

"Me too."

"You're doing good, Kate. You don't know it, but you look just a little better to me each time I see you."

"Thank you, Francis. I'm less hopeful than I should be, maybe. That's what Harry thinks. But you saying that means more to me than I can say. You have seen me at my worst, after all."

"Yeh," he said, and did not need to describe her worst, ravaged by chemo, her anger and fear.

"Thank you for bringing over Heidi's glasses. I mean . . ." she started; it seemed no sentence that began with Heidi's glasses needed to be completed: How, where, why, what were they doing? The art of losing isn't hard to master, thought Kate.

"Yeh," he said again. Yeh-yeh-yeh was the way Francis thought about a lot of the ordinary commerce of life, and all this was ordinary: old age, being sick with cancer, lost items, glasses, teeth. Francis never added words to the world; he felt there were enough as it is. But he did say, because he thought it would amuse Kate, "They were outside, in the grass beside the water hydrant. I think the dogs found them, I don't know where. Rowdy, probably."

"Oh, God," said Kate. "That animal never disappoints."

"He comes in and steals Dad's remote. It's not his fault. Dad feeds him."

Well, this was more than plausible: her son and Heidi might have been too . . . uh, *engaged* to notice. How perfect, thought Kate, to have this mystery solved by blaming the family's dumbest member. She almost felt bad for delighting in it.

"And thank you so much for bringing over some photographs. For Julien? I'll make sure he sees them."

"Yeh," he said.

"Can I have a peek?"

He raised his hands and let her slide the envelope from under them. It smelled sweetly of milk and manure; the farm had been a dairy for decades, and the perfume of the cows was in its bones. As she pried open the clasp, one of the prongs broke off; Francis, it seemed, hadn't looked at the pictures inside for years. She reached in and pulled out two old Kodak packets, the kind with the snapshots in back and the negatives in a smaller pocket in front. There were sixteen pictures, prints on heavy, slightly concave paper with scalloped edges; the negatives were missing. She looked at the image on the top and then slid the next one up enough to see it as well; she had never seen the place they captured but knew instantly what it was, where it was. This was not her business, she had disqualified herself at dinner; she felt like a grave robber uncovering a tomb, even just removing the prints from their ancient envelopes felt like prying the top off a sarcophagus. She filed the prints back in the first packet and then slid both of them into the manila envelope, reclasped it with the remaining prong, and replaced it under Francis's hands. He let his hands drop, as if he were a high priest enjoined by the knowledge that even if it took another fifty or a hundred years, these images could be seen only by one who believed in them. "I thought Julien might be interested," he said. "I want him to have them."

"Oh, Francis," she said.

"They were some of the first pictures I ever took. With the Brownie box my parents gave me. It used to take me weeks to save the money I needed for the film and the processing. I would make better prints, but I've lost the negatives," he said finally. "I wasn't as careful back then."

"Well. That doesn't matter."

"No," he said. "It doesn't."

"What matters is the hundredth of a second, as you were saying earlier today. The fact that all these years later, you can give that hundredth of a second to someone who would want it."

"Yeh."

"I'm sure he will be very grateful," she said.

Alice and Simon had continued to rest in their chairs; everything about the body hurts past age ninety, so remaining seated too long is not a hardship. A reassuring kind of sharp pain on the surface compared with the dull decay inside. All evening Simon had been surprising Alice, the way in which his mind lurched and weaved revealed a certain sort of, if not wisdom, then *wiseness*. She had perhaps misjudged him all these years, but it wasn't as if there was a great loss in this; it was only on this occasion that she ever saw him at all. She wondered which one of them would be attending the other's funeral. Julien and Céleste returned through one of the French doors, and for a few minutes after Hector and Lotte and a slightly unwilling Margaret had left—Margaret gave Alice a last, desperate look of alarm, as if she were being kidnapped—Simon had entertained them, mimicking Hector's disagreeably nasal and whiny tone: "Now we have to feel guilty about *the fish!*"

A few minutes later Harry came back, announcing that the others had scattered: Paul and Rosalie up to their room, where Daniel, it seemed, had been screaming for some time; Ethan and Heidi had gone off to catch up with J. and Simone to watch the fireworks on Kent Island; Eleanor was nowhere to be found, but there was no alarm in that. Perhaps Vittorio had arrived after all. Harry had caught sight of Milou killing time by perusing the bookshelves in the study. "Phew," he said, dropping back into his chair. A brandy, a glass of port would be nice—he had never stopped missing the ceremonies of drinking, even if the stuff no longer interested him—but if he did still drink, he'd have to stay sober in order to return Pop to Osprey Neck. On holidays, the sheriff—J.'s dad—had speed traps and sobriety checks set up from one end of Route 213 to the other. He'd grown to hate that drive. Why couldn't, why wouldn't, Pop just stay over; God knows, they had a bed for him.

"Phew," he said again. "A great weight has been lifted." They all understood that he was talking about the departure of Hector and Lotte.

"They are curious, aren't they," said Alice.

"I admire Lotte, a little," said Harry, laughing at his own pun. "She has no grace, but she shows how strong the will to endure really is. I think I admire Margaret in the same way. She's the Energizer Bunny."

While Harry explained to Céleste what he meant, Alice did everything she could to keep guilty thoughts away. Margaret, undaunted. Crushed by calamity at dawn; recalibrated, newly resolved by nightfall. Always looking ahead. "Ever Forward," as one of the inscriptions in the Retreat graveyard had it.

"It was me?" asked Céleste about the climactic end of the party. "*Ma faute?*"

Harry did not need to wait for the translation; this one was pretty easy. "No. Kate singled you out. She was annoyed at your father for putting Milou on the spot. You answered honestly."

Alice's heart fluttered. "Did Kate tell you that?"

"No, but I know my wife," said Harry. "I love my wife."

"I wonder if I could ask a question," said Céleste, looking directly at Simon. "Perhaps we're all too tired. It's about the visit to your brother's grave," she warned.

They had all by now gotten the very clear impression that when this woman offered a trigger like this, one should take it seriously. But Simon was not wary; it seemed this might be a continuation of the conversation they were having at the graveyard.

"Certainly," said Simon.

"It is perhaps too personal?"

Harry's father had always affected a zest for the personal, even impertinent, question, but there was now an odd color in his demeanor, a sense of willing resignation, acknowledgment that the time for this had come. "We're among family," he said.

"When you asked for your brother's forgiveness, what were you asking him to forgive?"

The question did not rattle Simon, but Harry was surprised that before he answered, he fixed his eyes upon Alice, and with the tiniest gestures and flutters, they were having a silent conversation. In the end, she was giving him license for something. In this interval it came to Harry that as much as he considered himself an expert, an unwilling expert, a force-fed expert, on those events in this place in 1939, there might be a part of the story that he had never heard, that in this day of missing pieces and encounters with the past, there might be still more surprises.

"You know the story?" Simon asked Céleste.

"Yes," she said. She gathered that the boys had been born in England, but during the Depression the family had come back to live at the Retreat for a few years. Sebastien had thrived in this place, and his mother, Edith, well, she had taken a lover. When Edward announced that they would be returning to England before the war broke out, Sebastien hatched a plan to hide out on the day they were supposed to depart. His father would have to leave without them, the war would start, and Sebastien and Simon, and Edith, would be free of him. "He tried to run away in Alice's sailboat, but he didn't really know how to sail, and he drowned in the Bay," she concluded.

It had been a longish summary, surprisingly accurate, and, for Harry, chilling to hear from the mouth of this stranger, French accent—French phrases, indeed—and all.

"But you knew nothing about his plan, yes?" she asked Simon. "You were eight, *plus ou moins*? You had no part in it."

"That's correct. No one knew anything about it. Especially not Alice."

"Then what was there to forgive?"

Yes, thought Harry: his father had been the blameless one, the injured party, the survivor who had to carry the weight of his brother's sorrows and his mother's sins; that had been his duty and his fate. He waited for the answer.

"It was August," said Simon at last. "Sebastien's plan was to get the boat ready in the darkness and then leave just before dawn. He came into my room"—and here he gestured to indicate that this room was directly over where they sat, a room not much used—"to give me some sort of goodbye, thinking he'd see me in a few days and I would be grateful for what he had done. Of course, what he didn't know was that I was happy to be leaving the Retreat, going back to England with our father. I loved my father, bastard that I came to understand he was. We were supposed to be sailing on the *Normandie*, and Father had promised me petits fours and Punch and Judy shows."

"As you had when you came over on the *Normandie* three years earlier," Harry said.

"Yes," said Simon curtly; he was telling Harry to bug out, that he had no need for prompts and reminders. For this story especially his son did not need to act like an aide in the memory unit of Osprey Neck.

"It was about three in the morning. I don't know what I sensed, but from the moment Sebastien stirred"—he gestured above and behind his head, toward Sebastien's room, which was now a bathroom—"I was awake. He came in, said something about 'Toad,' which was his not completely loving nickname for me, and then left. As soon as I heard the waterside door close, I went to the window. In the moonlight I could see him walking down the terraces toward the water, and then I heard some thumping from the dock. That's when I figured out what he was doing." He stopped speaking. Milou had wandered in from the study, Kate from the kitchen, and Eleanor from somewhere, and they had taken seats.

"I've never told Harry this. The story he grew up with was incorrect and incomplete in this respect. I have always told him that I knew nothing was going on until I woke up that morning in a house in full alarm. I never saw much reason to tell him any of this."

Harry did not respond, other than with a slight shrug.

"I called out for my mother"—here, the final gesture over his shoulder at the last room implicated in this tale, now as then the parental chamber—"and she came to me. I told her what I thought Sebastien was doing. She went to the window and stood there for several minutes; I can see her now, in her nightgown by the moonlight, a very young woman—I'd call her a girl today. She had no more sense of what to do than I did. I can understand that now." He stopped for a long time, took a drink of water; he still had half a glass of wine, and Harry was surprised he didn't drain it.

"I was panicking, picturing what might happen to Sebastien, alone on the water in the night. I asked her what she was going to do about it, and at last she turned to me and said not to worry, as if she'd known about it all along. She didn't—I'll take that belief to my grave—but that was her tone. She soothed back my fears. Sebastien was just acting out—however they said 'acting out' back then. 'All will be well. There's no danger on these waters. Get back to bed. Thank you for telling me. Here, let me tuck you in.'"

He stopped speaking again; he had a wounded look, like a dog that doesn't understand the source of its pain, but as much as he was reliving this event, as much as he was now the small boy being sent back to bed, there was little emotion in his voice. No tears forming in the candlelight. Just puzzlement, as if the past is filled with things that probably should be understandable, but aren't.

"Go on, Simon," said Alice.

He smiled to her. "I told Alice all about this later that morning, before Sebastien's body had been discovered. She and her mother had come over to comfort us while we waited. It still seemed that Sebastien would be found alive, and we agreed that there was no reason for me to tell anyone about my mother. We didn't want to get in trouble, or get her in trouble. And then my father appeared on the bottom terrace with Sebastien's body in his arms. Alice and I have borne that secret ever since, borne it well. Besides, that morning everyone was busy blaming Robert Baby, the Black farmhand, for Sebastien's escape. Sending out the posse to bring him in. Which was how things were done back then."

Harry wanted to say it was how things were still done, but the privilege of participating in his father's story, the burden of interpreting his enigmas, the punishment of reliving his tragedies—he had been removed from all that. He could feel the weight being lifted. It was Kate who asked Simon why he thought his mother had done it.

"That's the question I have asked myself for more than eighty years. She did truly think no ill would come of it. Sebastien was a very capable and resourceful kid. And, well, these waters aren't the North Atlantic. I don't think Sebastien's safety was ever the slightest bit in doubt for her."

"But?" said Kate.

"But . . . I believe she hoped Sebastien's plan would succeed. Crazy at it was, she might have believed she could persuade my father to leave without us. I think, as she stared out the window, she saw a small amount of genius in what Sebastien was doing. She had ceded every bit of parental authority by then; Sebastien lived his own life. She calculated. She bet the farm on her son's life."

Harry could not help but emit a groan. He groaned because this made sense, everything about it: a new light shone on the ruined person Edith had become, the Lost Mother, the shocked and numbed shell that was all Harry had ever known of his grandmother on his infrequent trips to Chicago.

"And yet, you ask your brother for forgiveness," said Céleste, the person who started this, "when you visit his grave. Because what you think you should have done, that night, was to betray your brother and defy your mother and wake your father. Your family was broken in two, and at that moment, you had to choose sides."

Simon nodded: the story was finally so ordinary in its hardships that it could now be taken to its conclusion by a complete stranger. As he sat there, all time compressed to an instant: the present of these events in 1939; the present of this moment around the remains and clutter of a banquet; the present of a future in which there was no more of the story to tell.

"Yes," said Alice. "Even that morning, before Sebastien's body was found, Simon knew he might have been able to stop it all, that his father would have run to the dock and made Sebastien give it up. He was crying, we both were, and I told him he was right to do what his mum had told him to do. Simon has lived with that since he was eight years old. I have told him over and over again that he must acknowledge that none of this was his fault, but, Simon, dear," she said, now focusing on him, "you always made one of your jokes about it. I almost believed you didn't care."

"Well. I almost believed it too."

Harry stood up. "You know," he said to the others in the room, "it's time to call it a night, but let's just give Pop and Alice a few moments together. Right?"

Céleste followed Kate into the kitchen with a handful of glasses. What a mess; but one thing Céleste did have to—well, not *envy*, not *admire*, *bien sûr*, but perhaps, marvel at—*s'émerveiller*—about Americans was their kitchens. Their dishwashers, even if they were all made in Korea or Germany; these dishwashers standing open, these giant caverns of clean, a dinner for fifteen was nothing to them. Their refrigerators: the remains of a huge fish, an enormous bowl of uneaten peas, just shove them in and eat them tomorrow. Or throw them in the trash. She thought about Armand and their daughters; in a few hours they would be eating breakfast in the tiny kitchen in Montpellier. She missed them, but as she took pleasure in the sweet image of the three of them sitting around the table with their bowls of café au lait and hot chocolate, she knew that it was a kinder, more peaceful scene without her. She was tired of being disagreeable. The American women she had met on this trip, with their narrowed eyes so ready to feel insulted by an innocent question, so without style, so trashy. And they all carried guns! No. When Céleste got home, she vowed, she would be nicer. Her family would be asleep now; for a second she was a spirit, an angel, visiting each of those heads on those pillows. She'd be less impatient, more loving, when she got back. Maybe she had been too strident at dinner, *qui sait?* Of course they had met Americans of good heart on this trip, many fine vignerons with all the sense of ancient tradition and pride she could ever find in France. Of course. But like so many of the vines at home in Languedoc, now so stressed by the heat and sun, by everything from unprecedented late frosts to biblical drought, the Americans' survival would depend on their own traditions. And she wasn't sure America had what it took. Wasn't sure America had any traditions at all.

While thinking these liverish thoughts and admiring the kitchen appliances and offering her thanks and goodbyes to Kate, Céleste noticed that the other man—in all the arrivals and departures, she had inferred for a time that he was Eleanor's boyfriend and found them an unlikely couple—had left, but the envelope was on the table. She was thinking she should remark on it, but just then her father and Harry Mason came in from the porch.

"*Alors, Papa,*" said Céleste. "*C'est l'heure de partir.*"

"You must be exhausted," said Kate. "You woke up in Detroit?"

"Yes," said Julien. "You have been kind."

"I wanted to apologize for what I said at dinner. About—"

He interrupted. "It seems that we all have opinions about the past. I took no offense."

"Well," Kate said. "*Attends une minute.*" She went over to the table and picked up the envelope. "Francis wanted you to take this."

"Papers?"

"No. Some photographs he took when he was a boy, maybe in 1960. Photographs of a place that doesn't exist anymore. He thinks they need to go with you, 'back to France,' he said. I think he meant back to Beal. That would be his way," said Kate.

"But they must be very rare. Very valuable to you. We couldn't accept them."

"You have to," said Kate, imagining the look on Francis's face if she returned the envelope to him and told him they wouldn't take it. "For his sake. Francis has lived a checkered life, frequently enough led astray, as we say. But there are good people who love him because of his kindness and generosity. Being generous is what keeps him alive. Each time he gives something away, he gets, in return, the strength to resist the bad side. Francis knows that if, in the end, he has nothing, he will have lived a good life."

"Well, *c'est formidable, mais—*," said Julien.

"Just take them," interrupted Kate. "Take them and remember this evening."

When they reached the hall, the group was engaged in farewells. Maybe Kate was "projecting," as Rosalie often used to accuse her of doing—"it's my magical power," Kate had once responded—but everyone seemed more exhausted than usual, wrung out. Was it always this way at the end of an evening or had this homey event asked more of them than she knew? "'My poor house, and I do equally desire,'" Kate mouthed. She was ten minutes from pillow time, to hell with the dishes, to hell with brushing teeth, etc.; she knew she'd have a hangover in the morning, knew she'd have to probe Ethan to see whether she had disgraced herself. Harry and Paul were helping Alice down the steps and into her old Chevrolet; Milou had pulled the car forward but was back in the hall saying her goodbyes. In the dim shadows of the foyer, the features that gave Milou her odd beauty became harsh, almost demanding, angry even. Kate knew why Alice loved her, but this Eastern Shore was not Milou's place; whatever happened to Weatherly, she would never settle here, or—perhaps more accurately—settle *for* here. If Kate had the chance, she would tell Milou that Céleste was right.

✺

"What a night," said Alice to Milou once they had driven off.

"Are you okay? That story with Mr. Mason?" Milou asked.

"Oh yes," she said cheerfully. "These things once seemed so important," she added, implying that Simon's story was one of those things that had long ago lost its power.

Milou didn't entirely believe this veneer. "Aren't you happy to have it told?"

"Oh, I suppose. For Simon, certainly. But neither Simon nor I spend much time looking at the past. We're looking ahead; we know what's to come, but we don't know how it will come. We don't know who will be there."

Milou heard this leading comment with a start, but for the moment she concentrated on her driving. They were headed down a long, straight stretch, with the fields of young corn on the right and thick woods on the left, and she had learned that when deer in the fields saw her lights, they would bolt across the road to hide in the trees. A car was coming the other way, and she was blinded a bit; a light was on inside the car, and as it passed, Milou caught a view of that girl, Heidi, in the passenger seat. Oh, she had found her irritating, but had to admire her gall, that gesture, walking in full view across the center of the party; Milou wouldn't have done that.

"I will be there, Alice."

"You'll be at my side?"

"Of course I will."

"You will be holding my hand?" She was thinking of Simon's gesture earlier in the evening; the idea of a last touch of life.

In answer Milou reached across the seat and took Alice's slender, fragile hand, driving that way for a few hundred feet.

"But they say you are planning to give Weatherly to me."

"Who says that? Is that what you and Céleste were talking about?"

"No, not about Weatherly. Kate said something earlier, but it's not the first time I've heard it."

"Does Margaret know?" asked Alice. For a second she was horrified that something so private, something held so tight in her inscrutable hundred-year-old heart, could rise to the level of gossip at the Food Lion.

"She hasn't said anything to me, but of course she knows. Margaret has survived by not knowing what she knows."

"Oh," said Alice.

"You can't do it, you know that. You can't give Weatherly to me. You can't do that to Margaret. Maybe she'll just turn around and sell it, but that's her business. This is her world, not mine. Can you picture me at a dinner like that ten years from now? Thirty years? I have to go home. That's what Céleste and I were talking about."

"She gets to the point, that girl. It must be the American blood in her," said Alice, but from the first, delicious moment when it occurred to her that she could leave Weatherly to Milou, she had been drunk on the idea; the more forbidden it was, the meaner it seemed. Well, you drink, Alice supposed, because your parents didn't let you. But time to sober up, before it was too late. Margaret, her Historical Society, her pretenses, driving through town in that silly car. Margaret was a fixture, more at home in this life than Alice had ever been. Margaret was a ninny, perhaps, but in this town, at that table, artless but never out of place. Alice had come to recognize that Margaret understood the subtle strengths of her rickety position; she had seen her ride that pony—for whom else would Billy McCready drive his tow truck ten miles out of his way on the Fourth of July?—and she could not fault Margaret for it.

Alice said nothing more for the rest of the drive—it was only ten minutes anyway—but when Milou came around to help her into the house, Alice gave her a hug. "It was my joy to have you for this time. As of tonight, I have emptied my heart and my life to you. After I die, please go home and marry someone you love as much as I love you, and if you have a daughter, consider naming her Alice. I have always liked the way you pronounce it."

"Ah-leese? Like that?"

"Yes," Alice answered, thinking that with everything all set, it wouldn't be long now.

On the ride home from the somewhat desultory Kent Island fireworks display, neither Ethan nor Heidi had much to say. It had been a dispiriting event; watching it from the middle of a crush of cars in a high school parking lot lacked wow and wonder. They found J. and Simone in J.'s father's pickup as they had planned, but J. had a group of Black friends on lawn chairs in the truck bed, and though they were friendly enough to Ethan, their Fourth of July and his Fourth of July were not the same; they were celebrating a different July 4, 1776. Ethan could only nod when J. asked how "the whale" had been. Simone wasn't pleased with that; she'd felt ridiculed when she fell for the joke at the beach and had decided since the visit to the river that she didn't like Ethan and wanted "J." to stop hanging around with him. It was time for Jeremy to grow up, to refuse that white family's petty gifts, to become a man, to become a *Black* man.

While they drove, Heidi had turned on the dome light of

the car—this was the sort of selfish and inconsiderate thing she would do even as he squinted at the deer, ditches, and drunk drivers in the road ahead—and was flipping through her book of drawings.

It was time, she thought; she hoped this wouldn't be too awkward. Heidi accorded herself the belief that she hated awkward moments more than most people; this especial phobia, as she thought of it, compelled her sometimes to be more abrupt than she meant to be. "I think I should go home tomorrow," she said.

She waited for his response as he passed an oncoming car on the straightaway into the Retreat and was surprised when it finally came. "Yeh," he said. He had already figured out that inviting her to this family event had been a mistake, which had nothing to do with history or North vs. South, but everything to do with him, to do with the role he would play in his family until he was the last one standing.

"Yeh? Like, that's it?" she said.

"Probably makes sense. Tomorrow the traffic will be lighter on the bridge."

The bridge; the goddamned bridge, thought Heidi. These people organize their lives around it. "That's not what I was talking about. I mean . . . you haven't paid any attention to me all night."

Ethan didn't dispute this. She was right: anytime she had said something to him tonight, whether at cocktails or later when they were reunited at the table, it felt like an interruption.

Ethan wasn't getting the point that *she was breaking up with him*, or maybe, just maybe, he was already past it. "I don't care about the traffic," she said.

She wouldn't, he thought; she wouldn't be driving. He turned onto the farm lane and then pulled the car over. "We've had fun but, well . . ." He stopped for a moment. "Well. I guess I think I don't have room for a relationship now."

He doesn't have "room for a relationship"! This was not going the way it should. "What does that mean?"

"It means that with my mom's health, and things going down between my parents, or whatever, and Rosalie—you don't know Rosalie, but something is up—and this is my job, it always has been; that's why all four of them conceived me, so I better stick around and do what I can do . . . and maybe I'll be taking some time off from school—" This was not something he had thought of before, not something he thought would ever happen, and as it turned out, not something he did, but he liked the way it raised the stakes on the moment. "And it's not fair to you."

"Jeez," she said, beginning to feel that Ethan might be carrying weight that she knew little about. "You'd do that?"

"You wouldn't understand. You didn't grow up in a family. You could be orphaned tomorrow in a freak accident with a potter's wheel, and it wouldn't change your life one bit."

When they got back, Ethan was surprised that his father was still there and not taking Pop back to Osprey Neck. He was outside on the landing, with the dogs; Ethan suspected that all three of them had had a pee together on the lawn. Heidi darted upstairs. Later, they spent the night in the same bed, and he hated that he had outsmarted her on their breakup—or thought he had—and he loved her warm body and soft hair, but Ethan, singer of songs of despair and delight, knew that teenage love affairs, ego, and bruises and the thrill of sex play out in double time, like a play with a wedding in the morning and a mortal wound by nightfall. It could end with a few lines of chitchat about bridge traffic, and even though their hearts might be twisted with the astonishment of lost love, and even though one of them might go back to college and do everything they could—which she did—to trash the other, what he was undoing was nothing compared with two people being pried apart one ripped tendon at a time, as might be happening to his sister and her husband. On the way upstairs he had heard through the door of their room the miserable murmur of two people trying to be decent to each other at this time, on this day, at this moment when they realized something was wrong; it would take years to play out—another child, a move to Silver Spring—but what Ethan heard unwittingly through the door was the real horror of falling away from the bonds and plights, not two kids deciding that though they could happily imagine continuing to fuck each other—and did, later in the fall, twice more, a brief, pointless reunion—there was no future in it, and a future was what they wanted.

But back at the front door, before all that, Ethan was surprised to find his father. "I thought you'd be dropping Pop off," he said.

"He's staying here tonight. In the sleigh bed room."

"You're kidding."

"No. I'm not."

"Like, what?" said Ethan.

"Like"—Harry mimicked—"he hasn't slept in this house since August 27, 1939, and when I was getting ready to bring the car around, he said he'd always thought he would spend one more night at the Retreat before he died, and he figured this was the night."

"Yeh, but still—" said Ethan.

"It's a bit of a story. Something happened tonight for him. I'll tell you. It's all good." He paused. There was a full moon; the light all day, Harry thought, had been beautiful, memorable, each part of the spectrum offering its own truths. In this spooky molten moonlight anything can happen, a dream. The dogs were having their final prowl through the back park. "Look at Rowdy," he said. "So in the moment. He isn't afraid of history."

"Dad. He's a dog. He doesn't know what history is."

Harry looked around and noticed that Heidi had disappeared. "How was your night?" he asked.

"Oh. Okay," said Ethan.

"Trouble in paradise?"

"I wouldn't call it trouble, and I wouldn't call it paradise. You and Mom?" he asked, as long as people were supposed to be honest at candlelit hours like this, when age and experience and hopes all become equal.

"Whatever trouble we have, I would call it paradise. I want you to have the same thing in your life." As he had once already this evening, he gave Ethan a hug and a kiss and sent him off. He went into the kitchen to put away the first load of the dishwasher, filled in the second, and left things somewhat pulled together. As he was turning out the lights, he noticed one of Heidi's spiral sketch pads on the table. It was love and loyalty for Ethan that allowed him to violate his principles and flip through it, which he never would have done if he thought Heidi was still his son's girlfriend. She was a stranger now; this sketchbook was like something he found on a subway seat, but when he came upon the drawing of Kate leaning against the kitchen counter, he gasped. However faithfully the girl had charted the indignities of age, she had also captured—stolen, perhaps—the look in Kate's eye, which was both uncertain but resolute, the same resolve that had so ripped at his heart before dinner, so fleeting, so spectral. It was an image to be treasured and suppressed, the kind of thing only a husband of nearly forty years should be able to see, not this naïf, this child with a pencil. He glanced around guiltily and then rather violently ripped it out of the pad, leaving a froth of evidence captured in the wire, and he didn't mind when, the next day, before Ethan took her to the train station, Heidi volunteered sourly, "It was for you anyway."

He gazed at his ill-gotten prize and fell into conflating this drawing of Kate at sixty-three, with only a fuzz of hair, and his own images of the young woman she had been when they met. He lost himself for a second in those early days, those first few dates back in Palo Alto and Berkeley, and it struck Harry that he had never doubted she had fallen for him, he had never dangled between ecstasy and despair, never questioned his certainty that if he assented, she'd drop out of graduate school to marry him. What a cocksure little shit he had been; his father had been completely correct to say he'd better marry her before she figured that out, and it was Harry's extraordinary luck that once she had figured it out, once she figured out how much of his professional success was driven by a terror of being found out, how much of his charm was simply booze, she stuck around long enough for him to grow up.

He had it in mind to say some of this to Kate, but when he made it to their room, he found her asleep. He had recovered from that moment of despair behind the pecan tree; it was just one more event in the journey. Whatever apologies were due to her for being married to him all this time, whatever summing up of the evening, whatever continuation of their discussion of tradition vs. history . . . well, there'd be no surprises in any of it, nothing learned, just the talk of two people at a sacred remove from the world, with time yet to get it all right.

At about the same time, Julien and Céleste, finally checked into the hotel on Kent Narrows after being told there was no record of their reservation, gave each other kisses in the corridor—"*Ne fume pas dans ta chambre, d'accord?*" he reminded her—and departed to their rooms. She watched television for a few minutes, clips of holiday celebrations from coast to coast. A concert in

Boston, an orchestra in a concert shell playing, as the reporter had it, the "War of 1812 Overture." She went back outside and smoked her last cigarette on a pier; even at this late hour the dock bars were thumping and the channel was clogged with boats flying Trump flags. There were cascades of explosions, and she couldn't tell whether they were from strings of firecrackers or bursts of bullets from assault rifles. Oh, she thought, they don't know how much trouble they're in. She called Armand and caught him before the girls had woken up, and when he asked what she had done today, she said they had done nothing, really. Just a dinner with some people her father knew. When he asked what all that noise was in the background, she said it was just the sounds of America going to hell.

In his room, Julien undressed, carefully hung up his blazer and trousers, scratched a little spot of mud off the cuff of one of his pant legs. His shoes were likewise muddied from that expedition to the graves, and it still, after all these years, irritated him that he could not leave his shoes in the corridor of a hotel, even a Holiday Inn Express, and find them polished and buffed the next morning. A particular man. He put on a set of handsome silk pajamas and then sat down at the sparse little desk at the corner of his room and, for a moment, looked out the window at the water in the distance and the marina and crab decks just below him. He saw the tiny glow of a cigarette on the pier and knew it was his daughter. Then he reached for the envelope Francis had wanted him to have and with the care, restraint, and reverence of an archivist, he found the packets of snapshots—*Memories for the Future* they proclaimed—and when he took them out, he saw instantly that the first photo was the house on the corner in Tuckertown that he had seen earlier. Next, there was another house, a much more modest shack in disrepair, probably unlived in, and then Julien realized that the large oak at the far left was the same tree on the far right of another of those photographs. He realized then that the boy had simply walked down the lane and turned square to capture each house, to frame each without distraction, giving each the honor and respect it was due, and so, over the next hour, overlapping a truck here, making a less certain guess there, Julien could lay out the panorama. In the center photograph was a steeply gabled farmhouse with the round attic window where his great-grandmother as a child had loved to observe the comings and goings of her world. Julien saw no little face peering through the glass, but someone was in the porch swing, pumping exuberantly, just a blur in time.

Eleanor sat in her study. In the hot air she had changed into a short nightgown she had brought along to awaken Vittorio's interest; among the many, many inadmissible things she had not breathed to either her family or friends—except to Rosalie earlier that evening—was that they had sex very rarely, and, *well, let's just let it hang out*, he couldn't come without his own hand doing the majority of the work. The house was now quiet, asleep around her; all over the Eastern Shore the Fourth of July was over. People had observed this remembrance of history in their own ways, with pride, with mild interest, with pugnacity, with dismay, with fear, and if they were lucky, this would all happen again next year in much the same way. The air was still, too hot and humid to be called calm: everything slowed in this air; one held her breath for things to come. This is how the days had ended for Mary Foxley, with the uncertainties of the next day held in abeyance. Was it not right to accord her the peace of a similar evening, three hundred and fifty years ago? In the end, wasn't it unfair to drag her into the swamps and potholes of America's present condition?

She should be allowed, thought Eleanor, to live and die in her own time, and since she was almost entirely Eleanor's creation, that is what Eleanor was going to allow her to do.

Her computer was open in front of her; she flipped through the final few pages of her novel, or novella, or notes. The wedding, the waterborne festival, with the families of the bride and groom and the neighbors and various royal and colonial dignitaries arriving in shallops and batteaux and doggers and hoys and whatever other terms they used for boats back then. Music might have been playing. (On what instruments? She'd found nothing about music in her Chesapeake reference collection, but there must have been music.) Anna Maria, her red hair flowing as always (this red hair thing: was it perhaps getting a bit icky?), walking up the allée on her brother's arm to marry Richard. Some dancing: little girls in white—Mary Foxley's daughter Rebecca Wilmer had four girls of her own by then—sitting politely in a line watching the guests dance. Servants and, yes, slaves around the edges. The real wedding cannot have been anything much like this (and was it a Catholic service or an Anglican one?), but Eleanor thought that Mary Foxley, for her last act, deserved a feast and a festival, so she wrote it that way.

Were these pages good enough to end the novel? Did they say enough and do enough? Probably not, and perhaps it didn't matter. The thought had been with Eleanor for months that it was time to move on from this project, maybe time to move on from fiction altogether; in many ways being crowned the literary star of her class at William & Mary had laid waste to her life; perhaps her twenties had turned out to be nothing but a false start. Her friends from Columbia who had seemed so fresh and so chosen now seemed too smart for their own good, burdened by the techniques and attitudes of an art form they could never master. When they chanced to meet on the street in Manhattan, at the farmer's market in Brooklyn, they chatted but avoided the question in each other's gaze: *Anything published?* In those earlier days, they could look through each other's eyes right into the ambitions consuming their souls. How certain they were, such swagger in their opinions! But what remained of Eleanor's work was this new person in her life, a person imagined so minutely for the past two years that she had become a companion for her, a companion so much more reliable than any living creature, and she was afraid to let her go.

She glanced again over the lines of her gay and festive final chapter, with a finger poised over the delete button. (Oh, she did have about ten other copies hidden on thumb drives, cloud accounts, emails to herself, but this one was, as composers say, the autograph.) Apple, she thought, should invent a *poof* for times like this; what is the sound of abandoning one's life dreams? It's a whimper of capitulation, a plea that the man with the axe strikes a swift and clean blow. But no. Not tonight. She would decide in the morning whether these pages of this novel were good enough. In the bright light of day is when the surface of fiction gets made, when things can be polished, nudged into alignment; at night, things run too deep, too impulsive and wild. Instead, her eye moved from the draft to a small note she had begun earlier in the day after the trip to the beach, an address to Mary Foxley, and since her project had started in the middle of the night in the dread second person—sorry, Monroe, but your manuscript was a *dog*—she was satisfied that her novel, if it ever came to that, could end that way as well.

You came alone, didn't you? Alone, in mind, because if you didn't, it is hard for me to imagine how you survived. You were prepared to lose all, not because that is what you expected, but because no matter what, you knew you were going to lose something. You followed your husband because that was your duty, and you left your father behind *because that was your fate. Your husband was a dreamer, and you were placing your hope not in dreams but in actions, because that is who you were, isn't it? You brought your son with you because you thought he could survive the climate, but you left your daughter behind because you knew she could not, and though you never saw her again, you knew she had survived to become a lady in a carriage, a mother of sons. You occupied a property from which the native people had been driven, you built an estate with the toil of indentured servants, and you may have tried to avoid it—*Did you? Did you?*—but the legacy you passed along to your son Richard could not endure without enslaved African labor. That was your life. God help you, you made a place to live it, and you handed it on when you died, and what else can we demand of a woman on her own in the wilderness? There is nothing you did that I cannot at least understand, if not excuse, but that is an admission that will have to be kept between us. Between you and me.*

10

Each ripple lapping upon the shoreline is a piece of time spent; the waves carve away at the future. The coarse sand, the stones and pebbles of oxblood and ginger, receive the water as if being nourished, but it is not so: they are being diminished, rearranged. The sand between your toes, the handful of pebbles sifted through the fingers, you see a little less of them than you saw yesterday. One year, as was the case on July Fourth 2019, there is enough sand to roll out the towels, to sink an umbrella stake, to luxuriate in the shore life; another year, like the following year, at the height of the Covid outbreak and the presidential campaigns, it is all rock and clay. The grasses, the bulrushes and the spartina and the invasive phragmites bounce ornamentally in the passing wakes, but they are always on the move; they will seed and root where it suits them best, and even now they are retreating to slightly higher ground, leaving the sand and stones to their fates. Wasn't there a secret duck pond on this stretch of shore once, with an inlet that breathed with the tides? The oaks and cypresses do not have the advantage of mobility; they're in it for the long haul, but the long haul is not in it for them, the waves are winning, the exposed elephant-gray roots harden in the sun. What year was it when the last of the loblollies fell on Hail Point?

As it turned out, the pages of fiction so much discussed that July Fourth never did become a novel. Eleanor went back to her copywriting day job and continued to decline invitations for weekends because she "had to work on the book," but that fall, as a sort of grim joke, she applied to several Ph.D. programs in history that she was certain she would not get into, Yale, Berkeley, Columbia, that sort of thing; if a path ahead is blocked, it's better to know it soonest. And then two things happened to Eleanor. In March she was admitted, with funding, to Columbia; apparently someone from the MFA program had put in a strong word for her, and to her last days Eleanor worried that it might have been the former teacher she had so maligned, Alexander Braithwaite. And then, in April, her mother died. Not of her cancer, directly, but from Covid, that opportunistic microbe thinning the herd of the weakened and compromised. Perhaps it was a grotesque injustice, because in the last few months of Kate's life she had experienced a sort of rebirth; each day she'd been more willing to believe that she had won her fight with cancer. Her hair had seemed to come back fuller than ever, gone were the overalls and bandanna, and she was actually allowing Harry to suggest that they make plans for a trip to Paris. It was not to be, although the joy was never going to be in the trip itself, but in the looking forward to it, in the belief that it could happen. They buried her in her family's plot in Connecticut, honoring a wish she had made known years before she was hooked up to a ventilator; permanent rest on Harry's Folly was never going to work for her. It amused her to think that she would end up beside Lotte for all eternity. *How can you just lie there? You always were so lazy.*

For Eleanor, facing her grief seemed to require that she grow up, become a person of fact, of reality as she could see it from where she sat, and off she went to graduate school. As much as it might have astonished her, even slightly disappointed her, though the job was a plum, she ended up on the tenure track back at William & Mary, just at the time when interest in the crucible of American history—the Chesapeake Bay—had opened up new questions for new scholarship. Her view was that the kernel out of which America grew, its unavoidable legacy, the history that had to be reckoned with, was the Bay, with its enslaved labor and concentrated capital and unsustainable agriculture, and not the equitable and tidy towns and white-clapboard meetinghouses of New England. The year 1620 was a pretty little tale, a script for countless primary school pageants, but 1607 was the year that mattered in American history; New England was the myth, but the Bay was the real story of America's birth. Still, though it earned distrust, even disdain from her more progressive younger colleagues who were now engaged in a full-scale war with the American past, Eleanor did not scold; she did not blame the Chesapeake and those who turned it into the Tobacco Coast; she did not renounce Mary Foxley.

Kate had been right, that July Fourth, to say that Harry was content to live with the ghosts, that his family's past was lifeblood for him, and in those years after he lost Kate he continued to live at the Retreat, shuffling here and there in that immense ark all too happily alone, so happily that he lived well into his nineties. His father's genes, perhaps, but it didn't hurt that he spent his days in the warm, comforting company of the dead. But this could not go on forever. "What are we going to do with the Retreat after Dad dies?" asked Eleanor, a question that Rosalie took to mean, *What are* you *going to do with the Retreat?* As if it were Rosalie's problem, because she was the oldest and still worked in real estate. A think tank retreat or, even better, a wedding venue, she had thought for a while before Eleanor pointed out that no one except neo-Nazis and Russian oligarchs might want to get married in a house that had once been the manor of a slave plantation. "Well, what do you think we should do?" Rosalie snapped back. "If the house is unoccupied, no insurance company will be willing to cover it. Did you ever think of that?" No, Eleanor had not ever thought of that.

There had been hurricanes on the Chesapeake recorded by English settlers since the Great Hurry Cane of 1667—Eleanor had always intended a gripping account of surviving that event as the transition into the second third of her novel—and watermen and coastal landowners of more recent times remembered Hazel and Agnes and Isabel as great moments of change. But now the storms began to hit routinely, began to make it clear that Mother Nature, who had created this estuary when the glaciers receded ten thousand years ago, was reconsidering the whole thing. On the rivershore of the Retreat, the surges crested the low banks behind which the family had gathered on that last July Fourth before Kate died, and the rising waters drove unchecked across the fields of corn and soybeans and wheat. The organic grain farmer who leased the land from Harry gave up, took his operation inland. "She's as poor as Caroline" was the old saying on the Eastern Shore, but sandy, well-drained, landlocked Caroline County now had the last laugh. Have you tried any of their wines, the chambourcin, the tannat blends?

Paul might once have been among those who were expected to know about the changes in the climate, but after he was denied tenure—the greatest thing that ever happened to him, he thought, no offense to academe—and he and Rosalie divorced—in no way a great thing—he became involved in a doomsday seed preserve in Ohio and soon turned into something of a national authority on the extinctions of plant life. Despite those doleful words, "doomsday" and "extinction," Paul Gottlieb remained an optimist; he believed in the planet, he had faith in the marshes where all this would get worked out, and he trusted that creation's plan was robust enough to survive the threatening present. Paul never lost his love of the Chesapeake, and he was Eleanor's big catch for a conference in Williamsburg—"The Past *Can* Be Prologue: The Bay Has a Future." His talk was fine, a full house, but he spent the three days of the conference panting over Eleanor, doing everything short of throwing her against a wall and smashing his face into hers. "Why haven't you married?" he asked. "A man or a woman, who cares?" She answered, "Because no one I liked enough has ever asked." Paul heard this, stood back and dropped his arms, and offered himself, even the self that had gained thirty pounds since that July Fourth. "Paul," she said, "if the rocks melt with the sun, I will still not have sex with you." Did Eleanor know, as Kate would have known, that the source of this expression was a poem by Robert Burns?

When Harry died, they interred his ashes not under a stone at the entrance to the graveyard beside Simon's, but, as Harry had directed, way in the back, slightly to one side of the general area long assumed to be where servants—either paid or enslaved— were buried. No one in the family was happy with this, such a politically redolent act, even if, they conceded, no system of the ethics of burial they knew of had ever quite confronted such a unique test case. What if, as seemed possible, the small shaft dug for his cremains pierced right through the heart of a person that had been lying there unmarked for three hundred years? What if they found bones? (They didn't, as it happened.) They argued,

"Why *claim* this space in *their* plot; do you really think this is a gesture of *solidarity and respect*?" Harry could not be moved; it was all dust to him. He directed that there was to be no urn, he was to be buried in no "trash receptacle," as he said to the funeral director, who took offense at this; his ashes were simply to be poured into the hole. He had begun to think, in his endless ruminations about the questions that had been posed at that dinner on the July Fourth before Kate died, that his sense of obligation and duty to the place was in many ways an unwilling burden, and he wished to lie among the likewise unwilling, the conscripted, the enslaved. I know, I know. Say what you will, figure it your own way, but that is where the remains of Harry Mason rest today.

As for those who had once been enslaved, not in the pretty manner of duty and faith, but with iron shackles, to those spectral repressed voices that had murmured in Kate's ears—the philosopher had it right: "haunting belongs to the structure of every hegemony"—what answer? Oh yes, Rosalie contracted a distinguished historian of American slavery to prepare a public, searchable website that tracked family lines and relationships of enslaved Africans at the Retreat as best as could be done. Did that atone? The one remaining slave quarter was given a new roof at a historic trust's expense, and it was opened for public access twice a year, as the trust demanded. Hmmm. But what about those few acres made available, as Heidi proffered at that dinner on July Fourth, to the descendants of slaves, perhaps a line of house sites somewhere, given away by lottery? "And exactly what acres did you have in mind," Rosalie had retorted. She cited easements as the difficulty back then, but thirty years later the problem was different.

By the time of Harry's death, the water levels were routinely cresting above the low seawall along Mason's Creek that had been put in so confidently at the beginning of the twentieth century, and several of the farm buildings on the creek were demolished before they could flood. The French House, where Oral and Alice French had lived after the Civil War, had to be moved to drier ground, at great expense, but when done, it occupied the highest hundred square yards of land on the farm. The Handy House, as they called it after Bo and Francis Handy, was barely holding on. But the Mansion House and the family graveyard, sited by Richard the Emigrant on what passed, in Tobacco Country, for a promontory, were still dry.

The unexpected solution to the "problem" of the Mansion House after Harry's death—after a few years of fretting and teeth-gnashing and lying to the insurance company—was that Ethan and his wife and two children moved in. Nothing would have seemed less likely to any of them even a few years earlier, but the Retreat had, for three hundred and fifty years, always seemed to find a tenant for itself. "My poor house, and I do equally desire." What fun is it to haunt an empty shell? Ethan was by then earning a decent amount from his fiction, and his wife, Mariama, a Senegalese woman he had met in the Peace Corps, was running a successful business promoting contemporary African art. *Oui, Céleste, ma chère, ce dépotoir* finally did get high-speed internet connectivity, as France had largely done by 2010, and there was no reason not to set up shop at the Retreat. Yes, a very collectible Chippendale piecrust table—*things brown, silver, and porcelain were back!*—had been sold to at least delay the financial disaster of owning such a place, but Ethan had turned into a capable steward. Neither Rosalie nor Eleanor would ever have supposed such a thing when Ethan lived in Brooklyn in a cramped, dark loft, but just as it had once been the surprisingly right thing for his parents, so it was for Ethan and his family.

Ethan had long recognized that there was a natural feature

in the Retreat's holdings, a depression that began as a small inlet off the end of Mason's Creek, ran across the field, and caused a dip in the state road—at one time teenagers from town called this dip the "launching pad"; if they hit it at about seventy, all four wheels would leave the road. This was the exact spot, on that July Fourth decades ago, that he and Heidi, coming home after the fireworks, passed Milou and Alice Howe on the way to Weatherly, blinding both drivers for a second. The dip continued as a slight fold into the woods, where even in the driest summers the lady ferns thrived and the footing on the moss was spongy, and then the land dropped ever so slightly to join a similar lick off the next creek upriver, where the spartina and phragmites were waiting.

The day finally came—it seemed like a single day to Ethan, as if the weirs or bulkheads at either end of a freshly dug canal were pulled down to allow the water to flow into it—that the two creeks joined. It was not that sudden, of course. First the licks of spartina and bulrushes and phragmites began to cut deeper and deeper, then a nameless storm surge drove the waters of both creeks inland and they made the first contact. Then, for a number of years, while motorists complained bitterly, one's drive down the neck went into about a hundred feet of broken pavement, often with standing salt water, and finally the county built a sort of causeway over this section. There was a custom in Maryland to give names to quite trivial fingerlings of water, under a bridge or overpass, even a sluiceway that went through a large culvert, but no one knew exactly what to call this new feature—in truth, it was hardly the only place where this problem existed—so the road crew erected a generic sign saying simply WATER. Water and more water. When all this was done, what finally happened was that the Retreat—haven, hermitage, call it what you will—

became an island. Maybe that's what it had always been, a place to hide, a world apart.

A number of years before this watershed event, but after Ethan had moved himself and family into the Retreat, he was going into a restaurant in New York—he was there to meet his editor, had come up from Maryland on the Amtrak, was feeling good on a fine summer day—when he held the door for a pretty and strangely familiar-looking woman coming out, and after they scrutinized each other enough to be sure, Heidi exclaimed, "*The Way We Were!*" Ethan didn't get the reference; he hadn't taken Hollywood and the American Culture at Vassar as she had done. "Robert Redford and Barbra Streisand, meeting up on the street years later," she said. "But you don't have your wife with you."

She was very smartly dressed, and one reason Ethan had to do a double take to recognize her was that she wasn't wearing glasses. He told her this.

"Oh. I had Lasik surgery," she said. "My husband didn't like my specs. I still feel naked without them."

"I hate him already," said Ethan.

She smiled up at him ruefully. Was he always this tall? she wondered. Always this handsome? "I've read a couple of your novels," she said.

"I've been lucky with them. But I've stayed pretty close to home. You wouldn't say that I've spread my wings, which is something you tried to get me to do."

"Jeez. Did I actually say 'spread your wings'?"

She still says "Jeez," he thought. How sweet is that! "No. I think the word you used about me was 'boring.' I took it to heart."

She did not apologize or dispute the word, but she hesitated on what she was about to say, then said it. "I love the one about the dinner on July Fourth. Was it presumptuous of me to see myself in it? I didn't mind, by the way. If it was."

"You're the only girl I ever dated who lost her glasses having sex in a hayloft."

She laughed; in maturity as in youth, not a hint of *pudeur* on the subject of sex. "I have no right to, but I feel proud of you."

"That's what I am saying. If there is any pride to be had, you have more right to it than you can imagine." He left it there, letting the memories seep into both their heads, letting the past lay its claim on how things worked out. "And you? Do you still draw? I keep expecting your name to pop out of the arts section of the *Times*."

"Sorry. I became . . ." She faltered on what she had become; instead, she made her own reference to past events. "I went to law school."

"Good choice, probably. I'm sure you're a fine . . . attorney."

"I keep at it. I'm tough. In fact, I am just leaving a lunch where an opposing lawyer told me not to be a bitch."

Ethan was not surprised to hear any of this. "In other words, you won the case."

"Yeh."

That was it, as far as this could go, and he leaned forward to give her a peck on the cheek, which she returned, and it turned into a full hug and then a rather long hug, whether as celebration of what they had both become or consolation for what they had not become, neither of them could be sure.